TIGHTROPE

Trelawney is back with a vengeance – and what a vengeance. Antony Melville Ross's first spy novel *Blindfold* was greeted with excited expectations from some of the most discriminating judges, summed up by Sheridan Morley: 'Not since Fleming's *Casino Royale* all of thirty years ago has there, I think, been so impressive a debut.' His second, *Two Faces of Nemesis*, in which Trelawney played only a minor part, consolidated this reputation. But in this, unquestionably his most brilliant performance, Trelawney and his bewitching partner Jane Trask are in the forefront of the action, which takes place in England and the United States. The skill and speed of the plotting keep the reader on the edge of his chair.

What makes the book something quite out of the ordinary in spy fiction is that it reflects the chaos and irrationality of the world we know from our newspapers – the world of hostages and terrorism, of mindless destructiveness and cruelty. Adding to this the known and predictable ruthlessness of the cold war produces a story with a kick like a mule. Its strength is increased by the discipline and vigour of the writing.

Books by Antony Melville-Ross

BLINDFOLD
TWO FACES OF NEMESIS
TIGHTROPE
TRIGGER
TALON
SHADOW
COMMAND

ANTONY MELVILLE-ROSS

Tightrope

COLLINS
8 Grafton Street, London W1

William Collins Sons and Co Ltd
London · Glasgow · Sydney · Auckland
Toronto · Johannesburg

British Library CIP data

Melville-Ross, Antony
   Tightrope.
   I. Title
   823'.9'1F

ISBN 0 00 221968 9

First published 1981
This reprint 1985

© Antony Melville-Ross 1981

Made and Printed in Great Britain by
William Collins Sons and Co Ltd, Glasgow

For Tim and Camilla
with love

PROLOGUE

The rain had stopped, but the wind probing across the rooftops as if uncertain of its direction alternately pushed and sucked at his damp clothing, never allowing his skin to accustom itself to discomfort. He directed a mental obscenity at the television weather forecaster who had promised him a dry night, flexed his fingers, then eased the pressure of the rifle resting in the crook of his left arm. This was the sixth night of waiting, but he felt no impatience. The money he was being paid was more than good and he had once waited for over three weeks to earn half the amount.

The sound of traffic along Portland Place behind him was fairly constant, but in Weymouth Street below nothing moved and very little had moved for the past six hours. He lay motionless until, an hour before dawn, a dim red light glowed twice on the roof of the building across the road.

The street lighting was medium to poor and, with the naked eye, it took him a moment to pick out the lone shadowy figure over two hundred yards away, but through the image intensifier on the rifle it stood out clearly. Taking a pencil-torch from his pocket he shielded it with his hand and pressed the button once. One, two, three flashes in reply. Affirmative.

The figure was approaching the junction of Weymouth Street and Harley Street now. When it had crossed the intersection he shot it through the chest, shifted his aim to the head lying on the pavement and fired again. Then he placed the rifle against the base of a chimney-stack and crawled rapidly away wondering, without much interest, who he had just killed.

CHAPTER ONE

The Minister's Private Secretary tightened the knot of his pearl-grey tie and said, 'I'm sorry, Trevelyan, but there's no question of my disturbing him now. He's due at . . . Well never mind about that. It's hardly your business. I have my orders and as you don't rate immediate access that's all there is to it. You people seem to be under the impression that you can come waltzing in here and . . .'

He stopped talking when his visitor snapped, 'Paper and envelope!'

'What?'

'Give me a piece of paper and an envelope. And you might as well get my name right. It's Trelawney.'

The mistake over the name seemed to unbalance the other. He looked confused, frowned briefly, then took a sheet of government stationery and an envelope from a drawer and waved them irritably in Trelawney's direction. His irritation increased when he saw Trelawney glance at the highly polished surface of the desk, take a wallet from his pocket and rest the paper on that.

'Oh, very cloak and dagger,' he said.

Without replying Trelawney sealed his eight-word message in the envelope, scrawled 'Most immediate. Minister's eyes only' on it and dropped it into the wire basket marked with an 'in' tag. He waited, then tapped it with a forefinger before saying, 'Most immediate. That means now. Will you take it in or shall I?'

The Secretary looked at the envelope, then up at the big man with the broken nose, very blue eyes and grey-flecked black hair. He frowned again, moved his shoulders in a gesture of resignation and got to his feet. There seemed to be something about the big man which left him no choice.

Twenty seconds later the Minister pointed a finger at a chair. Trelawney walked to it and sat down. Neither spoke until the door had closed behind the Secretary then, 'Why the delay in letting me know about this?' the Minister asked.

'It took time for the report to reach someone in the police senior enough to know who he was, sir. Then I had to go and identify the body.'

'I see. Any additional information?'

'Not yet.'

'Hmm. I take it that your presence here means that Rafferty is away.'

'Yes, sir. He's on holiday near St Andrews. Walking and playing a little golf.'

'Then you'd better get him back in one hell of a hurry, hadn't you? Oh, never mind. I'll do it myself.'

The Minister stopped the movement of his hand towards the telephone when Trelawney said, 'It's been taken care of. He'd left his hotel when I called, but I asked the local police to pick him up and take him to RAF Leuchars. They have a plane standing by to fly him to Northolt. They'll be coming down the North Sea, but there may still be some broken glass. I told them not to hang about.'

'Bugger the glass. You did absolutely right. When he . . . Trelawney?'

'Sir?'

'You've got all this moving very quickly. What did you use for authority?'

'Your name, sir.'

'Did you indeed? All right, but don't make a habit of it. Now, when Rafferty lands at Northolt how are you getting him into London?'

'Helicopter, Minister. I've got clearance for it to land in Regent's Park. It's close to the Department building.'

'Horse Guards' Parade. It's close to here,' the Minister said and picked up the telephone.

Trelawney lay back in his chair, half his mind probing for reasons and finding none, the other half recording the Minister's voice cancelling that morning's appointments, altering the helicopter's landing place, speaking to the Prime Minister. Slowly both mental activities subsided leaving only images of the exit wounds left by soft-nosed bullets in the human head and body. The click of the telephone being replaced on its rest brought him back to the present and he was thankful for that.

The Minister pointed a finger at Trelawney much as earlier he had indicated a chair. 'I don't know where you stand in the Department's pecking order,' he said, 'but, as you appear to have taken charge at this stage, what do you propose to recommend that Rafferty does when he gets here? He'll be coming into this cold.'

'That he talks to Sir Charles Barry.'

'Historical background?'

'Yes, sir.'

'The old boy won't have any up to date information, you know.'

'An historical background doesn't usually contain up to date information,' Trelawney said. 'It's...' He paused, shook his head angrily and added, 'I beg your pardon, sir.'

The Minister half smiled. 'That's all right. We must both be a trifle jumpy. That was a particularly fatuous remark of mine. All right, so it's Barry to start with, unless Rafferty has any different ideas, then he'll want to see the recommendations of the Selection Board I imagine.'

'If you please, Minister, and the members of the Board themselves.'

For a moment Trelawney thought that that line of investigation was to be denied the Department and was concluding that it didn't matter because they'd find out the names for themselves when the scowl of concentration left the Minister's face.

'Professor Morris, General Shand and Vice-Admiral Bembridge,' he said. 'The General's dead, but the other two are still with us. Know them?'

'No.'

'Well, the Professor was Charles Barry's predecessor. Must be over eighty now, but very much all there. The Admiral...'

One of the three telephones on the desk buzzed softly. The Minister said 'Yes?' and 'Thank you', then turned back to Trelawney.

'You appear to have used my name to good purpose. Your superior is east of Newcastle at Mach 2 point something.

What's that? A map reference?'

'No, sir. It's broken windows,' Trelawney told him and received a snort, part irritation, part amusement, in reply.

'Of course it is. I don't know what's the matter with me today. I've watched that figure 2 come up in Concorde often enough. Oh well, I expect you've got things to attend to. Bring Rafferty straight up when he arrives.'

Trelawney got to his feet.

'About Professor Morris and Admiral Bembridge, sir.'

'I'll ask both to receive a senior representative of the Department as soon as possible,' the Minister said.

CHAPTER TWO

The big Airedale had the man by the left sleeve of his jacket seconds after the gate clicked shut behind him. Its forelegs were splayed for maximum purchase on the turf beside the brick path, its eyes stared unblinking menace and a low rumbling forced its way past the cloth in its mouth.

The man sighed and began to transfer articles from the pockets of his jacket to his trousers with his free hand. When he had finished he unbuttoned the jacket and slipped it from his shoulders. The dog whirled and loped purposefully away towards a clump of trees, its prize trailing behind it on the grass.

When it was hidden from his sight the man strolled along the path towards the cottage, noticing how well the clematis had established itself on the walls since the last time he had been there eighteen months before, how far the work had progressed on the almost completed garden. He wished he could leave now, get into his car and return to London, not involve them again in a world they had left behind after so many years of dedication to it. It was 'them', he supposed, not just 'him'. He hoped so anyway. They belonged together.

'Mr Rafferty! How very nice!'

She was kneeling, half concealed by a flowering shrub, secateurs and garden twine on the ground beside her. He cupped his hand under her elbow as she stood up unsteadily, seeking for balance. Her hair was white and her face marred by the well-remembered lines of pain, but somehow she looked younger. Not her proper age of course. She could never do that after what they had done to her, but there was natural colour in her cheeks and the evidence of suffering etched into her skin had receded from her eyes. He was glad about that and that it was 'them' because, obviously, she was happy which meant that they were together.

'Hello, Lady Barry,' he said.

In rapid succession she frowned, smiled, frowned again, then laughed softly.

'That's what they think I am down here, but I'm still just Martha Cartwright. Just a guest.'

'A permanent guest I hope.'

She blushed, something he had never seen her do before and there was almost girlish pleasure in her embarrassment.

'I'm not sure that I approve of your hope, Mr Rafferty,' she said, paused, then added defensively, 'But he does get in the most frightful muddle when I'm not around.'

Rafferty nodded. 'Yes, he always did, didn't he?'

It struck her suddenly that everything he had said so far had been spoken tonelessly as though he had lost the ability to hear his own voice. She stood for a moment looking at the lanky, grey-haired man who for so many years had been the Department's senior field operative and was now its Deputy Director, noting the lack of expression in the normally sardonically humorous face, the hint of whiteness about the compressed lips.

Not yet ready to know the reasons, '"Dropitsir" took your coat I suppose,' she said.

She, he knew, had given the dog to Barry and named it after his repeated commands had failed to achieve the surrender of some object by the fiercely determined puppy. It had been a golf club, hadn't it?

He nodded again. 'Yes. He's still the perfect butler.'

'Well, you taught him to do it, so you only have yourself to blame. I'm only too thankful he doesn't try it with anyone else, but fancy his remembering after all this time. Did you empty your pockets?'

'I emptied them.'

Ready now for whatever the answer might be, 'What's the matter, Mr Rafferty?' she asked.

Rafferty looked down at the small figure standing before him, her chin raised as though she were defying him to strike her.

'Is the boss here, Martha? Sorry. I've always thought of him as that. I mean Sir Charles.'

'Gone to the village for a bag of cement to finish the terrace.

He'll be back soon, but what is it? I've never seen you like this in all the years I've known you.'

He looked round him at the pretty cottage with its pretty garden which she and Barry had restored together. His jacket lay beneath 'Dropitsir's' paws in the middle of the lawn now and the dog was watching him hopefully, ready to thwart any attempt at recovery. Then his gaze returned to the little old lady who had been pretty too before the Gestapo had almost killed her all those years ago, who was still pretty in her own gently charming way.

'The Director was shot this morning,' he said.

Quite slowly the colour drained from Martha's face and he took a step towards her, but she shook her head.

'Dead? Julian Havelock-Templeton?'

'Yes.'

He found himself listening to the silence which was not silence, hearing her breathing and the peaceful summery hum of insects in the hedges. The quiet non-silence dragged at his nerves and he flexed his shoulders to dispel a sensation he did not permit himself to experience. Martha brushed a wisp of white hair from her forehead with a gloved hand leaving a smudge of loam in its place. The sight reminded him of Ash Wednesday.

'Oh dear.'

Martha had breathed the words rather than spoken them and to Rafferty's ears they held a world of sadness. He thought that strange, strange enough to ensure that he kept his expression carefully neutral. He didn't speak.

'I . . .' Martha said and stood staring at the dog as though she was uncertain what it was, then in a sudden spate of words, 'Well, we can't just stand here. Come inside, Mr Rafferty, and sit down. There's a joint in the oven, I must . . .' She left the sentence unfinished, turned away and hobbled towards the front door of the cottage. Rafferty followed her slowly.

Standing relaxed in the middle of the sitting-room he watched her pass through into the kitchen, heard the opening and closing of the oven door then, very faintly, the click of a switch.

'Drinks on the oak chest in the corner, Mr Rafferty. Do help yourself. I shan't be long.'

'Thank you,' he said, but stayed where he was until the faint sounds of movement upstairs reached him. He moved quickly, silently then. The red indicator light below the oven was glowing, but the metal was still cold and the oven empty. The clock above it registered five minutes to one and he frowned.

A glass of tonic in his hand, Rafferty walked on to the flag-stoned terrace and sat down with his feet dangling over the edge, staring unseeingly at that part of the brick retaining wall at one end which was unfinished. Through the window of an upstairs room he could hear drawers sliding open and shut.

'Now what?' he asked himself quietly, but did not notice 'Dropitsir's' growl of encouragement. He was thinking that his order to senior Department personnel that morning to travel in pairs might prove more useful in his own case than he had anticipated and that Trelawney, waiting in a second car less than a mile away, might now have something better to do than provide him with cover.

CHAPTER THREE

The little town of Blandford Forum was crowded and Rafferty slowed to a crawl, stopped, waiting for a tangle of cars and farm trucks ahead of him to sort themselves out.

'Market day,' he said.

Barry moved impatiently beside him. 'I can see that. Can't you *do* something?'

Rafferty glanced at his wing-mirror. Trelawney's black Lotus was three cars behind. He turned and looked at Barry. The beard, eyebrows and hair were as shaggy as they had always been, but they were white now.

'Nothing comes to mind, boss. This is a car, not a Harrier jump-jet.'

'Why didn't you use a helicopter?'

'Oh quite,' Rafferty said. '"Mystery Helicopter Lands in Remote Dorset Village" splashed all over the front page of the local paper is just the publicity you need. Martha too. Putting the finger on my friends has always been my thing. Ah, the log jam seems to be breaking up. I'll see if I can weave my way through while you're thinking up the next silly question.'

He waited interestedly for an explosion, but none came and Salisbury was behind them before Barry spoke again.

'Get this thing moving, Rafferty. I *must* be in central London by three-thirty.'

'We're doing ninety right now, boss, and the M3 isn't so far ahead. I'll cut in the after-burners as soon as we're on it. Meanwhile, would you mind telling me what the tearing rush is all about?'

'Yes, I would,' Barry replied. 'Just keep motoring and don't call me "boss". If you recall I stopped being entitled to your particular term of respect over a year ago.'

'Well I'll say one thing for you,' Rafferty told him, 'nobody could accuse you of being bogged down by consistency. I never met anyone before who issued orders with one breath and denied his right to do so with the next. Still it takes all kinds, so I'll re-phrase what I said a moment ago. Tell me, Colonel Sir Charles Barry, what the tearing rush is all about. Tell me why you have to go to London at all. Tell me why Martha had to remember that she had a non-existent joint in the oven so she could get away from me and pack your bag before you knew you wanted to go anywhere.'

The tyres of the careering Jaguar whimpered on the cloverleaf slip road, then motorway was streaming under the car. Barry thought it was like watching a speeded-up film and wondered as bleakly as he had ever wondered anything what the final reel would show. He didn't speak.

The silence between the two dragged out for a full minute before, without a trace of emphasis, Rafferty said, 'I'm not asking you, boss, I'm telling you to tell me.'

Barry continued to stare at the road, but without seeing it now. He was picturing the man beside him, the skin like taut leather on the angular, flat-planed face, the long narrow-shouldered body so apparently defenceless that men had died because they saw it as such. Physically Rafferty hadn't changed. Not even the grey hair suggested ageing to Barry because it had been that shade for the quarter century or more that he had known him. The personality was nearly the same too. Irreverence had always been Rafferty's hall-mark, a light-hearted conviction that authority was something specially designed for his own particular amusement. The difference this day lay in the absence of humour from the disrespect and that, although he had never encountered it before, Barry supposed was understandable.

'Give me three hours in London,' he said. 'Three hours alone. Then I'll come to the Department and tell you.'

'Very kind of you. Any special reason why I shouldn't pull into the next service area and make you tell me there?'

'Three hours, Patrick. Please!'

Rafferty thought that he could count on his fingers the number of times that Barry, in all his years as Director of the Department, had called him by his Christian name. Its use had either accompanied an apology or indicated extreme distress. He had always found it touching. This time he was interested, but unmoved.

'Very well. Three hours,' he said. 'Now, aren't there some questions you should be asking me?'

West of Basingstoke on the M3 the inevitable police car appeared in Trelawney's mirror. It was a long way behind in the overtaking lane and he felt mildly surprised that one hadn't shown interest sooner. He slowed at once, manoeuvred through the traffic on the two inner lanes and stopped on the hard shoulder. When the police car joined him there he was leaning back against the side of the Lotus writing in a notebook. He tore the page out and put the book and his pen back in his pocket as the police observer walked up to him.

'Are you aware that you . . .' the man began, then stopped talking when Trelawney said, 'Just a minute, officer. Here are the registration numbers of my car and the dark blue Jag I'm supposed to be covering. You'll have seen that go by half a mile ahead of me. Here's my identification.'

He held out the ragged-edged page in one hand, an open wallet showing a not very informative Home Office pass with his photograph on it in the other.

The policeman looked down at both, then up at Trelawney.

'And?' he said.

'Check out those numbers and ask your people to give us a clear run through to London. I'm only "Tail-end Charlie" on this job, so don't ask me what it's about, but it seems we're in a hurry.'

'We noticed that,' the observer told him, took the paper, walked with it to the police car and gave it to the driver, then he looked back at Trelawney.

'You'd better get after your chum. We'll be right behind you. If these numbers are kosher we'll flash our lights and you'll know you've got your clear run. If they aren't, you and I'll be having another little talk.'

'Thanks,' Trelawney said, 'but I ought to warn you that I'll be moving along a bit.'

The other smiled. 'Don't worry your head about that, sir. My mate and me'll keep you in sight even if we have to pedal.'

Back in the overtaking lane Trelawney calculated that the exchange had lasted forty-five seconds. Allowing a similar period for stopping, awaiting the arrival of the police and getting back to where he now was meant that Rafferty's Jaguar would be about three and a half miles ahead. Accelerator flat on the floor, headlamps on, he passed a fast moving Ford Capri, stubbornly holding its position in the same lane, at a relative speed of fifty. For a moment he thought he was going to take a section of the central anti-glare screen with him, then he was clear. The Capri's lights flashed angrily as his 130 mph slipstream hit it. 'Temper,' he said, then smiled when the Capri pulled sharply over to let the pursuing police car by.

Twenty-five seconds and a mile later the police car's headlights blinked in his mirror. Long, long, long – Long, short, long – OK. He waved an arm in acknowledgement and watched the car drop rapidly behind, the blue warning light on its roof extinguished.

Barry said, 'Do you know the type of gun used?'

'Yes. L1A1 7.62 mm standard Army rifle.'

'How do you know?'

'The cops found it,' Rafferty told him. 'It was left where it was fired from on the roof of an empty building off Portland Place near his home. Two shots. Both hit. Chest while he was walking, head when he was lying on the ground. Range exactly 150 yards.'

'Good shooting at night. That may help with the identification.'

Rafferty looked for some sign of the Lotus in the rear-view mirror. There was none, but he wasn't worried by that. No prowl car had shown any interest in his hurtling progress, so he knew what had delayed Trelawney. He eased the pressure of his foot on the accelerator fractionally.

'You think so, do you?' he said.

'Don't you?'

Rafferty sighed softly but didn't speak until Barry repeated the question, then he said, 'Oh listen, it's a very good gun with an excellent image intensifier. At that range my old mother could have done it if she didn't have arthritic wrists.'

'Prints?'

'Nary a one. It was a professional job.'

'Have you asked the Army to trace . . .'

'Boss, forget the gun. The police are taking care of all that and the best of British luck to them. I'm not interested in it. I don't much care who fired it either. If the cops find the man, he won't know anything. He'll have received his orders by telephone and been paid cash through the mail. I want to know *why* and when I do I'll be that much closer to knowing *who* gave those orders.'

Rafferty was silent for a moment, then went on, 'All of which you know perfectly well. It's your late successor you should be interested in, the man I came to see you about. I want background material. You should want information on his recent activities. As, apparently, you don't, I'm stuck with an inference.'

'That I already have that information?'

'Quick thinking,' Rafferty said.

'Well I don't,' Barry told him angrily. 'I have one potential lead and need three hours to follow it up. You have already promised me that.'

Rafferty nodded, but didn't speak. The black Lotus was clear in his mirror again and he pressed the accelerator to the floor. The occasional police cars they passed paid them no attention and he was weaving through the dense outer-London traffic before Barry spoke again.

'Are you carrying a gun, Rafferty?'

'Gun and rig under your seat, boss. I put it there because I knew "Dropitsir" would have my coat off me. Anyone special you want me to wave it at?'

'I'd like to borrow it.'

Immediately Rafferty was back on the terrace of the cottage in Dorset watching a reluctant dog surrender his jacket to Barry, hearing the soft voice of Martha behind him.

'Mr Rafferty?'

He had turned.

'Yes, Martha?'

'Please bring him safely back to me.'

'Why should you doubt it?'

For long seconds she had stared at him wide-eyed, then said, 'I don't know. Just do it. Promise me you'll do it.'

He had inclined his head towards her, saying nothing, but it had seemed to be enough. She had given him a small, bleak smile and looked away.

'Help yourself,' Rafferty said and watched out of the corner of his eye as the burly white-haired figure beside him contorted itself to reach under the seat. Barry struggled out of his jacket, strapped on the harness, put the jacket on again, then asked, 'Would you let me off at Hyde Park Corner?'

Fifteen minutes later Rafferty did so and watched Barry walk towards the public subway, then he took the hand-set from under the dash.

'Al?'

Trelawney's voice said, 'Yes, Raff?'

'Can you see him?'

'Yes.'

'Right. Follow him. I'm going straight to Thayer Street.'

As he drove away, Barry disappeared down the subway steps and Trelawney abandoned his Lotus, bonnet open, the two nearside wheels on the pavement.

CHAPTER FOUR

Rafferty handed the keys of the Jaguar to the garage supervisor and said, 'Where did this thing and the Lotus come from, Lee?'

'Mr Trelawney told me to hire them early this morning, sir. Said you might be needing to get about a bit fastish. Him too. Mr Young fitted the radios.'

'I see. I thought they were a bit fancy for our budget. You tell the police they're on the Department's list?'

'Yes, sir. Mr Trelawney said to.'

'Okay. The Lotus is probably being towed to a police pound about now. It was left at Hyde Park Corner and I doubt they'll leave it there snarling up the traffic even for us. Have somebody bail it out and bring it back, will you?'

'At once, sir.'

Rafferty nodded, left the garage and walked the hundred yards to the Thayer Street block which housed the Department. He went through the glass doors and along the narrow foyer which might have belonged to an apartment building. At its end he turned left and presented a fake American Express card to a man sitting in an armoured glass cubicle out of sight of the street.

'Afternoon, Sergeant.'

'Good afternoon, Mr Rafferty sir,' Sergeant Cole replied, took the card and slid it under the opaque glass top of a grey metal box on the ledge in front of him. For a second the glass glowed with mauve light, then the box ejected the card like a ticket dispenser and the sergeant handed it back to Rafferty.

'Right, sir.'

By-passing the lifts Rafferty went down the stairs to Requirements Section in the basement. For once he didn't stop to marvel at the chaotic conditions in which Young, the Section Head, liked to produce his sophisticated mechanical, chemical and electronic devices, but picked his way through the detritus of past achievement or present endeavour to the office area at the back of the big room. Young was standing at a draughtsman's light-table, tapping the angle of his jaw with a slide-rule and stabbing at a pocket calculator with the index finger of his other hand. He jumped when Rafferty spoke his name.

'Cor, you don't half move quietly, Mr Rafferty!'

'Sorry. Let me have another gun, would you?'

'The one Mr Trelawney drew for you this morning worn-out already, sir?'

'Yes, you know how it is. They don't make them like they used to.'

'That's what I always . . .'

'Just get it!' Rafferty said.

The gun signed for and in place under Rafferty's jacket Young watched him walk away. He'd never heard Mr Rafferty snap before, no matter how bad the situation was. Of course it had been a tragic day, but it wasn't as though Mr Havelock-Templeton had been close to Mr Rafferty the way Colonel Barry was. Sir Charles Barry he corrected himself, shook his head worriedly and turned back to his calculator.

Rafferty went out through the open steel door of Requirements Section and back up the stairs to the foyer. He glanced thoughtfully at Sergeant Cole in his armoured-glass box, ignored the lifts again and climbed to the first floor. There wasn't much there except the big conference room with a walled-off space for a projectionist at one end, but he examined the windows carefully, looked at the closed-circuit television 'eyes' and the sprinkler system outlets in the ceiling. On the floor above he did the same thing in Records Section, Photographic and Documentation Section and in the three small rooms set aside for any emergency medical treatment which it might be difficult to explain to a hospital. Some people greeted him quietly, others nodded, most avoided his eyes. There was no mistaking the overall air of tension.

When he reached the third floor he stood, undecided, listening to the sounds of typewriters, telex and cipher machines coming from interior and exterior offices. He shrugged and took to the stairs again. Short of a concerted attack by armed men, a possibility he was not prepared to overlook, the building was as secure as modern technology and Young's ingenuity could make it.

On the fourth Rafferty walked the length of the corridor, crossed the Director's empty room and stopped in the doorway to the office Martha had worked in for so many years.

He stood there for a moment looking at the occupant, then asked, 'You all right, old thing?'

The 'old thing' was a girl of twenty-six with a plain, rather stupid face, a squat figure and a ready smile. She had Honours Degrees in three disparate subjects, an Olympic Bronze medal for swimming and spoke seven languages, three of them like a native. The smile came at once, but it was more a rictus than an expression of pleasure.

'Hello, sir,' she said. 'Yes, I suppose I'm all right. I feel . . . well, I feel like I imagine one usually feels when one's employer is shot down in the street. Like panic stricken.'

'Want to go home?'

She shuddered and shook her head.

'All right. I'll arrange for one of the boys to go with you when we shut up shop tonight and I'll ask Angie to stay with you if you'd like that.'

'Yes please, sir. Pretty feeble, aren't I?'

'No, just normal,' Rafferty said. 'Any messages?'

'Yes, Mr Grenville, the Minister's Private Secretary, called,' she glanced at a pad on her desk and at her watch, 'seventeen and thirty-five minutes ago. He said that you or Mr Trelawney were to call him the moment you got in. Shall I get him for you?'

'No. Anything else?'

'Yes. A Mr Leo Volchak called. He . . .'

'*A* Mr Leo Volchak, for God's sake! Didn't Mr Havelock-Templeton tell you anything? Call him now.'

'Yes, sir, but I don't know who or where he is. He said you'd know.' She hesitated then added, 'I'm awfully sorry.'

Rafferty smiled, his first unforced smile since earlier in the day when the Scottish police car had stopped beside him and the leggy blonde who required him to play golf with her in return for her favours.

'Well don't be. It isn't your fault,' he said. 'Call the Russian Embassy, give my name and ask for him.'

He waited for the connection sitting in the Director's chair and when the Russian came on the line, said 'Good afternoon, Mr Volchak. I imagine you've been reading the evening papers.'

The reply was in good English with a heavy, rather guttural accent.

'I'm very glad to hear you put it that way, Mr Rafferty. My purpose in approaching you was to offer our sincere condolences and to give you our absolute assurance that the crime was none of our doing.'

'It never occurred to me that it would be,' Rafferty told him. 'I think the more advanced services grew out of that sort of thing some time ago. At least between themselves and at such a level. Wouldn't you agree?'

'Yes, Mr Rafferty, I would. May I take it that you will inform other – er – interested parties of what I have said?'

Rafferty promised that he would, put down the telephone and heard the click from the adjoining room as the tape-recorder cut out. A moment later she appeared in the doorway.

'Disclaimers yet!' she said then, when Rafferty didn't speak, asked, 'As I was supposed to have known anyway, may I know who that was?' Her tone was overly bright.

'The London Station Head of the KGB. You'll find him on the Embassy list as a water-pick maintenance man, or something bloody stupid. They still like playing that game. I don't know why.'

'Do you believe that it wasn't the KGB?'

'I believe that it wasn't the CIA,' Rafferty said. 'Now, you go to Hospital Section and lie down until I send for you. That's an order.'

The man with the thinning red hair and World War II RAF style moustache was sweating heavily. He tried to tell himself that it was due to the closeness of the air in the disused cupboard under the stairs he was crouching in. It was more comforting to do that than admit that he was afraid of the voice whispering in the telephone receiver at his ear. Well, not the voice so much as the terrible retribution for inefficiency he had been assured it could order.

He shook his head in nervous irritation and said, 'I tell you I can't be sure. It's a possibility and that's all.'

'You were hired to be sure,' the receiver whispered at him.

'Christ!' the red-haired man said, 'I only finished installing the stuff two hours ago. Then there was this line to you to rig. There's a lot of traffic interference and I haven't got accustomed to the sounds of the building yet. All buildings have their own language. Creaks and clicks when the temperature . . .'

'Shut up and listen,' the receiver told him.

The man sighed, put down the telephone and fitted the padded ear-pieces in place, pressing them to the sides of his head with his hands. For four minutes nothing moved but his eyes, then he pushed the ear-phones back, letting them hang around his neck, and picked up the telephone.

'All I can say is that I think there may be someone there. I can't . . .'

'You're getting repetitive,' the voice said. 'Keep listening.'

The line went dead.

An hour later a light blinked in the base of the telephone rest.

'Anything positive?'

'No.'

'Then get this. She left ten minutes ago and should be with you any time now. Start recording, listen with one ear and give me a running commentary.'

'Right,' the listener said, but eight minutes went by before he spoke again.

'Sound of key in door. Door opening. Door shut. Footsteps – female I think. Crossing living-room. In bedroom now. Bathroom. Definitely female – sharp heel-clicks on tiled floor. Water running. Water stopped. Back in bedroom. Pretty quiet. Faint rustle, like material. Could be undressing. Same. Same. Tell you when there's any change.'

The telephone receiver broke a long silence.

'Well?'

'Still the same. Seems to be taking her time. No – wait. Shower running. Didn't hear her move. Must be barefoot. I suppose I was wrong about there being someone there before her.'

'When I want you to start supposing I'll let you know,' the voice said. 'Call me when something happens.'

The red-haired man nodded vigorously in the cupboard under the stairs, then wiped the sweat from his face and neck.

'Mr Trelawney for you, sir, from a call box.'

Back in his own room, Rafferty said, 'Put him on, Liz. Yes, Al?'

'He's at 308 Wilton Crescent.'

'Okay, get back and cover it. I'll have three men round there right away. Place them two front, one back, if there is a back, then get yourself here as soon as you can.'

'There's something else, Raff. One of the names on the indicator board in the foyer is Fiona Langley. She's one of ours. Know her?'

'Think so. Brunette in Records with a vacuous expression and a permanent pout. Wears sun-glasses all the time. That the one?'

'That's the one.'

'In that case stay there,' Rafferty said. 'When Barry leaves you follow him with one of the others. I think he'll come straight here, but tag along. The remaining two cover Langley and follow if she goes out. If she heads for Heathrow or anywhere like that they're to bring her in.'

He broke the connection, depressed the key marked 'Conference' and three others. The acknowledgements came at once and he started talking again.

CHAPTER FIVE

Colonel Sir Charles Barry lay back in the deep armchair, relaxed, motionless. Neither his eyes nor the muzzle of Rafferty's gun resting easily on his knee moved from the wide archway leading to the bedroom where the woman was undressing. She had let herself into the flat and walked straight to the bedroom without a glance in his direction, her hands loosening the loop of hair at the nape of her neck, a toss of the head sending the hair cascading about her shoulders. Then she had removed the large black-tinted sun-glasses she often wore at work to rest her eyes from the use of contact lenses which turned their colour from natural blue to brown. For a minute or two she had moved out of his range of vision and when she returned he had seen that the mouth-distorting toothless dental plates had gone too.

It unsettled him a little to note that even at his age her beauty produced a quickening of his pulse rate and that it quickened further as she took off her clothes. This she did with a clear sensuous enjoyment and studied grace as though performing for an audience. When she was naked she disappeared from his sight again and he heard the sound of water running in the shower. Waiting, still motionless, he thought that, with the possible exception of Jane Trask – Jane Trelawney now – she had to be the most beautiful woman he had ever seen. Odd that the Department should possess two such. Then he frowned, angry with himself for the comparison. There was no 'possible exception' about it. The accolade went to Jane Trelawney who wore amused compassion in her eyes like a blessing. The bitch-goddess in the shower had never heard of it and, as if in confirmation, his pulse slowed nearly to normal.

The shower cut off abruptly and, a moment later, she was back wearing some pale-grey translucent creation he was unable to put a name to. It was neither house-coat, nightdress nor negligee but, he decided, whatever it was narcissism could hardly be stretched further. It was only then that it occurred to him that she might be expecting somebody. He frowned for the second time, angry again with himself for his failure to have perceived something so probable. Old, he told himself. Too old to be allowed out alone and a voyeur to boot. No, at least he wasn't that. It was shock value he was after and that would be the greater now.

She had made up her face and was brushing her hair when he said, 'That'll do, Fiona. I want to talk to you.'

Without turning towards him she replied, '*Dear* Sir Charles. So patient and so good at picking locks. I do hope you enjoyed the cabaret.'

He very nearly asked, 'You mean you saw me?' but stopped himself in time and said, 'Come here.'

She got up from her dressing-table at once and stalked across the bedroom to the archway, very tall in her high heels, the undefinable garment coiling about her like smoke. When she was four paces inside the living-room she saw the gun and stopped, an expression of surprised amusement on her face.

'Sir Charles dear, there's no need to go to those lengths to protect your honour.'

He ignored the remark and said ponderously, 'At the first sign of anything I might interpret as leading to an act of aggression on your part I shall shoot you dead.'

'Would sitting down be interpreted as leading to an act of aggression on my part?' She still looked amused.

Barry gestured with the gun towards a chair. She moved slowly to it and sat down.

'What does the Department employ you as officially nowadays, Fiona?'

'A senior clerk in Records.'

'I see. That appointment is cancelled with immediate effect. You will not be required for that duty or your real one again and you will not attempt to leave this flat until I send an escort for you.'

Lightly she asked, 'And if I do?'

'You will be shot painfully, but not fatally.'

Fiona Langley settled herself back in her chair, crossing one leg over the other, letting the material slit to the hip fall away.

'Well,' she said, 'at least it's comforting to know that I'm wanted alive.'

Barry's reply was low, but clear. 'I hope for your sake that tomorrow brings you no cause to reconsider that thought.'

'Very sinister, Charles. I may call you "Charles", may I not? But would it be too much to ask what this is all about? I might even be able to save you the trouble of having me tortured. After all, it isn't really your scene, is it?'

'No, it's not,' Barry said. 'The infliction of pain and mental anguish is a proclivity of yours which I found it difficult to live with, but you will not find us wanting in determination and ingenuity. As you say, however, you may be able to save us the trouble.'

'Try me. You can always confirm what I say under narcotics.'

He nodded. 'Yes, we can always do that.'

So much, he thought, for his shock tactics, the sight of her elegant leg an impudent reminder of how easily she had turned them on him. It didn't matter. If she was prepared to talk interestingly enough his purpose would be served. He had to make her do that.

'Not so long ago you killed someone, Fiona. Who was it?'

'As you seem to be back in the hot seat why don't you look in Havelock-Templeton's safe and find out?'

'Be very careful,' Barry said. 'I'll answer that one question and no more. Any evasion on your part thereafter and . . .' He raised the gun in his hand, then let it sink back on to his knee, feeling mild embarrassment at the theatricality of the role he had cast himself in. 'Mr Havelock-Templeton's records, as far as you are concerned,' he went on, 'contain nothing but your name against certain dates. He has now been killed. Nobody knows why, but it is reasonable to assume that it was in retaliation for something.'

Barry fell silent for a number of seconds wondering if Fiona Langley's suggestion that he look in the late Director's safe had been a trap, if she was aware that her name was never recorded as anything but a junior employee and that the bulk of her salary was paid out of non-accountable funds. Too late to bother about that he decided and began talking again.

'The appearance of your name and your true function which is known only to Directors of the Department past and present form a link which one cannot ignore. I ask you again. Who did you kill?'

Fiona Langley shrugged and said, 'A man called Vernon Whiteoaks. May I have a cigarette?'

The cigarette box and a table lighter were beside her and Barry had examined both as he had almost everything else in the apartment.

'Go ahead.'

She lit a cigarette and looked at him through the smoke.

'Name ring a bell with you?'

'Yes, but very faint. Continue.'

'The Leeds sex murder. My God, what a place for sex! Remember now?'

'Yes,' Barry said, trying unsuccessfully to conceal his disgust.

A faint spark of resentment glowed for a moment in her eyes. Then it was gone and she said, 'You know, you don't have any right to look at me like that. I've had to do similar things on your orders.'

'I don't have to like your methods.'

She sighed before saying quietly, as though talking to herself, 'He doesn't have to like my methods. Vernon Whiteoaks, I ask you. It's the sort of name they dream up for a serial in women's magazines.' Then, more loudly, 'Perhaps you'll understand a little better when I tell you that he was a Pole called Dyboski who made his way into this country via a Displaced Persons camp in 1946. He was a teenager then. After a time he had become a British subject, changed his name, worked his way quite a way up in the Trades' Union movement at local level, then disappeared to the DDR for three years. That's East Germany, in case you've forgotten.'

With heavy patience Barry said, 'I haven't forgotten,' and Fiona Langley went on, 'Well, that's a relief. Anyway, he came back from East Berlin in 1971 with two things. A clear mandate as Liaison Head and Paymaster to the Communist infiltrated Unions and detailed plans in the long term for the disruption of industry plus, in the event of war, for crippling the ports. We haven't had a major war yet but, as you've been buried in Dorset for so damned long, the world may have passed you by a little. Why don't you spend an hour or so in a library while you're in London? Get out the newspapers for the seventies and see how well he's done the rest of his job!'

'Thank you, Fiona. Perhaps I should do that. And so it was decided that he must go?'

'So I assume, as I was ordered to help him on his way but, before you start whimpering again, let me explain one of the facts of life which seems to have escaped you.'

Barry said nothing and the woman continued, 'You don't go around assassinating Trades' Union officials. Not in this country you don't. It's liable to lead to repercussions on a national scale. In a case like Whiteoaks you look for a weakness and if it doesn't exist you make one. I had to make one. It took Whiteoaks two weeks of exposure to me, Sir Charles, to discover that he was a kink, a masochist, and one night for me to indulge him too far. Certain newspapers had a lovely time when he was found and from then until now nobody has mentioned the word "politics".'

'But there has still been a repercussion. Why?'

She mashed her cigarette angrily to shreds in an ashtray and said, 'I haven't got the remotest idea. Now go away and stop pestering me and when you're feeling more self-righteous than usual try to remember that it's people like you who create the need for people like me!'

'I must admit that there's truth in that, Fiona. You and I have a lot to answer for in our respective parts of judge and executioner. Pilnyak, Miller, Veit, Olsen, Guthrie. Even some of our . . .'

'Oh really, Charles! Do we have to go wandering down memory lane *now*?'

'No, I suppose we don't,' Barry agreed and sat for a moment as though lost in thought, then he leaned suddenly forward. 'There *was* no repercussion, was there, Fiona? Not from outside. Tell me, why did you kill Mr Havelock-Templeton?'

'He kept me waiting at a hamburger bar where we had been conducting an illicit affair,' she said.

Barry put his left hand in his jacket pocket, produced a small object and held it towards her.

'Recognize that?'

'It's the heel of a woman's shoe.'

'Your shoe, to be precise.'

'Really? I didn't know you were a fetishist and I thought they preferred the whole shoe anyway.'

'It would be convenient to have the rest of the shoe and its fellow, but they seem to be missing.'

She smiled at him as though he were an endearingly precocious child. 'Never mind, Charles. I'll let you choose a whole pair. There are about thirty in the cupboard in the bedroom. I'm sure you'll find something to please you.'

'This heel,' Barry said, 'was found on a rooftop thirty-five feet from the rifle that killed Mr Havelock-Templeton. I imagine that you have burnt the shoes themselves. It doesn't matter. The two prints on this are smudged, but identifiably yours.'

With slow, careful movements Fiona Langley took another cigarette from the box beside her and lit it, then inhaled slowly before saying, 'I see. What a remarkably corny frame-up.'

'Additionally,' Barry told her, 'you were seen to leave the building next to the one from which the shots were fired about four minutes after the shooting and five seconds behind a man of whom we have an indifferent description. The description of you, on the other hand, tallies exactly. Not surprisingly considering your appearance.'

'Which of my appearances?' she asked him.

Barry ignored the question.

'Why did you kill him, Fiona?'

'I didn't, as it happens.'

Patiently Barry said, 'Surely I don't have to explain to you that it is immaterial who pulled the trigger. You and this man are accomplices, one to the other. Each of you bears equal guilt and will continue to do so unless you care to tip the scales in your favour.'

'By turning Queen's evidence and telling you who he is?'

'As you say.'

'No, Charles, not as I say. The police could make me that offer, but you cannot, so take yourself and your stupid suspicions and go to the devil!'

Barry looked and sounded anxious when he said, 'If you were following this man, if you tried to stop him and failed, you would tell me, wouldn't you? You aren't afraid to admit to failure, are you? You don't doubt my authority, my re-appointment as Director?'

She looked at him with mocking arrogance.

'Goodness me, what a lot of questions! I don't think I'll bother to answer any of them. That "little boy" line may go down well with Martha, but don't try it on me.'

He nodded tiredly and got to his feet, the gun still pointing at her. 'Very well, until tomorrow. I'm genuinely sorry that it has to be this way, but the choice was yours. As I told you, don't try to leave and don't bother with the telephones. They don't work any more.'

'Why tomorrow?' Fiona Langley asked. 'Take me in now. You never know. I might do away with myself during the night.'

'It's simpler to hold you here,' he told her, 'until Dr Teller arrives from Canada. He's our insurance that you'll tell us what we want to know. We might be clumsy enough to kill you. You know Dr Teller, don't you?'

'I do not.'

The reply didn't surprise Barry. He had never heard of a Dr Teller either, but thought that the whole exchange had gone very well.

'You will. I'm very much afraid you will, only too well. As to doing away with yourself, nobody who loves their body as much as you do yours would entertain the thought for a moment.'

She stood up slowly then, her arms hanging relaxed at her sides. The arrogance had not left her face and now it seemed to spread to the posture of her body.

Barry glanced at her naked right hip and leg, then up at her face. His voice grated when he said, 'I can hardly wish you a good night, but I recommend that you gird your loins in both senses of the term.'

CHAPTER SIX

'Door shuts,' the red-haired man said. 'I suppose he's left.'

'You and your supposing will get you killed one of these days,' the receiver told him quietly then, more loudly, 'Listen!'

'Sorry. Only silence. Still silence. Wait, there's movement. Her footsteps I think, like she's walking up and down. Now she's talking to herself. Words indistinguishable.'

'I won't warn you again,' the voice at his ear said. 'How the fucking hell do you know who she's talking to? Just listen, damn you.'

'Yeah, yeah, sure. No change. Ah! She just said, "I'd like to strangle the old bastard with his own beard!" Quite loud that was.'

'All right. Give it five more minutes.'

The listener took his watch from his wrist and placed it in front of him, watching the sweep of the second hand, ears straining. At the end of the fifth revolution he said, 'She's still in the living-room, but sitting down. I heard a chair or something give. Nothing else.'

'Very well. Connect me to the tape-recorder. Start from where this Sir Charles character first speaks and run it right through. Break in if anything interesting happens and I don't mean her going to the bog.'

The man sat, pulling at his handle-bar moustache, watching the slowly revolving spools. He was sweating again, less from fear of the voice now than the information the tapes carried, the words he had listened to and tried to transmit as they were spoken. He hadn't liked what he had heard, not one bit. Who were these people who talked about murder and torture, judges and executioners? That stuff about a department and directors too. Government? Couldn't be, not with her admitting to whipping that poor bastard to death in Leeds. Jesus! That had been a case and no mistake! 'An orgy of perversion' one paper had called it. Maybe some way-out religious sect, or perhaps the Mafia. Did the Mafia operate in England? Did even *they* do that sort of thing? The idea of getting out at once came to him, but he discarded it. The power represented by the voice on the telephone still frightened him enough to keep him where he was.

The light on the phone rest winking brought him back to himself. He hadn't noticed that the spools had stopped turning.

'Did you get it all?' he asked. It seemed best to take the initiative.

'I got it all. Keep listening and report everything to Samms here. I'm leaving now.'

'How long am I expected to . . .'

'You're getting a little deaf, friend,' the voice broke in. 'I just told you to keep listening. You'll hear from me when I want you to stop.'

'Butterflies subsided, Sue?'

'More or less, Mr Rafferty,' Sue Mitchell said. 'They gave me a pill and I lay down for a bit.' She still sounded tense.

Perhaps, he thought, a little light diversion might help.

'You can get me Mr Grenville, the Minister's Private Secretary, now.'

'Yes, sir.'

'By the way, which phone did he come through on?'

'The black one, sir.'

'Right, call him on the scrambler.'

When the connection was made, 'I understand that the Minister wants to speak to me,' Rafferty said and heard Grenville reply, 'Well, actually no. He's out at the moment, but I want to be in a position to brief him on your meeting with Charles Barry when he gets back.'

Rafferty's eyebrows shot up, but he kept his surprise out of his voice.

'Oh, that. Wasted effort, I'm afraid. The old man's getting a bit past it. Can't remember names or people. He thought I was a surveyor from the County Council when I first arrived and showed me the plans for his septic tank. I straightened him out on that, then he started calling me Chadwick. Still was when I left.'

'You're not expecting me to believe...'

'Dribbles a lot too,' Rafferty went on. 'Sad really, but there's plenty of life in him. Cadged a lift back to town to go to his club.'

'That's the Naval and Military, isn't it?'

'No, The Playboy,' Rafferty said.

There was silence on the line for several seconds before Grenville spoke again, his voice resentful.

'You people appear to take a childish delight in making it difficult for me to do my job. I had trouble with a man of yours called Trelawney this morning. If this lack of co-operation continues you'll leave me no choice but to report the situation to the Minister.'

'Oh please, don't be hard on Trelawney. He's pretty sound really.'

'Sound! By God, I hope nobody ever describes me as "sound"!'

'I shouldn't think you need worry about that,' Rafferty said. 'Now as soon as your boss gets back you go and tell him all about it. He'll crucify you when he hears that you've been yelling the names of people in this organization over an open wire as you've done twice to Miss Mitchell this afternoon. I hope I'll have time to come and watch you dangling.' He had spoken with cold, slow emphasis, waited interestedly for a reply then, when there was none, replaced the receiver. Again the click of the recorder in the next room switching itself off came to him and, absently, his eyes turned in that direction. The girl appeared in the doorway. Part of his mind recorded the fact that she looked less strained, but most of it was occupied with Grenville.

'Phew! I feel better for listening to that,' she said. 'First you made me laugh, then you made me feel safe. I shan't need my hand holding tonight now. But tell me, are the names of people here all that secret?'

'What?' he said. 'Oh. No of course they're not. We're probably all on file just about everywhere, but I don't expect Grenville knows that. He just needs to learn to mind his own business.' He paused before adding, 'Look, Sue, I'm rather expecting Sir Charles to be with us for a few days. I'll be going back to my own room so he can use this one. Will you look after him?'

'Of course, but won't he be bringing the famous Martha I'm always hearing about?'

'No.'

'Is it true that she won a George Cross during the war?'

He lit a cigarette, wishing the girl would stop pestering him with questions. There was so much to do, so much to think about. Particularly so much to think about but, he decided, a minute answering this one might be well spent, might stiffen her. It was so often the highly intelligent ones who needed stiffening and she hadn't had the happiest of years. First her lover and then, a few months later, her boss. The former, a Department trainee called Matthews, had died during a practice mobile surveillance job in a twelve-car pile-up in fog on the M23 in Surrey. Nine people had been killed in the crash and it had never been established by the police who, if anyone, had been at fault.

Rafferty, together with the rest of the Department, had been unaware of Martha's history until, to her scarlet embarrassment, Barry had made it public at the dinner the senior staff had given them both on their retirement. For more than thirty years, with Barry's help, she had kept her secret. First she had changed her name by deed-poll before accepting an appointment as his confidential secretary, then ascribed her crippled state to polio as a child and arthritis in later life. Strange, Rafferty mused, that the little old lady, who had been old for so long, should still be in her early fifties.

'Yes,' he said. 'She made herself into a demolition expert. Specialized in bridges and railway lines. Blew a lot of Nazis to blazes in occupied France and Belgium before the Gestapo got their hands on her. They smashed her toes and fried her insides with some heating contraption trying to make her talk. They didn't succeed. Not bad at eighteen I'd say.'

Some of the colour had drained from Sue Mitchell's cheeks while he had been talking, but her voice was reasonably steady when she spoke.

'It's all relative, isn't it?'

'What is?'

'Trouble. I thought I'd got some.'

'Yeah. Well, don't get all awed about it. She never won any Olympic Bronze.'

She smiled and was turning away when he said, 'Sue?'

'Sir?'

'Open this safe, please.'

'Yes, sir.'

She turned the dial this way and that several times, did something with the handle, turned the dial again and pulled the heavy door open. He hadn't bothered to watch her.

'Shall I tell you the combination, Mr Rafferty?'

'No. Do you remember what it was when Mr Havelock-Templeton took over from Sir Charles?'

'Yes, I do.'

'Okay, write it down here, then fix your face and go on home.'

Her hand moved involuntarily to touch her lips.

Rafferty shook his head. 'Mascara's run,' he said. 'Comes of getting emotional.'

At his own desk once more Rafferty looked up when Barry came through the doorway, pleased to see that Sergeant Cole had not permitted even the ex-Director access without an escort. He nodded his head at the clerk in dismissal and gestured Barry to a chair.

'Ready to tell me all about it, boss?'

Barry sat down, took a pipe from his pocket and stuffed tobacco into the bowl. Some of it fell on the desk top. He blew it off and flakes settled on Rafferty's trousers. Rafferty smiled faintly, leaving them where they were, thinking it was good to have Barry around again, wishing that the circumstances were different,

'Yes,' Barry said, 'but do something for me first, would you, Rafferty? Get a man, two if you can spare them, along to 308 Wilton Crescent. They . . .'

'Fiona Langley is already under surveillance,' Rafferty told him and watched the forward thrust of Barry's beard which was one of the very few indications of surprise he had ever been known to give.

'Which means that I am too, eh?'

'Does it? I don't see the logic in that. Is there any reason why I shouldn't be able to fit a name to an address? The address of one of our people?'

Barry looked at his unlit pipe, then back at Rafferty.

'None at all, but I've just as good as told you that I've been to see her, haven't I?'

'Yes, you have.'

'Was I followed, or spotted by your surveillance team?'

'Those questions are pointless and the answers none of your business, boss.'

Angrily Barry dropped his pipe on to the desk and more strands of tobacco fell from the bowl.

'You don't know how wrong you are,' he said. 'If I was followed, the chances are you don't know about her. If I was spotted by one of your stake-out men then you do, which you shouldn't!'

'All right,' Rafferty said. 'As I don't have a spare week to unravel that one I'll tell you that you were followed. To me Langley is a Records clerk and that's close to being a grace and favour job too. Used to be Foster's secretary until he committed suicide. She was living with him when that happened and went completely to pieces. For some reason I never understood Havelock-Templeton insisted on finding a job for her when she'd pulled herself together again.'

'What do you think of her physically?'

'I don't.'

'Well, do it now, man!'

Rafferty moved his shoulders in a gesture of resignation. 'Very good body, but that mouth! Looks like a cross between a goldfish and a teenager waiting for a kiss.'

Barry pulled gently at his beard then, as though satisfied that it was securely in place, gathered up the scattered crumbs of tobacco and pressed them into the bowl of his pipe.

'She wears peculiar dental plates,' he said. 'Brown contact lenses too when she hasn't got those dark glasses on.'

Rafferty watched the start of the well-remembered pocket-search for matches, pushed his lighter across the desk and asked, 'Arch supports and elastic stockings as well, boss?'

His pipe going Barry handed back the lighter before saying, 'Changes her hair colour. Quite simple things that alter her appearance completely. In fact, Rafferty, Fiona Langley is a blue-eyed, raven-haired knock-out who is so damned good-looking that it hurts even an old fool like me. She is also an ice-cold, frozen-hearted bitch who for the last six years has carried out all the Department's more difficult liquidation assignments.'

'I see. The Director's appointment presumably.'

'Correct. Not even the Minister knows. Obviously, the circumstances being what they now are, you had to know.'

'Obviously,' Rafferty said. 'Until somebody tells me different I *am* the Director.' He ignored Barry's sharp glance and went on as though thinking aloud, 'How very interesting. So the peculiar Fiona has been our chief instrument for "termination with extreme prejudice".'

'For what?'

'It's an expression the American security services use to describe an official killing. Don't you remember?'

'No.'

'Well they do, but don't ask me why.' Rafferty smiled briefly then went on with untypical briskness, 'When I gave you the news this morning you assumed that the killing of Havelock-Templeton was a reprisal for something we had done. As I was unable to suggest what that could have been, you decided to contact the only person in the Department who might be privy to secrets withheld from me. Further, you were extremely anxious to reach her flat well before the time she would return home, presumably for the purpose of searching it. What did you find and what took place between the two of you?'

'I found that the place was bugged,' Barry said. 'Two in the living-room lamps. One behind the bed-head.'

'Wire or radio?'

'Wire, but I didn't find the outlet.'

Rafferty reached towards his desk-speaker.

'Young, I shall need you tonight to do a wire trace.'

'Very well, Mr Rafferty sir.'

'I don't know how to put it delicately, but will you be able to bug the buggers?'

'Easy if I can get at their wire,' the box said. 'I'll just piggy-back straight off it.'

Releasing the key Rafferty turned back to Barry.

'And then?'

'She arrived, I led her to believe that I had been reappointed Director and asked her about her recent activities. Apparently she had been instructed to – er – dispose of a man some months ago and had duly done so. This man was a . . .'

'Just like that? She told you just like that?'

'I had to apply a little pressure,' Barry said. 'Well, as a matter of fact I threatened her. Then I accused her of killing Havelock-Templeton, or being the murderer's accomplice. She denied it of course, so I told her that she had been seen leaving the building just after the shots were fired at almost the same time as an unidentified man and that the heel of one of her shoes . . .'

Barry stopped talking when he realized that he had lost his audience. '. . . you to pull those men off 308 Wilton Crescent at once,' Rafferty was saying to the desk-speaker.

Then Trelawney's voice. 'And if she wanders?'

'She wanders. I think somebody's going to hit that place tonight, hopefully after dark. That's when I'd do it anyway and don't bother to tell me that there's no such thing as a calculated risk, because I'm taking one. I don't want whoever it is frightened off by people lurking about in the street. I'll want you, Geddes and Fenner, plus a couple of marksmen for the roof. Pick 'em yourself and have Young assemble everything you think we might need. I'll get back to you.'

'I hoped you'd see it my way,' Barry said.

Rafferty ignored the statement. 'You were talking about the heel of her shoe. What about it?'

'So I was.' Barry reached into his jacket and drew a woman's shoe with no heel from the holster he had borrowed from Rafferty. A complete shoe came from under the harness strap, then he produced the missing heel from a side pocket and placed all three objects in a row on the desk. 'You've seen them put them on. Stick their toes in, bend the leg back at the knee, hook a finger round the heel and pull the...'

'Yes,' Rafferty broke in. 'So her fingerprints are on it and I imagine it was supposed to have been found somewhere near the rifle on the roof, all of which you spelt out for the benefit of whoever was listening in.' He took a large buff envelope from a drawer in his desk, dropped the shoes and the heel into it and pushed it across to Barry. 'As you pulled the heel off yourself I expect you'll want to get it fixed for her. Those things cost about fifty-five quid. They're by Raynes.'

Rafferty lay back in his chair and yawned. The day which had been a long one, was only now about to start and the nights before with the girl at St Andrews hadn't been entirely restful. He yawned again and said, 'Then you told her that she was under house arrest or some such. That's what you wanted the men there for. You knew she'd notice them.'

'You're very quick, Rafferty, but then you always were.'

'Marvellous, isn't it? Now tell me who she killed.'

'A man named Vernon Whiteoaks in Leeds. Remember the case?'

Rafferty said, 'Yes, I remember it. I took all the Sunday papers for three weeks over that one. I've got a very prurient mind you know,' but he neither sounded nor looked amused. He paused before asking softly, 'What sort of people are we?' Then in his normal voice, 'Okay, why?'

'Because those were her orders I imagine.'

'And she said nothing about a reason for them?'

'In my day it was extremely rare for her to be given a reason. I can't speak for Havelock-Templeton of course.'

If Rafferty noticed the evasion he gave no sign of it. He yawned for the third time and said, 'Hell, I'm tired. You must be too. How about some sandwiches and coffee?'

'Thank you. I'd welcome them.'

Rafferty looked at his watch and stood up. 'Liz'll have gone home hours ago. I'll see what I can find.'

He closed the door behind him, walked along the passage and opened another. Seated behind her desk his secretary looked up at him.

'Any luck, Liz?'

'I'm afraid not, sir. They say there's no secret writing. No nothing. Just the numbers. Typed on an Olivetti "Lettera 32" if that's any help. The pages have been photographed and "Codes" are working on them now. Oh, one thing. There are no fingerprints except Mr Havelock-Templeton's and they aren't where you'd expect them to be if he'd put the paper in the typewriter.' She picked up a folder and looked at it curiously.

'Somebody just invented gloves,' Rafferty said. 'Thanks, Liz. Would you mind making some coffee and sandwiches for Sir Charles and me? Don't take them in. I'll be back in a couple of minutes. You aren't supposed to be here.'

He took the folder from her and walked quickly along the corridor to the Director's room. The big safe opened unprotestingly when he worked the combination he had re-set using the figures supplied to him by Sue Mitchell and that, he thought, was just as well. It had a number of ways of registering disapproval when tampered with by an unauthorized person, one of which was to destroy its contents.

Its interior was so tidily arranged that it appeared to be almost empty. Four or five neatly stacked folders, a thin sheaf of papers stapled together at the top left-hand corner, a larger bundle secured with a ribbon and, finally, three notebooks. A far cry from Barry's day, he thought. Then, if Martha was to be believed and he didn't doubt that she was, such items as tobacco, newspapers, library books and the day before's uneaten sandwiches were cleared out by her before Barry arrived for work. Once there had been a fishing creel with a tin of live maggots in it.

Rafferty had examined the contents of the safe when he had altered the combination and had decided that, with the possible exception of the folder containing the numbers he now held, there was nothing either relevant to the present situation or of a particularly sensitive nature there. He put the folder amongst the others, closed the door and spun the dial.

Barry pushed his tray aside and said, 'That's better. Never did like missing lunch. Dinner too, considering the time. When are we moving in?'

'You're not moving anywhere,' Rafferty told him. 'Rightly or wrongly you set this thing up. I'll take it from there. Which reminds me, I'll have that gun back. Miss Langley may need it.'

His expression and movements grudging, Barry took the automatic from his hip pocket and placed it on the desk.

Rafferty stared at him speculatively for several seconds before saying, 'Look, boss, if you want something to do why don't you go through Havelock-Templeton's safe? I've had no time. You might find a clue to what the hell this is all about.'

'Very well. What's the combination?'

'I don't know. That's the Director's private safe. I can phone Miss Mitchell, but can't you remember? You used it for long enough.'

'It'll have been changed when I retired, Rafferty.'

'Oh, I see. No, as a matter of fact it wasn't. I was there when Havelock-Templeton told Miss Mitchell he was leaving it alone. Didn't want to confuse two sequences and set the alarm off.'

'Damned poor security,' Barry said, but to Rafferty's ears the remark lacked conviction.

CHAPTER SEVEN

'If you'd stop kicking me in the ear I might be able to cut this glass,' Rafferty said and Young's 'Sorry, sir. Foot slipped,' came to him faintly from above his head.

When he pulled the pane of the lavatory window out of its frame, guiding it to one side clear of the nylon ladder, the cords attached to rubber suction cups at the top corners took the strain. He watched as the glass disappeared upwards into the darkness, then slid through the opening he had made.

The lavatory door opened silently in response to the infinitely patient movement of his fingers on the handle, as did the bathroom door after it, and he found himself looking into an empty bedroom. The wide archway Barry had described to him was to his right. He moved forward until he was framed by it and stood looking at the woman, grateful for Barry's cautioning words. 'She doesn't look the way you know her, Rafferty. Don't waste time on a double take.'

She was sitting, dressed as he had been told she still might be, reading. The lighting in the room was soft and an anglepoise lamp illuminated the book resting on her thigh. Rafferty thought that she resembled a very expensive call-girl waiting disinterestedly for a client to arrive. He placed a finger across his lips, took one step forward and found himself staring into vivid blue, wide-open eyes. Recognition on her part was almost instantaneous and the eyes narrowed as alarm left her until they were almost obscured by her heavy lashes.

Rafferty kept his finger against his lips and made jabbing motions towards the wall with his other hand. Fiona Langley stood up, walked to the record-player and placed a disc on the turntable. When music flooded the room she turned, moved to his side and took the automatic he held out to her.

His mouth close to her ear, 'Got the general picture?' he asked.

'It's beginning to develop. I'm target Number Two. Barry set me up so they'd have to make their play tonight.'

'Right. Have you said anything since Barry left?'

'A few obscenities. They'll have done no harm.'

'Good. I'm going to let Young in in a minute to trace the bug lines. When he's finished he'll go and Trelawney, Fenner and Geddes will be coming through. Latimer will stay as telephone link to the roof. Anyone else shoves their nose in here you shoot him. Clear?'

'I'm flattered,' she whispered. 'With you and Trelawney I've *really* got the heavy mob looking after me.'

'Don't get cute with me, lady,' Rafferty told her. 'Nobody's looking after you. I understand you can do that for yourself rather well. You're part of an operational team. Now, collect whatever it is you need to make you look the way you do at Thayer Street. Some clothes too. Take the lot into the kitchen, change and stay there till I tell you to come out. Move.'

Fiona Langley grinned, blew him a kiss and walked away. When, clothes over her arm, sponge-bag in one hand, gun in the other, she disappeared into the kitchen Rafferty returned to the lavatory and helped Young in through the window.

Young ignored lavatory, bathroom and bedroom, passed through the archway and walked straight to the floor-length curtains covering the living-room's single large window, then he turned and beckoned to Rafferty.

The wire ran from the edge of the wall-to-wall carpeting vertically up the seam of the curtain's outer edge between it and the wall, then was lost to sight in the darkness behind the pelmet.

Young managed to convey his contempt for amateurs in a whisper.

'Standard trick for a quick job, sir. I'll just nip upstairs, find out where that goes and patch in to their outside line.' He tapped the rubber-covered box hanging by a strap from his neck. 'Won't take long.'

Rafferty shook his head. 'No, that's all. Sorry I brought you out unnecessarily. Send the others down when you go up.'

'What shall I do then?'

'Go home and invent something.'

'All right, sir.'

Young walked quickly away. Anything Rafferty said was all right as far as he was concerned. He'd spend a couple of hours working with his micro-chips.

Trelawney's big frame appeared in the archway, Geddes, shorter, slighter, mild-mannered, at his shoulder. Behind them Rafferty could see Fenner's tubby shape. All were wearing "Thames Gas" engineers' coveralls and Geddes was carrying a metal tool-box. Rafferty crooked a finger at Trelawney.

'Latimer?'

Trelawney jerked a thumb in the direction of the bathroom.

'Good. Who's on the roof?'

'Stirling covering the buildings opposite. Reid general look-out.'

Without acknowledging the softly spoken words Rafferty pointed at the curtain and said, 'Wire runs up this edge and through the ceiling. I think there must be a relay man on the other end in this building. Probably have been too difficult to isolate the Post Office line to here in daylight or they'd have bugged the phones, but patching in to an external cable wouldn't be hard. Take Peter and Jack and look. If he's there try to keep him operating under your control. I'll have Langley create a scene in a few minutes. You may be able to hear him reporting it.'

Trelawney gestured with his head at Geddes and Fenner. Both joined him at the door, then he looked at Rafferty standing by the record-player. The music stopped. For thirty seconds Trelawney crouched, his ear pressed to the door, before raising a thumb. When a new disc started to play he opened the door and led the way into the deserted passage outside. Rafferty closed the door after them, easing the Yale lock gently home, then walked to the kitchen.

Puzzled, Trelawney stood at the door of the apartment directly above the one he had just left listening to the faint sound of voices and occasional laughter coming from inside. Several people, he thought, and at least two of them women. He glanced upwards but, as he knew, there was nothing there but flat roof. Would there be room for a man in the space between roof and ceiling? Possibly. He looked left to where Fenner was waiting at the bend of the stairs forming a link between him and Geddes near the bottom. Then he looked down.

The tiny pile of sawdust, where somebody had drilled through the door-frame at floor level, caught his eye first then the wire pressed down between carpet and wall. It was leading back the way he had come and he followed it towards the stairs. A third of the way down them it disappeared through a hole in one of the treads.

As he passed him Trelawney said, 'Come on,' to Fenner and to Geddes, 'Stay there and cover Langley's door. I think we've found the bastard.'

The passage continued for only a few feet beyond the foot of the stairs, an ornate console table with nothing on it occupying the end, but there was room enough in the side wall for a door. Trelawney took a gun from under his coverall, swung the door inwards and found himself standing in a long, narrow service room. It was empty except for a sink at the far end.

With only the indirect light from the passageway to see by it took him a moment to notice the irregular-sided piece of hardboard giving access to a space under the stairs.

Fiona Langley made a lot of noise with ice, clattered bottles, knocked the arm of the record-player screechingly across the disc, swore and burst into tears. Still sobbing she looked at the broken needle and slid a cassette into place. When the music began again she stopped crying, shouted, 'The fucking, slimy, treacherous, sadistic old bugger!' and threw a glass into the open fireplace. It shattered with a satisfactorily explosive sound.

She looked over her shoulder at Rafferty, read approval in his expression and leant against the wall, relaxed, waiting.

Kneeling beside the small hardboard door Trelawney heard a male voice say, 'Samms, I think she's falling apart. Case of the screaming abdabs. Yelling and throwing things about . . .

What? . . . Yes, okay. Standing by.' Then the sound of a telephone being replaced on its rest.

He put the gun down beside him, pulled the door open and reached for the face that twisted towards him, taking it by the outside of the upper lip on either side of the nose with his thumb and folded forefinger. Feeling the slipperiness of a moustache he tightened the pincer grip and the man squealed thinly, then said in a high, distorted voice, 'Jesus! That hurts!'

'Yes,' Trelawney agreed, 'it does, but it's better than a bullet in the groin. Now come out of there!'

At Trelawney's jerk on his lip the man left the cupboard as though ejected by an explosive charge, tears mingling with the sweat on his face. Fenner stepped over him and peered into the cupboard. 'Ear-phones and recorder one side, telephone the other,' he said, then, 'Wait a minute. There's an attachment for the telephone on the recorder but, unless the phone's bugged which seems pointless, we aren't on the air now.'

Trelawney still had hold of the man's lip. 'You! Is that right?'

'Christ, yes! For pity's sake let go!'

'Quite sure?'

Increased pressure brought a sharper squeal. 'I promise! You have to lift the receiver to talk like anywhere else!'

The gun back in his other hand Trelawney released his grip on the man.

'What's your name?'

'Hall. John Hall. Are you the law?'

'You should be so lucky,' Trelawney told him. 'Crawl back into your hole, Johnny boy, and do whatever you're supposed to do. Do you call Samms next, or does he call you?'

The mention of the name seemed to shake the man as much as anything had done and he sighed quiveringly.

'If I hear anything from Flat 14 I call him. If not, I'm to stand by for him to call me.'

'When?'

'About midnight he thought.'

'Okay,' Trelawney said. 'That gives you about seventeen

minutes to live. We'll consider an extension if you behave perfectly normally when that call comes through.'

Reid was short, slightly built and dark. Stirling, not much taller, had a barrel chest, big hands and ash-blond hair. Each treated the other with sorrowful contempt, but they operated as a pair with the easy accord of identical twins.

'That's interesting,' Reid said. 'A taxi's pulled up at the house with the decorators in. Two men getting out of it.'

Stirling's eyes continued to scan the roofs and windows of the buildings across the road, his rifle cradled in his arms just below the top of the parapet he was kneeling behind.

'Half the houses in the street have got the decorators in. Very exclusive neighbourhood this is. They don't spring-clean, they have the whole place done over. You referring to any particular one?'

'Yes. 314. The one we used for getting up here. They're going into it now. Could be a case of "great minds".'

Stirling grunted. 'If you're having one of your tidal brain-waves why not ask Latimer to consult Rafferty's great mind? The telephone's right beside you.'

Reid made a tutting noise, then, 'Don't get your knickers in a twist, mate. We can wait and see. A couple of flats in there are still occupied. They could be going to one of them.'

'All right,' Stirling said. 'Just don't nod off and let them shoot me in the arse while I'm looking the other way. I've got a job to do.'

The light in the phone base began blinking again at four minutes to midnight.

'Easy now. Take it very easy,' Trelawney said. 'Think about your life expectancy. Pick it up and we'll both listen to Samms.'

The man who called himself Hall lifted the receiver.

'Yes?'

'What kept you?'

'Trying to make out what she's doing.'

'Skip it and get this. They're coming in over the roof. At exactly . . . What's your watch say?'

'Eleven fifty-seven and – er – twenty seconds.'

'That's near enough. At exactly twelve four and a half you go to the front door and attract her attention. They'll take care of...'

Trelawney grasped Fenner by the collar of his coverall, drew his head close to Hall's and left the service room with controlled, near-soundless strides. The door of Flat 14 opened at his knock and he found himself looking at Rafferty's gun.

'Unknown number coming over the roof at any...'

'They were,' Rafferty said and put his gun away. 'Two men. Unfortunately Reid had to shoot one of them. Let's hope he wasn't important. But I gather you found the relay man. Any idea what's supposed to happen next?'

'No, but Jack Fenner may by now. I'll find out.'

On his way back to the service room Trelawney paused beside the stooping figure of Geddes rummaging in his toolbox. He spoke to him briefly. Geddes nodded and ran up the stairs, his tools clinking.

'It was to have been a "snatch", not a killing,' Fenner said, 'with Junior here helping them get her across the roof to Number 314 and into a car he's got garaged nearby. According to Samms, if that's who I was listening to, total elapsed time for that, including fetching the car, would be fifteen minutes. Adding another three for Junior to get back to this phone brings the time to twelve twenty-three. That, give or take a minute or so, is when Samms expects to hear "mission accomplished".'

'And so he shall,' Trelawney told him. 'Go and tell them in the flat, will you?'

CHAPTER EIGHT

Rafferty stood in the doorway linking the Director's room and his secretary's looking at Barry asleep on the sofa where Martha had snatched periods of rest when the pressure was on. Somebody had brought him pyjamas and bedding from Hospital Section. He was snoring gently.

Pulling the door to Rafferty walked to the big safe, worked the combination and took out the small stack of files. The one containing the numbers was still there. He felt no surprise. If the numbers constituted a pit, Barry would be the last person to fall into it, but it had been necessary to try.

The door to the passageway opened, Trelawney looked in, nodded at Rafferty and went out again. Rafferty followed him, said, 'Come to my room,' led the way along the passage and sat down behind his desk. Trelawney sat on it.

'I've called Jane,' Rafferty told him.

Trelawney smiled his thanks. That was typical of Rafferty. Wives, husbands, bed-mates of whatever standing, provided they were aware of their opposite number's occupation, were contacted by him as soon as possible after any job involving risk. This night, with everything on his mind, he would have found time, in addition to Jane, to call Hilda Geddes, Marion Reid and the small, diffident woman Fenner lived with whose name everyone but Rafferty had difficulty in remembering. Latimer was unattached as was Rafferty which left only Alice Stirling. Believing her husband to be an aircraft incident inspector she was never told anything. Stirling wanted it that way.

'We've tidied up at Wilton Crescent,' Trelawney said. 'Nothing left except the wire in the flat above. I expect someone will find that under the carpet some year or other.'

'Any trouble over the shooting?'

'No. There was a party going on in the same flat. One of them came out and said he thought they'd heard shots, but

Peter had found a pipe or something to bang with a spanner by then and told them he was fixing a gas leak.'

'Mmm. Samms let anything slip when Hall made that last call to him?'

'Nothing of much help,' Trelawney said. 'His words were "Drive them to the New Forest. You'll be holding her in a derelict house for twenty-four hours before I arrive. Jim'll give you the location. The three of you enjoy yourselves. I want her in a receptive frame of mind when I get there. Now pack up your equipment and get out of that place".'

Rafferty wrote 'Twenty-four hours' on his scribbling pad and sat looking at what he had done. Twenty-four hours of repeated sexual assault? It made no sense with everyone apparently in such a hurry. There were much quicker ways. But then the hurry had been triggered off by Barry's re-emergence on stage like some elderly demon king. Until that had happened Samms had been prepared to wait, to listen, to observe. Then Barry had forced him to act swiftly, but now – twenty-four hours?

He glanced up at the sound of Trelawney's voice.

'He's sacrificed his ears, Raff. All he can do is watch to see who goes there to investigate her non-appearance here in a few hours. He'll have her place staked out from nine onwards and will want to be around to see what happens, not down in the country.'

'Are you reading my mind?' Rafferty asked.

'No, only those three words you've written on your pad.'

And Barry says *I'm* quick! Rafferty thought. I was almost there, but Al beat me to it and he knows almost nothing. Not that I know much, but he has this ability to make bricks without straw. Always has had. That first assignment of his for the Department when he was put into Libya only as a red herring, but had picked up the threads of a conspiracy and woven himself a violently successful mission. Rafferty sighed silently. He seemed to be into clichés this day. Red herrings. Bricks without straw. What in the world had straw got to do with the manufacture of bricks?

'Aren't you clever?' he said.

'Am I right?'

Instead of answering the question Rafferty asked one of his own.

'What have you done with everybody?'

'The man Reid killed is in Hospital Section. The one with him and Hall, if that's his name, are down the passage. Geddes and Stirling are guarding them. I sent Fenner, Reid and Latimer home.'

'What about Fiona Langley?'

Trelawney grimaced. 'She's sitting in my room pouting and snivelling. I can't think of a less attractive combination. What's the matter with the bloody woman?'

The urge to share his knowledge with Trelawney was strong. He looked so rock-like, so competent propping himself with one thigh on the edge of the desk. For the first time in many years a breath of misgiving touched Rafferty. In all his adult life he had never experienced the need to confide in, or rely on, others. Why now? Impatiently he brushed the query aside and the temptation with it.

'She can't stand violence in any form, Al. Hid in the kitchen and – well, snivelled as you say. I had to drag her out to make that scene for Hall to report.'

'Oh, that reminds me,' Trelawney said. 'Hall wasn't just listening in on the flat, he was recording too.' He took a large tape from the pocket of his jacket and put it on the desk. 'Do you want to play it through?'

'Have you listened to it?'

'Sorry. No time.'

Keeping the relief out of his voice, 'Don't worry,' Rafferty told him, 'I'll listen to it later. You go home now. I'll be busy for a while with those two characters you've got on ice.'

'Can't I help?'

'No, I don't think so, thanks.'

Questions hammered at Trelawney's brain like an excited crowd of people demanding simultaneous and individual answers of someone addressing them. It required a near-physical effort to shut out the clamour. He made it in the belief that Rafferty would tell him what was going on when he was ready to do so and stood up.

'Very well,' he said. 'I'll take Langley home with me for

Jane to nurse. She can't go back to her flat, I don't imagine she'd be too enthusiastic about sharing Hospital Section with a corpse and you don't need her sobbing on your shoulder.'

Rafferty heard himself say, 'Leave her. Get some sleep. I'll be calling you in early.' He had spoken without conscious thought and knew instinctively that his reaction had been right, but it was not until the door had closed behind Trelawney that the reasons for it were clear to him. There were two of them – the first a reluctance to have her in close contact with Jane Trelawney.

That Fiona Langley knew Jane by sight was certain; the reverse less so and, even then, it would not be as the woman he had first seen only a few hours before. Rafferty allowed a picture to form in his mind of Fiona Langley under the calm regard of Jane's long, black-fringed grey eyes, eyes that would see right into her, ignoring the effect of the toothless dental plates which distorted the perfect mouth, padded out the delicate concavities below the cheekbones and turned her face into a parody of itself. He was sure, without knowing why, that one enchantress would recognize another regardless of camouflage. Close at hand the white witch would know the black and needing every weapon in the Department's armoury he wanted to keep that knowledge to himself at least until . . . until when?

'Until I know what I'm trying to do,' Rafferty said aloud and turned his thoughts to the second reason. That was much simpler. He had a job for Fiona Langley.

She was sitting in one of the armchairs in front of Trelawney's desk shaping her nails with an emery board. He sat down in the other.

'I'd like you to do something for me, Miss Langley.'

Her eyebrows lifted questioningly above the rims of her big black-tinted glasses and sank slowly out of sight again.

'Yes, Mr Rafferty?'

He explained what she was to do.

'That's easily arranged, Mr Rafferty. I'll go and collect some props from my flat if I may.'

'No, I can't risk your being seen,' he said. 'Write down the things you need and where they are. In the circumstances I think I had better fetch them myself.'

Across the passage Rafferty leant in the doorway of an unfurnished room looking at the two men. One was small, almost wizened, no good for what he wanted. It would be too implausible. The second was taller, about five foot ten and reasonably built. He'd do.

'Which one's Hall?' he asked.

'The bigger one, sporting the handle-bar moustache,' Geddes told him.

'Okay. Take him away. You go too, Stirling. This little chap and I want to talk in private.'

He moved into the room, watched Hall and his escorts leave and closed the door behind them, then stared at the floor for several seconds as though lost in thought. The sound of the small man shuffling his feet seemed to bring him back to himself.

'How old are you?' Rafferty asked.

'Who? Me? I'm forty-eight.'

'There, you see? It isn't difficult, is it?'

'What isn't?'

'Answering questions,' Rafferty said. 'I've got a lot to ask you. Keep on the way you've started and we'll have practically no trouble at all. What's your name?'

'I want to see a lawyer.'

'Yes, I expect you do, but I'm afraid we're not the police. You might almost say that we make our own laws around here. Some of them anyway, like whether or not you reach your forty-ninth birthday.'

Belligerently the small man said, 'Now I've got it! This is the crummy Secret Service government outfit that tart who done Whiteoaks works for. And who might you be? James bloody Bond's bloody father?'

Rafferty smiled at him approvingly. 'That's very astute of you? How did you manage to track her down?'

'Don't you go getting condescending with me, mate! Our lot's astute all right. We photographed her with a movie camera, that's how we tracked her down. We photograph all the birds our lot go with in case they need checking out. That one needed it if anyone ever did. Took two months to find the bitch what with us covering all the Mickey Mouse organizations in London, but we done it. She'd fixed her face different somehow, but you can't disguise a walk, specially not a walk like hers and how do you like that?'

'I like it very much,' Rafferty told him. 'A most beguiling switch of the hips. Not overdone. Just right.'

'Oh my Gawd, a comedian.'

'Yes, I'm said to be excruciatingly funny. What's your name?'

'Get stuffed. I'm not giving you any more information.'

'Oh I think you will. Hall will be undergoing interrogation shortly. You're third. Sorry not to put you higher in the batting order, but you look weedy enough to die on us before we get what we want.'

'I do, do I? And who's bloody second if I may ask?'

'Of course you may ask. I don't mind giving *you* information. It's Samms,' Rafferty said and saw the truculent mask dissolve into shock.

He swung his foot at the inside of the man's knee then and stood looking down at the small figure alternately gasping and retching on the floor before adding, 'And, if you still want to improve your mind, that's the medial condyle of the femur causing you discomfort.'

He let himself out of the room.

The tape Trelawney had given him revolved slowly, making no recognizable sounds. Rafferty stopped it and pressed the fast forward key. When the recorder began to twitter at him he stopped it again, reset the tape and listened to the exchange between Barry and Fiona Langley. At its end he sat for several minutes without moving then, very softly, 'Oh boss,' he said.

Fiona Langley's list of requirements was lying on his desk. He put it in his pocket and walked out of his room, turning towards the lifts. Confronting Barry would have to wait.

CHAPTER NINE

Barry woke immediately at the touch of Rafferty's fingers on his shoulder, levered himself into a sitting position on the sofa and swung his legs to the floor. His feet carried the blanket with them and it settled in a pile around his ankles.

'What happened at Langley's place?'

Rafferty stood, looking down at him, saying nothing.

Frowning, Barry asked, 'Someone get hurt?'

'Yes. One of your Trades' Unionists grew a third eye-socket. Reid's a very good shot.'

His frown deepening Barry said, 'What are you talking about, Rafferty? What Trades' Unionist?' Then, his voice sharpening, 'Did you say one of *my* Trades' Unionists?'

Ignoring the questions Rafferty spoke in a near whisper. 'You weren't exactly open with me about your talk with Miss Langley, were you? I've learned a great deal more about what was said now. Why did you hold out on me?'

'Hold out on you? My dear Rafferty, I have no idea what the woman has been saying to you, but if you prefer her version to mine I can't be held responsible for that.'

Rafferty closed his eyes, shook his head wearily, then looked at Barry again.

'It's no good, boss. I know you've had to lie to me in the past. Withhold information too. You've had to do it to all of us because that's the way the system operates, but you aren't in the saddle any longer, so don't try it now. What you and Langley said to each other was recorded on tape. I've listened to it.'

'I see,' Barry said in a dull voice. 'I'll get dressed if you don't mind, then . . .'

'I do mind,' Rafferty told him. 'There's a lot to do and it's got to be done quickly. Open up and I'll see if there's any way of keeping you and Martha out of whatever this is all about.'

'Martha knows absolutely nothing of . . .' Barry stopped talking, blinked and went on, 'In view of what you have already witnessed that was an ill-considered lie. I promise you it will be my last – of any sort.'

'Just talk,' Rafferty said.

Barry nodded and pulled the blanket up over his knees.

'I can't quite remember what I did say. Where the disparities are.'

'Then let me remind you. At one point you said quote Apparently she had been instructed to dispose of a man some months ago unquote. On the tape you accuse her of having done so. How were you able to do that?'

'Guesswork,' Barry said. 'I assumed that Havelock-Templeton's death was a reprisal, a back-lash, and in view of the severity of that back-lash I further assumed it to have been payment in kind. An eye for an . . .'

'You're simply repeating back what I said to you, boss.'

'Naturally, because that's the way it was. I thought you must have forgotten.'

'Did you really? You're the one giving every indication of having difficulty in remembering. I'll give you another example. When I asked you who she had killed you told me Vernon Whiteoaks in Leeds, but when I enquired about a reason you said, and I quote again, "In my day it was extremely rare for her to be given a reason. I can't speak for Havelock-Templeton of course". That wasn't very forthcoming in view of what she'd told you, was it?'

Barry remained silent and Rafferty went on, 'If it's not too much trouble perhaps you wouldn't mind explaining your failure to mention the name Dyboski and the man's activities. Then, when you've finished doing that, I'd like to hear your opinion on what the howling hell Havelock-Templeton thought he was doing in usurping the functions of MI5 and Special Branch in a fashion I don't think they'd particularly appreciate.'

Still Barry didn't speak and Rafferty grasped the front of his pyjama jacket, twisting the material, then shaking him slowly to and fro.

'I find myself in the middle of a shooting war, Colonel Sir Charles Barry. Three people have died in it and prisoners have been taken. As the ranking general of one of the opposing forces I have a certain curiosity about what's going on. Because what has happened and what has been said are so unnatural, so far outside any guide-lines we have ever been given, I cannot consult our political masters or our natural allies without placing the future of this place at risk. Amongst other things that means that the Central Records Office is closed to me.'

Rafferty had not stopped his slow shaking, nor did he do so when he went on, 'Can you imagine it? "Listen, George, a St Bernard just brought in a dead body and a couple of live ones. I'm sending you prints and mug shots by messenger. Let me know if you've got anything on them". Christ Almighty!'

He released his grip on Barry, straightened and said, 'When we started this one-sided conversation you made a mistake while trying to protect Martha. I agree you admitted to lying, but you can start off right now by telling me *what* you claimed she knows absolutely nothing of.'

Barry straightened his pyjama jacket, ran his fingers through sleep-tousled hair and said, 'All right.' For a few seconds he sat, picking at the blanket, then began to speak.

'Retirement's a funny thing, Rafferty. I'd had a pretty full life. The Army, the war, then directing this organization. The war taught me Intelligence work and a lot about Burma and the Japanese, but that hardly made for a catholic education. This place gave me a much wider view, but too little time to see more than half a dozen moves ahead in whatever the game was and there were usually several of them running concurrently. Well, you know what it's like yourself now. Anyway, it wasn't until I retired that I had the leisure to think my own thoughts and I found that an intensely depressing occupation.'

He glanced up, almost defensively, at Rafferty's face as though anticipating impatience, but there was none to be read in it and he talked on.

'First I looked at the world situation.' Barry spread his arms as though encompassing a globe. 'That brought on frustration because I was no longer in a position to play the small part I had grown accustomed to in doing something about the mess it was in. Can you understand that?'

'I can.'

Barry's nod seemed to indicate satisfaction at having made clear a particularly obscure point.

'Then I considered our own mess, here in this country, and wondered if I couldn't do something about that. I'm trying to keep this short so I'll spare you a description of the thought processes which led me to the conclusion that the Unions are the most detrimental single factor to our national survival.'

'I'm glad about that,' Rafferty said. 'It would have been a replay of the oldest speech since the Gettysburg Address.'

Barry gave no sign of having heard him.

'Any pressure group which can topple an elected government of the right or the left as this one has shown it can is a danger to parliamentary democracy and it is infinitely more so when it is under foreign control. I have no quarrel with the Union rank and file or the leadership except for one point and that's their gullibility which . . .'

Rafferty interrupted him for the second time. 'They're playing our tune, dear. I never thought I'd live to hear it again.'

Tossing his blanket aside Barry reared to his feet then fell back on to the sofa at the gentle push of Rafferty's hand on his chest.

Furiously he said, 'If, as you claim, you have listened to a tape of my conversation with Langley, you have also listened to *our tune* within the last hour or so!'

'All right, boss, but you weren't singing along with it then.'

'Do you want to hear me out, or not?'

'I want.'

His surge of anger forgotten, Barry said in a wondering voice, 'I didn't know that Dyboski and Vernon Whiteoaks were the same person. My sources – well, I suppose they assumed I knew. Not that it matters.' He scratched absently at his beard from the neck to the point of the chin and Rafferty was reminded vividly of Trelawney's description – a cross between a colonel and an Old English sheep-dog.

'What sources?' he asked.

'Old friends at MI5. Others with the CIA. All sorts of people. I even had Rambaud from Paris staying at the cottage one weekend. It's surprising how much they'll talk to an ex-Director if you don't push 'em too hard and what one won't tell you another will. It wasn't very difficult to stick the pieces together.'

'And what had you got when the glue dried?'

'Dyboski,' Barry said. 'Or Whiteoaks as I knew him.'

'Just Dyboski?'

'Just Dyboski,' Barry repeated and broke his promise that he would lie no more. 'His name came up time and again so I concentrated on him.'

'And then Havelock-Templeton conveniently had him killed for you?'

'No, not for *me*, Rafferty. You see, knowing my feelings, he encouraged me in my – in my researches. We shared the same views on where the danger lay.'

For another hour Rafferty stood almost motionless looking down at Barry, asking questions, listening to the answers.

Finally he said, 'All right, we'll leave it for now. Did you find anything interesting in the safe?'

'Yes, a file with pages of numbers in it. Doesn't mean anything to me, but I expect your cryptographers will be able to tell you what it's about soon enough. I'll get it for you.'

In the Director's room next door Rafferty waited while Barry opened the safe, then took the file offered to him. He looked inside, shrugged and said, 'Make yourself comfortable. Sue Mitchell will be looking after you. Send her out for anything you want.'

'Thank you, Rafferty, but I'll be going back to Dorset on the first train.'

'You're not going anywhere, boss, and before you tell me that I don't have the powers to hold you, try leaving this floor.'

'I see. May I call Martha to let her know I'm all right?'

'I've already told her,' Rafferty said. 'She sends you her love, agrees that the safest place for you is here and says that you're not to worry about her.'

CHAPTER TEN

Despite his nakedness John Hall was sweating again. Sitting on the floor in the corner of the unfurnished room he alternately brushed his forehead with his fingertips and tugged at his red moustache. He had been doing so ever since they had taken his clothes away and the lanky man with the grey hair had started to question him.

'Let's try one more time,' Rafferty said. 'There are only half a dozen people with the name in the London telephone directory. It's none of them. Who and where is your friend Samms? I really would recommend that you tell me, otherwise life is going to get quite remarkably unpleasant for you.'

The nervous movements of Hall's hands continued, but a stubbornness born of fear remained stamped on his features and he didn't speak. Rafferty shrugged, walked to the side door of the room, opened it and Fiona Langley came in. She had prepared carefully for her part in the statutory leather dress and aggressive boots. Even Rafferty thought she looked extremely alarming and wondered what was going on in the mind of the man on the floor.

'This,' he told Hall, 'was your intended victim. You are now hers. I'm sure you'll remember hearing something of her reputation yesterday.'

Hall gaped up at the woman standing over him, then drew his breath in sharply as the toe of her boot thudded into the side of his right buttock.

'Stand up!'

He got to his feet, fear almost but not entirely obscuring his embarrassment at his naked state.

She turned to Rafferty. 'What do you want from him?'

'The identity and whereabouts of a man named Samms. I'll have him taken to the basement.'

'No,' she said. 'It would be better if I dealt with him in the country. I have everything I need there.'

'As you wish, but I don't want him killed.'

'I can't guarantee that. Has he had a medical?'

'No.'

'Then see that he has one to give me some indication of how far I can go.'

'Very well.'

'Thank you.' She looked at Hall again. 'But first I'll give him something to be thinking about on the drive down. Anticipation is half the battle.' Her tongue moved slowly around her lips as she unbuckled the heavy belt at her waist.

'Don't be stupid,' Rafferty said. 'You'd have a crowd here in two minutes.'

Fiona Langley smiled charmingly at Hall. 'He's right, isn't he? Never mind, Mr Hall. We shall have plenty of time together later.' She refastened her belt and walked quickly from the room followed by Rafferty. Hall sank down on to the floor again trying to offset the terror she inspired with what *they* had said they would do to him if he ever identified any of them. He was still doing it an hour later when a man threw his clothes into the room and said that the doctor was waiting to see him.

When the glass doors of the Department swung to behind him Hall turned left on Thayer Street in obedience to the pull of Trelawney's hand on his upper arm.

'Garage is along here,' Trelawney said.

Hall glanced sideways at him. The same big bastard who, he remembered, had dragged him out of the cupboard by his lip. Well, big or not he wasn't going any further with him. No drive into the country, wherever that was. Not to that woman. The hour he had spent thinking about her and his examination by a doctor who had been so interested in the condition of his heart left no doubt about that. As they turned on to the garage ramp he brought his heel sharply down on to Trelawney's instep.

Hopping on one foot, nursing the other in both hands, Trelawney felt his leg swept from under him. He spun in mid-air, grabbed for his assailant, missed and fell heavily. Something struck his temple with near-stunning force. Lying motionless he watched. Almost immediately Hall was out of his field of vision, then two cars moved slowly across the garage entrance in the direction he had taken. Four men, two on the near side of the road, two on the far, followed on foot.

Trelawney got up, waited three minutes for them to get out of sight, then walked back to the Department, brushing dust from his clothes with his hands. His head throbbed dully.

Rafferty said, 'How did it go?'

'All right,' Trelawney told him. 'That is if you consider being kicked in the side of the head "all right". Anyway, he's off and running with the boys after him. What do you want me to do now?'

'Go and see Professor Morris and Admiral whatsisname. Morris lives in Oxford. Be there at three. Then you'll have to make Lee-on-Solent by eight. Here are the addresses.' He held out a piece of paper before adding, 'Find out every last thing they know about Havelock-Templeton, no matter how trivial, then get back here as quickly as you can. Okay?'

'Yes,' Trelawney said.

He was half-way along the passage to his own room when he turned at the sound of Rafferty's voice.

'Al, come back in here, would you?'

Trelawney stopped in the doorway and leant against the frame looking at Rafferty staring morosely at nothing. He stayed where he was until Rafferty sighed, turned towards him and said, 'Portrait of a man making up his mind. Shut the door and sit down.'

Having done what he had been told to do Trelawney waited silently for another minute before Rafferty spoke again.

'I see no particular merit in allowing myself to be bound to secrecy by an unsolicited bequest. It is my intention to share my inheritance with you.'

'Generous of you.'

'It is, isn't it? But I have to admit to a degree of self-interest. Until Stirling comes through with Samms' whereabouts I don't want to leave this building, which is why I've asked you to do a job I should be doing myself.'

Rafferty made an unnecessary rearrangement of the objects on his desk and Trelawney watched the movements of his hands curiously. They were as untypical of Rafferty as his earlier moody expression had been.

'I don't like any of this,' Rafferty said.

'I can see that.'

'Shows, does it?'

'Mmm. You'd better start reading the Will.'

Without taking his eyes from Trelawney's Rafferty reached out languidly with his left arm, picked up a tape-recorder from the top of the bookcase beside his desk and placed it in front of him. He looked down to align it precisely with the edge of the plate glass covering the desk's wooden top, then seemed to forget it.

'I fed you a line of bull last night, this morning, whenever the hell it was.'

'So what's new?' Trelawney asked.

'What's new is that it was unnecessary. I was startled by what I'd heard, more so by what I'd seen. It was also implied by our revered ex-boss that what I was hearing and seeing was for the Director's ears and eyes only, a restriction which, incidentally, included the Minister and on up. All very impressive. It wasn't until three minutes ago that I decided that I didn't buy it.'

'What took you so long?'

Rafferty sighed for the second time, then said, 'Don't you fool with me, Al. Of all people, not you. I've said I don't like any of this. I don't even know for certain what it is yet, but it stinks to such an extent that if it has anything to do with what it appears to have it means the end of the Department as we know it. It could even lead to . . .'

He frowned, shook his head and went on, 'Never mind that. I need your help more than I've ever needed it before. You can't give me that help with your head in a paper bag, so I'm going to tell you everything that has passed between Martha and me, Barry and me and Miss Langley and me. When I've done that I'm going to play you this tape.'

More than half an hour had gone by when the recorder clicked off. Throughout Rafferty's recital and the playing of the tape Trelawney had not spoken. Nor did he speak now and the sounds of the city invaded the room as though someone had turned up the volume. He jumped slightly when Rafferty said, 'Well, you'd better bugger off to Oxford, hadn't you?'

Trelawney stood up. 'Do I take it that nobody else hears of this?'

'I've been thinking about that,' Rafferty told him. 'It seems to be open season for Directors of this, to quote a new friend, "Mickey Mouse" organization, so I shall be lodging written reports with my bank and if that strikes you as an odd procedure you'd better take your imagination for a walk in the country.' He put the tape-recorder back on the bookcase and added, 'As you're next in line you might consider keeping a diary of your own.'

'I meant now, not "in the event of".'

'Yes, I know you did,' Rafferty said. 'Tell Jane. Nobody else. Just Jane.'

It was no longer possible to operate in pairs. Too many of those capable of providing efficient cover were involved in tracing Samms, or were standing by for Rafferty's orders when the man was located. Trelawney's eyes moved ceaselessly. Ahead, both sides, then the mirrors. Left wing, right wing, interior. The M40 was busy, but not crowded and no car appeared to be emulating his frequent changes of speed and lane.

With Oxford still some thirty miles away he turned off in the direction of High Wycombe, driving slowly. Only a Shell tanker and a very small Fiat followed him. He parked in a side-road, watched them go by then took the Lotus back on to the motorway.

Having grown accustomed to the idea, he conceded to himself that his wife made a very logical addition to the team of three which Rafferty saw as the optimum number. It relieved him of the necessity for prevarication in her presence. Not that she ever questioned him, or he her, about their various assignments at least until they were completed, but openness would help. So, he thought, would her experience. A more than merely successful field operative for longer than he himself she had, over a year before, been brought into Thayer Street as a Mission Controller.

During those months she had never, for obvious reasons, run an operation of his but, to a certain extent, she would be running both him and Rafferty after he had explained the situation to her. Her job would be to act as a link, to administer, to collate information and, where necessary, to direct on the basis of that information.

Trelawney realized that this placed his life in her hands and was content on his part that it should be so. She had saved it in Libya on the very first occasion he had seen her and, for good measure, done it again on the following day in England. His concern was for the emotional strain the coming responsibility would place on her. But then she *was* supposed to be a professional, wasn't she?

The thought barely completed, he spoke aloud, his voice angry.

'*Supposed* to be a professional! Christ Almighty, she taught you what the word means!'

His declaration of faith made, he waited for it to make him feel less anxious about her. It did not and he left the motorway again by the slip road leading to Princes Risborough to give himself something else to think about. Nobody followed him. He rejoined the main traffic stream and drove fast towards Oxford, mulling over the rest of the thoughts Rafferty had put to him.

If appearances were to be believed Havelock-Templeton had been engaged in some kind of vendetta with the Trades' Union leadership, or some part of it which he considered inimical. It was hard to believe in those appearances but, in the absence of others, they could not be discounted. That the Minister knew nothing of the activity was obvious. Had he done so he would have put a stop to it, or, if a justifiable cause existed, he would have told Rafferty after Havelock-Templeton's death. He had done neither of those things.

Now it was essential that he remain in ignorance, at least until a logical case could be presented to him. For him not to do so would result in the immediate replacement of the topmost echelon of the Department and Rafferty was not prepared to let that happen. He had little faith in most of the owners of the covetous eyes forever watching for their chance from the sidelines and Trelawney could not but agree with his assessment.

As though it were an aid to concentration Trelawney shook his big shoulders and the Lotus wobbled in protest. He steadied it automatically, thinking about the likely reaction of the Trades' Unions to the diabolical murder of one of their officials by an agent of the government. Public outrage? Court action? Riots? A general strike? Any or all of those things. Even the seeds of civil war were there. But a counter-assassination? That made no more sense than the original killing.

As he drove into Oxford Trelawney was toying with the idea that Havelock-Templeton had been probing in the dark towards some objective the existence of which he was too uncertain about even to mention to anyone else, even to have Fiona Langley question her victim because he dare not tell her what questions to ask. Perhaps his probe had been designed to produce a reaction which might tell him something. Possibly it would have done that had it not left him lying dead in a London street.

Then it was time to look for Professor Morris's house.

CHAPTER ELEVEN

Oakhill Crescent belied its name. It was flat, completely straight and dispirited lime trees stood at regular intervals at the pavement's edge on both sides of the road. The houses were nearly identical, semi-detached red brick, hiding shyly behind over-tall laurel hedges. Late Victorian Trelawney supposed.

He drove the Lotus quickly along it, saw No 27 to the right and continued on his way. Three minutes later he approached the house from the opposite direction. On each run he saw no traffic, no people, one cat. The same cat. Stopping the car five yards beyond the open gateway to No 27 he reversed into the tiny driveway. It divided just inside the gate, one arm branching towards the front door, the other, at right-angles to the road, serving a side entrance. Trelawney parked there, locked the car and walked round to the front, his feet crunching in the thick gravel.

The man who opened the door to him was frail, but his stance was upright. He wore a beard, thin, patchy, tabby streaked with white. Trelawney wondered if a beard was a prerequisite for Directors of the Department. Havelock-Templeton hadn't had one of course, but he hadn't lasted very...

He pushed the absurd thought away from him and said, 'Professor Morris?'

'Come in, Mr Trelawney. Come in.'

With the door shut behind him, Trelawney asked, 'Don't you want me to identify myself, sir?'

The old man's eyes twinkled at him through his glasses.

How often he'd read that description, Trelawney thought, but never seen it happen before. The small bright eyes were definitely twinkling.

'Show me your card if you must, but I know all about you already. You see, I was one of those responsible for blocking your appointment as Director. Perhaps, as things have turned out, I was wrong to have done that, Alaric.'

Trelawney smiled. 'Only my parents ever called me that, sir.'

'Ah well, I'm much more than old enough to have been your father, so I'm sure you'll forgive the presumption. Let's go into the study. We'll have a sherry. I know it's three o'clock in the afternoon, but my doctor recommends it. Of course, what he means is at eighty-seven what difference does it make? There are . . .'

Following the chattering figure along the passage to the study at the back of the house Trelawney decided that the Professor had established his own identity neatly enough. Only his ageing mother and father, who he had weaned from the use of the name before he was fourteen, and the very few at the Department who had ever had access to his personal security file knew that Al stood for Alaric. He had made certain of that.

Trelawney disliked sherry at any time, let alone in midafternoon, but he accepted the glass handed to him uncomplainingly. As if his doing so had been a signal the chattering stopped.

'What do you want to know about Julian HavelockTempleton?' The question came abruptly, the voice that asked it far less old.

'Everything, sir,' Trelawney said. 'Everything you can remember.'

'Everything that Professor Morris could remember took him forty-five minutes to relate, three-quarters of an hour of precise facts delivered as though he were addressing a class of students.

'Tell you anything, Trelawney?'

'Not a thing, sir.'

'Then ferret, boy, ferret! I've given you his *curriculum vitae*. I don't know what else you're looking for. Drag it out of me!'

Trelawney nodded. 'Would you say, sir, that he was capable of acting without ministerial authority?'

Impatiently Morris said, 'That's a fool question. Of course he was. So was Barry. So was I. Come to that I don't recall *your* seeking authority from anyone before you killed a "double" in Cologne and left a trail of havoc across Libya on your first mission. Then in Bulgaria . . .'

'You have a very good memory,' Trelawney broke in, 'but you know as well as I that I'm talking about implementing a course of action requiring a policy decision, not a field operative's reaction to . . .'

In his turn Trelawney fell silent at a gesture of the Professor's fragile, liver-spotted hand.

'You're perfectly right, young fellow. One's inclined to let one's tongue run on at my age. But to get to your point, it is not always desirable to seek the Minister's approval.'

'Because he might refuse it?'

'No, not that. In certain circumstances there might be too little time. That is obvious. What is less so is that to approach him at all might place him in a position of considerable embarrassment. Any Minister is a political animal and all political animals come and go. We stay, you and I.' Morris paused for a moment before asking, 'I say, am I lecturing?'

'Go on, sir,' Trelawney said.

'Very well. A Minister may be thankful that action has been taken over a matter that would have troubled his and the Cabinet's conscience had it been put to them. Naturally, any Director would need to have had very excellent reasons for implementing such action without authority. Er – now I come to think of it "very excellent" isn't grammar, but I expect you follow me.'

'Of course. Are you able to say if Havelock-Templeton would have been less or more likely to act on his own initiative than you or Sir Charles Barry?' The look of impatience appeared on Morris's face again and Trelawney added quickly, 'I know that circumstances dictate actions and that there may have been no comparable circumstances but, if there were, I'd like to know about them.'

Morris interlaced his fingers, dropped them on to his thighs and looked down at them as though in prayer. For a full minute he was silent, then he looked up at Trelawney.

'No comparable circumstances. He wasn't Director for more than . . .' He consulted his fingers again then said,

'Parminter didn't release him until . . . You know Parminter, don't you?'

'Yes, Havelock-Templeton was one of his team until Barry persuaded him to join the Department. I believe Parminter was rather annoyed with Barry over that.'

'Do you? That wasn't what I heard. My version is that Parminter wasn't all that sorry to see the back of him. He was too interested in Barry, more interested in him than he was in his own master. There was a period when he would lend Barry specialists, even operational teams without consulting Parminter. One of those occasions ended in . . .'

Morris stopped talking, shook his head very slowly from side to side, then looked apologetically at Trelawney.

'I see what you're getting at,' he said. 'It's very boring to be old, you know. No, you don't know. Never mind. All I mean is that one is so inclined to overlook the obvious, so now let me make a positive statement. At a lower level Havelock-Templeton was inclined to take more on his own shoulders than I or Charles Barry would have done in his place. Does that help you at all?'

'Assuming that that character trait followed him up the ladder it may, sir. Would you consider him capable of – no, forget that. I mustn't ask you to conjecture. It would only fog the issue.'

'Quite. What next?'

'Nothing, thank you,' Trelawney said. 'I mustn't take up any more of your time.'

He got to his feet and the Professor stood up with him.

'You don't ferret very deeply, Trelawney.'

'I think the rabbit moved to an unlisted warren, sir. We'll have to find that first.'

'Very cryptic,' the other said then, as though school had been let out, began chattering again as they left the house together.

When they rounded the corner of the building Morris quickened his pace.

'My goodness! What a handsome piece of machinery. You don't see anything like that very often. I . . .'

'Stop where you are!'

The force of Trelawney's words was such that the Professor stopped within two feet of the Lotus's bonnet as though the air had crystallized immediately in front of him.

'Don't touch that car. Walk slowly backwards towards me.'

Morris did as he was told, felt himself grasped under the armpits and swung into the air. Trelawney set him down on his feet on the bottom of the three steps leading to the front door.

'Somebody been tampering with it, Trelawney?' The old man sounded breathless, but not alarmed.

'It's probable, sir. I'm going to look. On no account are you to approach the corner of the house and if you go indoors stay at the far end, away from flying glass.'

Trelawney turned on his heel then back again at the grip of a hand on his arm.

'I'll obey your two orders,' Professor Morris said, 'if you'll obey two of mine.'

Trelawney raised his eyebrows, waiting, saying nothing.

'If there is, say, an explosive charge attached to your car, be so kind as to leave it there. It won't have a time mechanism because they would have no idea when to set it for. It'll be heat activated, or a trembler device, or some such. I'm in the fortunate position of knowing just about everybody from the Commissioner of Police to the Chief of the Defence Staff. Leave it to me to arrange for its removal.'

'Thank you, sir. And the second thing?'

'Don't keep your appointment with Admiral Bembridge. I don't think he can tell you anything I have not.'

For a moment Trelawney stood, his expression undecided, and Morris added, 'Knowing what I do about you, you weren't followed here.'

'Point taken,' Trelawney said, walked to the corner of the house, then dropped to his hands and knees.

Ninety seconds later he reappeared.

'It's taped to the exhaust pipe, sir.'

'I see. Now, that fact established, would you mind telling me how you guessed?'

'I think he walked along that far tyre track, putting one foot in front of the other,' Trelawney replied. 'See where the sides of the depression have fallen in slightly. There and there. There too. Round the corner – no, don't go and look – you can see where he pulled himself under the car, then scuffed the mark over with his foot. The overturned gravel's damp.'

The old man nodded. 'Remarkable. Quite remarkable. I'd never have noticed that.'

'Nothing remarkable about it really, sir. Like Rafferty I enjoy staying alive. He describes himself as a life nut.'

'Does he indeed? Well, don't just stand there. Come inside and have another sherry while I do some telephoning,' Morris said.

CHAPTER TWELVE

Samms looked like a mutation. Unbelievably thin he measured six foot ten inches from the top of his small head to the soles of his feet. Even so the inordinate length of his arms placed then out of proportion to the rest of his body. Once he had worked in a circus side-show billed as 'The Human Praying Mantis'. Now he was standing, apparently oblivious of the intense activity around him, staring at Hall squirming on the cheap carpet.

He said, 'Leave that junk, Coleman. Help Harper carry the radio equipment down to the garage. Frankel? You see anything?'

'*Nein*, Mr Samms. A small girl wit' a dog only.'

'Keep looking.'

'*Ja*, Mr Samms.'

Gradually Hall's writhings eased until he lay on his side, knees drawn up, forearms pressed to his stomach. The air he dragged into his lungs made an ugly rasping sound.

'Then having lied to me on the phone you aggravate the offence by coming back here. That was naughty of you, Hall,' Samms said. 'Very naughty. I wonder how long we've got before the men in flak jackets arrive firing their nasty CS gas at us, and bullets too if we don't behave ourselves. Oh yes, you've been very naughty indeed, haven't you?'

Hall's breathing had returned nearly to normal, but he could only shake his head and Samms went on, 'If I were you I'd pray that they come before we leave. I'd have to shoot you then which would be much nicer than what's going to happen when we take you with us. But you know that, don't you? We must abide by our own rules, however unpleasant they are, for the sake of the others.'

A strange calm had settled on Hall. His voice was hoarse but steady when he said, 'I think I'd prefer that to her. In fact I know I would. Remember those films we took of her in Leeds when she was going with Whiteoaks? Well, that's not the half of it. You should see her close up, staring at you with no clothes on. She was going to have me taken somewhere out of town and give me the Whiteoaks treatment. I promise you I'd have talked, Mr Samms, and they'd have been on to you like Big Ben just fell on your head. Those people don't mess about and I had to warn you. Okay, okay, and save myself too, so I got away and did it clean.'

'Why didn't you stop running and phone in from a public box if you'd lost them?'

'Because they'd taken my money, that's why. My watch as well, so I couldn't hock it I suppose. Would you have liked me to call through the operator and have it recorded so they could check? Be your age.'

Samms walked across the room and back with a peculiar jerky gait that moved his long trunk forward at one step and back at the next. He stopped directly in front of Hall and stared up at the ceiling.

'How much longer, Coleman?'

'Ten, maybe fifteen minutes, Mr Samms.'

Still looking at the ceiling Samms said, 'You know what I think? I think they put the frighteners on you with this bird, then let you get away so they could follow.'

Hall shrugged. 'I'd thought of that and it's possible. Taking my money points to it, but it didn't work out. I took four hours getting here. In and out of half the public buildings in London, lifts up, stairs down, escalator rides, any subway with more than two exits. No way was I followed far, Mr Samms, but I still watched this street for half an hour before I approached the house.'

Samms grunted. 'Any idea where this naked piece was supposed to have been taking you. If the place exists we might hit that next.'

'What naked . . . Oh! *She* wasn't naked. *I* was. She was dressed in . . .'

In a near bellow Samms asked, 'Are you telling me that they took your clothes away? Out of your sight?'

'Yes.'

'Get out of them! Every bleeding stitch! And do it faster than you've ever done anything!'

Hall's clothing lay scattered about the floor, every seam of every garment slit open, buttons smashed with a hammer, the heels and soles of his shoes ripped off, their uppers slashed apart along the stitching.

'All right, you're clean,' Samms told him almost grudgingly. 'Get Coleman to lend you something to wear.'

Neither of them paid any attention to the seemingly plastic zip on Hall's trousers and that was to give Young of Requirements Section cause for quiet satisfaction.

'That's in Islington, isn't it?' Rafferty asked and Stirling's voice in the telephone ear-piece said, 'Yes, sir.'

'Any idea of numbers?'

'I drove past once, Mr Rafferty, and saw two figures. One very lofty and the other's wasn't Hall, so that makes a minimum of three.'

'All right, but let's think of it as a minimum of six. How are you going to play it?'

'Move in after dark if they stay which I don't think they're likely to do. Not after last night and Hall having been in our care. If one or two leave I'll have them followed, but if it looks like an evacuation we'll do the old front and back jam sandwich routine. I've got the ambulance standing by to pack 'em into.'

Rafferty was silent for several seconds before saying, 'I just hope there isn't more than one car.'

The receiver at his ear invited him to join the club then went on, 'If there is we'll have to settle for a tailing job.'

'I can't improve on that,' Rafferty said. 'Good luck.'

He replaced the receiver, picked up the internal phone and keyed two digits.

'Young here.'

'The gadget of yours did its job, Young.'

'Oh, I'm glad, Mr Rafferty sir. Was the blast containment effect adequate?'

'I meant your tailoring endeavours earlier today.'

'Ah yes. What was the audible range?'

'Adequate,' Rafferty said.

*

Straightening after tying the laces of a pair of shoes provided by Coleman, Hall felt his arms grasped and forced behind his back. Rope bit into the skin of his wrists.

Tiredly he said, 'Now what?'

'Mr Samms isn't all that sure about you yet, Johnny.' It was Harper's voice. 'He mentioned a court-martial. You take it real easy and I'll act as prisoner's friend if we get out of this place alive. Now walk down to the garage.'

The acceptance of despair settled around Hall like a warm, soggy blanket. It felt almost comforting and he recognized the danger in that, but was too emotionally exhausted to revolt against it. Too much had happened to him in too short a time and it wasn't fair because he had only tried to do what was best for all of them. No, that wasn't right – he *had* done what was best for all of them, told them to wait for radio bugs, micro-wave beam equipment to arrive, anything but the antiquated cat's cradle of wires they wanted him to install in the Wilton Crescent flat. They had explained pleasantly that there was no time to wait and, just as pleasantly, asked him if he preferred to do as he was told or leave the team the slow way.

He had done as he was told and he had done it quickly despite the discovery that the passageway outside the flat was paved with marble. That had involved him in breaking into the flat above because the corresponding passage there was carpeted and he could hide his wire. The second break-in had stretched his nerves because he had no way of knowing whether or not the place was occupied. They had tightened further while he worked there momentarily expecting the owner's return. Then the long hours of listening culminating in . . .

'Get in the back,' Harper said.

Hall stood looking at the Audi with no clear recollection of how he had arrived beside it. The back door of the car was open. So was the over-full boot with Coleman bending over it muttering to himself, rearranging the articles inside. Most of them looked like firearms, but it was difficult to see in the dim light of the single grimy bulb hanging from the garage ceiling. He contorted his body, edging his shoulders into the car, but it was impossible to maintain balance with his hands tied behind his back and he fell heavily to the floor between the two sets of seats.

'Sit in the middle,' Harper told him without offering to help.

Somehow Hall got his legs under him and worked his way up until he could topple back into a sitting position. Harper climbed in after him, then the boot slammed shut and Coleman got in on his other side.

It was even darker inside the car, but he could see Samms, his head touching the roof, in the front passenger seat. There was no driver.

'Look, Mr Samms,' he said, 'this isn't necessary you know.'

'We'll let higher authority be the judge of that, Hall. Now be silent.'

He sank back into lethargy, his mental activity limited to self-pity too unfocused to cause him more than mild distress. So tired. All those hours of walking rewarded by Samms ramming him in the solar plexus with his fingers as though they were a bayonet. Why should Samms do a thing like that? And that woman! God, she was scary, but beautiful too. His muddled mind had begun to weave a fantasy around her when the driver's door opened and Frankel got in.

'Is clear.'

'Go,' Samms said.

Frankel pressed a button on the dash, an electric motor whined and the garage door moved slowly upwards, the light increasing as it rose. He started the engine and drove cautiously out into the street, turning left.

Disinterestedly Hall noted the dozens of cars parked on the opposite side of the road at right-angles to the small garden in the middle of the square, the absence of moving vehicles except for one car approaching from ahead. He let his eyelids droop shut.

'This street is one-way, isn't it?'

Was that Samms speaking? Who cared?

'*Ja*, I don't like.'

Noted. Frankel didn't like. Then somebody said, 'Holy Mother of God!' and he opened his eyes again.

The car was close, four headlamps shining brightly even in the daylight, pointing straight at him. He screamed and threw himself sideways, trying to reach the floor past Coleman's legs, waiting for the impact.

It came from behind, a heavy jolting crunch that threw him back against Coleman's chest and let him see Samms' body whip like a sapling in a gale. In the second before the car in front struck them, a glancing blow which slewed the Audi through a half circle, he realized that Samms was dead. Nobody could wear his head at that angle and live. He began to laugh, great whooping belches of laughter that shook his frame so strongly that he didn't notice Coleman's frenzied efforts to push him aside.

Somebody else thought it was funny too. An asinine hee-haw-hee-haw of sound growing louder and that made him laugh all the more. Then the braying stopped. Hall gave a final explosive exhalation and fell silent too, staring at the big white vehicle with coloured lights flashing on its roof. There seemed to be men everywhere, some in ambulance service uniforms.

Simultaneously all four doors of the Audi were yanked open. One of the ambulance men said, 'No you don't, chum,' in a quiet voice and shot Frankel through the wrist. That started Hall laughing again. He was still doing it when they threw him on to the ambulance floor.

CHAPTER THIRTEEN

'Mr Stirling calling from "The Abattoir", sir. Would you take it on the scrambler, please?'

Years before Rafferty had given the training school in Hampshire that name and now nobody in the Department called it anything else.

'Thanks, Liz,' he said to his desk-speaker and picked up the green telephone.

'Yes, Stirling?'

'Five in the bag, Mr Rafferty, but I'm afraid one of them's dead. Very tall man. Probably the one I saw through the window. Whip-lash effect broke his neck when I shunted their car.'

'Any idea who anybody is?'

'Only Hall, sir. None of them has any identification papers and they're only just coming round from their injections. Oh, by the way, somebody seems to have been giving Hall a bad time. He was hysterical when we picked them up. Could be useful.'

'It could indeed,' Rafferty said. 'Get him awake and keep him awake, but nobody speak to him at all. Mr Trelawney will be with you by about – say four in the morning. Life at its lowest ebb and all that. He'll take it from there. Can do?'

'Can do. He won't want to sleep, not with me leering at him he won't. Got a wonderful line in leers I have.'

'Then leer away,' Rafferty told him, 'and well done over the Islington bit.' He replaced the receiver and looked at Trelawney sitting quietly on the far side of his desk. 'Did you get that?'

'Yes, most of it. Did he say five?'

'Yes, but one's dead. There will be seven, two of them dead, by the time you arrive. Peter Geddes is taking down the pair from Wilton Crescent.'

Trelawney said, 'Ho-hum. May I have a cigarette?'

Throwing one to him Rafferty asked, 'Why don't you send

someone out for a packet? That's the third of mine you've had in the last hour.'

'I've given up smoking.'

'I see.'

Neither spoke again until a quarter of the cigarette had gone, then, 'Raff?'

'Yes, Al.'

'I'm taking Jane out to dinner tonight. Kind of easing her gently into controlling this mission, whatever it is. But before I do I'd feel happier if I were certain that you had made the right choice of Controller. Part of me thinks you have. The rest isn't so sure. And as both points of view are subjective I don't trust either of them. It can't have been for her sake or mine, so . . .'

Irritation touched Trelawney at the sight and sound of Rafferty talking to his desk-speaker.

'. . . some slave out to buy Mr Trelawney a packet of cigarettes, would you, Liz? He smokes – er . . .'

'Rothmans, sir. I'll get them.'

Turning back to Trelawney Rafferty said, 'For my sake mainly,' and saw irritation replaced by puzzlement on his face. 'It's difficult to explain, Al.' He hesitated, then went on, 'No, it isn't difficult. It's just awkward telling a man things he doesn't know about his wife. At least, I shall be very surprised if you do know about them.'

Rafferty picked up a pencil and began to draw a series of stick-men on his scribbling pad. He gave one of the figures a hat and blocked it in.

'Jane's been the Department's darling for a long time now, a fact which I don't imagine has escaped your notice. Well, it's not exactly surprising, is it? People light up when she's around.'

He glanced across the desk, caught Trelawney's faint smile and returned to his drawing. The figure with the hat acquired a pair of shoes.

'What you almost certainly don't know is that the feeling went to the very top, to Barry himself. I didn't know myself until he told me when he retired, although I had sometimes wondered how . . . I couldn't quite see . . . Oh damn! Let me get this straight. Barry's a very humane man. Entirely ruthless while an operation was in progress, he'd crumble a little when it ended and the tension was gone. If it ended messily, even for the opposition, he'd crumble quite a lot. When that happened he'd go to Jane if she was in England.'

Rafferty continued to draw, but held up his left hand as if to ward off any protest.

'No, not for what you may be thinking. He just needed to be with her for a while. Sometimes he'd get his hand patted, at others a tongue-lashing, depending on what she thought he needed. She's very wise, you know. Anyway, he'd come back here his old self again having undergone some form of emotional catharsis. I say, I hope you don't mind my telling you this.'

'Not in the very least,' Trelawney said. 'It's rather – rather...'

'Yes, it is, isn't it? But you're wondering what it's got to do with the price of cheese. Right?'

'The connection *is* a bit obscure.'

Rafferty put his pencil down and lay back in his chair, looking at Trelawney.

'Without dropping everything, which is impossible anyway, we have three candidates available to control our joint endeavours. Carew, Addington and Jane. Of the three Jane is the most junior but, in my view, she is Addington's equal as a Controller. She also has wide experience of field work, which he does not.'

Liz came in carrying a packet of cigarettes and Trelawney said, 'Thanks, honey. I'll pay you on my way out.' She smiled and left.

'That leaves Carew,' Rafferty went on. 'He's in a class by himself. If he wasn't he wouldn't be Senior Controller but, for this catch-as-catch-can situation we're in, he suffers from a most undesirable trait. He's seniority conscious.'

'Meaning what?'

'Meaning that I doubt his ability to give me a direct order. It isn't his fault. Having a Director of the organization downgrade himself and be asked to run him is unprecedented and, consequently, outside his experience. You know the rules. An agent may refuse a mission if he lacks faith either in the Controller or the Field Director assigned to him. I can't refuse the mission, but I'm in the fortunate position of being able to choose who controls it.'

Rafferty got up, walked round his desk and sat on its edge close to Trelawney's chair.

'Al, when the telephone rings at some place where I've been holed up not knowing the score, only that the net's closing, I don't want to be deferred to, I want to be told that a diversion will take place at the end of the road in fifteen seconds and to get the hell . . .'

An abrupt chopping movement of Trelawney's hand silenced him.

'You're preaching to the converted, Raff. I've been there too, you know. Let's get back to the point and you tell me why you think Jane wouldn't be inhibited in the same way.'

Rafferty looked puzzled when he said, 'I thought I'd explained all that. When probably the most distinguished chief this outfit ever had has put his head in her lap, do you really imagine that she's going to be overawed by me?'

CHAPTER FOURTEEN

Trelawney returned his wife's wave then watched her move towards him, threading her way quickly between the crowded tables. He was admiring the way she walked, enjoying it as he always did. She had two walks. One a stalk when she was pensive, like a high-fashion model on a catwalk, but without awareness of self, and the other a swinging stride that threatened to break into a skip of exhilaration without ever quite doing so. She seemed to be exhilarated now and he stood up, smiling, seeing the heads of both men and women turn to follow her progress.

'Darling, I'm sorry for being late. The traffic's awful and...'

'Would Madam permit me to take her coat?'

Heavy dark-chestnut hair swung about her head as she turned to face the head waiter. Another waiter was holding her chair. A third hovered. She collected waiters as readily as she made heads turn.

Jane Trelawney glanced down at her off-white belted raincoat, flexed a knee as if to examine the high heel of one of her polished brown shoes and said, 'I don't think Madam should. Apart from these shoes she isn't wearing anything else.' She gave him a brilliant smile and added, 'It has a devastating effect on my friend here.'

The head waiter inclined his head gravely to show that nothing surprised him any more and held two menus close to his chest while Jane sank down on to the chair eased forward by his scarlet-faced underling. Only when the big man had resumed his seat did he dispense the menus.

'Madam. Sir.'

'Thank you,' Jane said. 'May I have an absolutely enormous Bloody Mary first, please?' She repeated the word 'enormous', drawing it out to indicate the size of the drink she wanted then went on, 'It's Cook's night out. That's me.'

He looked down at her and permitted himself the smallest

of smiles. It was difficult not to smile at so beautiful a woman even if she was mad. Mentally striking out the unspoken word he substituted 'eccentric' and felt better for it.

'At once, Madam.'

The colour still burning in his own cheeks Trelawney said, 'For God's sake, Jane, what's got into you? It isn't like you to embarrass waiters.'

'Embarrass them, darling? Don't be silly. I've made their evening. They'll be wondering if it's true and having all sorts of deliciously wicked thoughts. Just you watch the word spread.'

It already had he saw. The faces of two waiters several tables from them turned in their direction only to look quickly away when they met his glower.

'You're the one I've embarrassed,' she said. 'I haven't seen you like this since the day we first met in Libya when I seduced you.'

He shook his head. 'Your memory's going. You seduced me, I won't try to deny it, rather comprehensively, but that was the next day back here in England. I tried to buy that cottage once, but someone offered more than I could afford.'

'You're a sentimental old thing,' she told him, 'but your memory's at fault, not mine. I *raped* you at the cottage while you were all weak and defenceless. I *seduced* you the day before at the villa outside Tripoli when you recovered consciousness to find yourself naked and me there ironing your clothes. You nearly died of embarrassment, then went all monosyllabic and gruff and efficient and I knew you were gone, man, gone. Come on, admit it.'

A waiter arrived with her drink. She thanked him then asked, 'Wouldn't you agree that it's perfectly possible to seduce someone without laying a finger on him?'

'Yes, Miss – er, Madam. If you say so.'

When the man had gone Trelawney reached out and grasped her by the wrist.

'What is it, my love?'

Her long grey eyes opened very wide and stared into his like twin-searchlights.

'Not going to cry. Not going to cry. Not going to cry,' she said.

He tightened the grip of his hand slightly on her wrist and waited.

For a long moment she seemed to fight something inside her, then breathed out noisily, sniffed once and said, 'To put it mildly I really think I've been over-reacting.'

Trelawney continued to wait.

'A man tried to follow me when I left Thayer Street to come here tonight. That's why I was late.'

'Good show. How many does that make this week?'

'Tag me, Al, not pick me up.'

'Ah,' Trelawney said and the amused expression which had begun to form on his face faded. 'How did . . .'

'Oh, darling, they do seem to be awfully determined about you. First the bomb under your car, then trying to trace you through me. I don't seem to be as professional as I was, so please don't be angry with me when I say I'm frightened for you.'

Trelawney's black eyebrows nearly met over his nose as he scowled.

'I'll castrate bloody Rafferty for telling you about that bomb.'

'Company,' Jane said and the head waiter stopped beside them.

'Would you like to order, sir?'

'Not yet. We'd like another drink.'

'Madam doesn't appear to have touched hers, sir.'

'When I want you to keep me up to date on the state of the game I'll let . . .'

Slowly Trelawney dragged his eyes away from his wife's gaze, looked up and said, 'I beg your pardon. You're perfectly right. Ask them to bring me one, would you?'

'Of course, sir. A vodka martini.'

Jane resumed the dialogue as though there had been no interruption.

'Don't be cross with Raff. He told me simply to emphasize how careful we have to be and he was immediately proved right.'

'Yes, I can't deny that. Did you get a good look at this man?'

'Short, say five-seven, medium build, swarthy, receding black hair, brown eyes, possibly left-handed because his watch was on his right wrist, clean shaven, bad teeth, age about – I'm not sure – between thirty and forty.'

He grinned at her. 'I suppose you don't happen to know his name too.'

'Beshir Mahmoud,' she said, disengaged her wrist, felt in her handbag and dropped a wallet on the tablecloth in front of him. 'At least that's what his credit cards and driving licence say. Oh! Dates of birth are hidden in the licence number now. I forgot.'

She listened to the soft hiss of air expelled between his teeth, then his voice.

'Did you kill him or something?'

'Just "or something".'

Putting the wallet in his pocket Trelawney said, 'I'll phone the name through to Raff. He'll want to try it on the computer.'

He had risen from his chair, but sat down again at the dictate of a pointing forefinger.

'I love you,' she told him, 'even when you go into one of your lunatic "dot and carry one" phases. I called Raff as soon as I could get to a telephone. What do you think I am?'

Not answering the question he asked one of his own.

'Any witnesses?'

'I don't think anybody saw him go down, but quite a crowd gathered when he was lying on the pavement. I told them he'd collapsed right in front of me and someone went to call an ambulance. Of course I'd lifted the wallet before they arrived. You know, feeling his heart.'

Trelawney watched the approach of his second drink, thanked the waiter and said, 'So you think you don't seem to be as professional as you were?'

When she made no reply beyond an unsmiling twitch of her lips he asked, 'Haven't you really got anything on under that coat?'

She looked at him with gentle affection. 'You'll have to

sweat on that one until we get home. Not that it makes any difference. Raff wants you to brief me tonight and you're to leave for Hampshire at two in the morning.'

'I know.'

Jane gave a confirmatory nod of her head, then suddenly burst out, 'Darling, I'm so sorry. I *hate* women who behave badly in restaurants. It was nerves talking. Let's eat now, then not come here again. Not ever!'

Wearing a brown towel, turban-like, on her head and another round her hips Jane came out of the bathroom and looked at Trelawney sprawled fully dressed on the big bed. At first she thought he was asleep, then caught a glimpse of reflected light between his eyelashes.

'You're cheating,' she said.

'Yes. Did I ever tell you that you have elegant breasts?'

'Often. I've known breasts to be described in all sorts of ways, but I think "elegant" must be a Trelawney original.'

'It's apt,' Trelawney said. 'Come here.'

She crossed to his side, bent down and kissed him, but when he raised his arms she stepped back out of his reach.

'Really, you are the most frightful peasant,' she told him, took his shoes off and put them on the floor. 'Now go to sleep. You've got less than two hours.'

On her way to the dressing-table she glanced back.

'Will the hair dryer keep you awake?'

He shook his head, smiling.

When she had dried her hair, Jane sat without moving for fifteen minutes gazing at her reflection in the looking-glass, unaware either of herself or her image. She was re-running at high speed her own mental tape of her husband's tale which it had taken him five times as long to tell. It came to her virtually verbatim and the cadences his voice had employed in the construction of each sentence were there too. Her recall capability was very high.

'And that's all I know,' he had said. 'It's all yours now, with full mission control powers over Raff and me, plus anyone else available who you can use without letting them know what's going on.' He had paused before ending with, 'And that includes that adorable bundle of fun Fiona Langley.'

Jane blinked, stretched and turned to look at the sleeping figure on the bed. 'Poor sweet,' she whispered. 'I bet you did some knuckle chewing before you agreed to allow me to be put on this spot.'

It wasn't difficult for her to guess what had happened. Rafferty was a 'field' man. According to Barry the best in Europe at the height of his powers and one of the three best in the world. He had never sought a higher office, any position carrying responsibility for life other than his own, least of all that of Deputy Director. Then, when Foster died, Barry and Martha between them had manoeuvred him into the position of acting second-in-command, an appointment later confirmed by Havelock-Templeton on the negative grounds that the passing years had deprived him of his lofty standing in the 'field' league.

And Rafferty hated it.

He had, Jane knew, argued that her husband should be promoted in his stead, but without success. Too little had been known by the selectors and the rest of the Intelligence Establishment of an agent named Trelawney. Now bullets from an assassin's rifle had pushed Rafferty to the very top, into line for a knighthood which he would consider an anachronism, into the task of fighting an enemy without identity.

He was trapped, doubly trapped, because he could neither resign without explanation, nor appeal for outside help. The first move in the game, a revolting move, had been the Department's and it would not bear scrutiny, so he was forming a triumvirate consisting of the friend he trusted, the friend's wife whom, although he had never said so, he had been in love with for years, and himself. He was broadening his power base, enlisting talents he did not possess, giving back to himself some of the freedom of movement he had been deprived of. That way, she guessed he had reasoned, he could make his best contribution towards laying what, as yet, was little more than a ghostly adversary.

12.45 a.m. and cooler. She walked to the bathroom, trailing a towel from each hand, then returned wearing

Trelawney's dressing-gown, thinking about the little team of three, a triumvirate as she had described it to herself knowing that it meant a coalition of three men. She had worked and fought as an equal in a man's world for too long to care about the derivation of that word, or need anti-sex discrimination legislation to justify her use of it. A triumvirate was called for. So be it.

A pad and pencil lay by the telephone on her side of the bed. She fetched them, sat down at the dressing-table again and cleared a space of female paraphernalia to give herself room to write. She needed that room. Her approach to writing, head cocked, elbow and forearm supported on the surface in front of her, produced an endearingly child-like picture. That and the resultant formless scrawl were the only child-like things about her.

For an hour she stayed at her task, eyes, for the most part, looking inward. Only occasionally did her pencil move across the paper. When she had finished she had covered less than three of the small pages.

Trelawney woke at her kiss, sat up and took the cup of coffee she handed to him.

'Thanks. What have you been doing?'

'Thinking thoughts.'

'Oh. I hope my snoring didn't break the train.'

'For once you didn't snore. Perhaps you should see a doctor.'

He manipulated his broken nose experimentally and said, 'Don't worry. It'll come back.'

Five minutes later, 'I love you, Al darling,' she said.

Trelawney didn't hear her. He was driving through the thin night-time traffic in the direction of Hampshire.

Jane picked up the pad, shrugged out of the dressing-gown and slid under the covers he had been lying on. Then she began to read what she had written.

'Is Langley a Lesbian? Does it matter?' her scrawl asked. She reached for a pencil and added the words 'Might do. Think about it', then read on.

'What does she know that she hasn't told? Probably nothing, but what about what she doesn't know she knows?

Send her to Dr Williams today. What about Hall's phone? Al says no dial and no dialling tone, only empty silence when rung off. Direct line. Must have Post Office engineer on their books. Can't investigate. Too public. KGB Volchak – what time did he call Raff? Check against times of newspaper, radio, TV releases. May not fit. Martha and Charles Barry probably pawns (unwitting?) of H-T. What for?'

That brought her to the end of her first page. She read the second and third, then said aloud, 'My dear good woman, you have the most grasshopperish mind I've ever come across.'

When she lifted the receiver of the direct scrambler line to Thayer Street a voice said, 'Prideaux, Night Duty Officer.'

'Jane Trelawney, Mr Prideaux. Would I be right in thinking Mr Rafferty is still there?'

'Yes, Mrs Trelawney. I suggested he went home, but he says he has to finish his football pools. I'll put you through.'

Three seconds later, 'Hello, Jane.'

'Good morning, Raff. There are two things I'd like you to do and one thing I'd like you to tell me.'

She listened for any hesitation, any unusual inflexion in his voice, but there was neither when he said, 'Fire away.'

It was going to be all right. He had invented the game and was prepared to abide by his own rules.

'Fiona Langley slept with Dyboski for a considerable time. She may have heard things she doesn't remember now. I think Dr Williams should try to jog her memory.'

Rafferty said, 'You've got it,' and she smiled at the Americanism with its implied immediate acceptance.

'Secondly, you fed Leo Volchak the idea that he had read of H-T's murder in the evening papers. He didn't dispute it, but it would be interesting to know if the news *had* been released by the media before he telephoned Sue Mitchell.'

This time there *was* hesitation until Rafferty said, 'I ought to have my head examined. I'll get on to the editors as they come on duty. Now, you want me to tell you something.'

'Yes, the numbers file. Have the cryptographers broken the code?'

'Afraid not, Jane. They think it's a one-time pad system, or some such. They're still working on it, but they aren't hopeful. Anything else?'

'No, not now.'

'Then I have something for you. From now on you'll be collected and taken home by a Department driver. They'll change cars frequently. Leave yours alone. Okay?'

'You think they know where Al and I live?'

'No. If they did Mahmoud wouldn't have tried to follow you. Let's keep it that way.'

'You've got it,' Jane said.

CHAPTER FIFTEEN

Almost everybody from the Department who arrived at or left 'The Abattoir' did so in a commercial van without side windows. The one Trelawney was driving carried the legend 'Ground-Air Crop Sprayers Ltd'. It was very boring to handle after the Lotus, but he had no intention of touching that car again even if the Army bomb disposal people returned it in one piece. When a sign reading 'Ministry of Agriculture, Fisheries & Food – Research Station' appeared in his headlamps he slowed and turned left off the country lane, feeling the tyres vibrate over a cattle grid. A quarter of a mile along a twisting tree-lined drive he came to the house set in a sprawl of outbuildings.

''Ello, sir. Nice trip down?'

Trelawney switched off engine and lights and looked at the dim shape of the ex-Royal Marine Commando. The sky behind him was showing the first faint traces of dawn.

''Morning, Sergeant Pender. Yes, I thoroughly enjoyed it. Being an inveterate liar I always tell myself that this is the best part of the day.' He got out of the van and stretched his arms above his head. 'What's the situation down here?'

'Gettin' a bit crowded, sir. Stirlin' and Reid arrived yesterday with these five characters, one of them dead. Then about three hours ago Mr Geddes turns up with two more. One of them's a stiff too.'

'Okay,' Trelawney said. 'Do you know where the one called Hall is? I want to see him first.'

'This way, sir. Stirlin's been proddin' 'im awake all night, but I think Mr Osaragi's taken over now to give Stirlin' a spell.' Pender led the way into the house and pointed to a door. 'In there, sir. I'll be 'ere if you want me.'

Hall was standing, backed into a corner of the room, staring at the small figure of the chief instructor a few feet in front of him as though mesmerized. He paid no attention to the opening door, but Osaragi turned towards it.

'Trelawney san. It is good to see you again.'

'And you, old friend. How's this one been behaving?'

'With complete decorum, but I think he wishes he were not here.' The Japanese smiled and added, 'But I will leave you so that he may tell you all about it.'

When Osaragi had gone Trelawney stood for a moment as though lost in thought then, with no warning, struck Hall's face with the back of his hand. It was a straight-armed swinging blow which caught him high on the cheekbone and dropped him sprawling twelve feet away. For long seconds Hall lay where he had fallen, then rolled on to his back.

He said, 'I earned that for kicking your head.' There was resignation approaching apathy in the sound of the words.

'No, it wasn't for that,' Trelawney told him. 'It was to teach you basic manners.'

'Manners?'

'Yes, you stood up a lady. She really is very upset about it, so as soon as you're ready I'll take you to her and you can tell her how sorry you are.' Trelawney paused for effect before adding quietly, 'And everything else you know.'

Hall's body seemed to grow rigid then, as though a spring had been released, he jack-knifed into a sitting position and clasped his knees to his chest. When he spoke his voice was so tightly controlled that it vibrated like a wire under tension.

'It isn't! It simply can't be!'

'What the hell are you talking about, Hall?'

The wire snapped, Hall's head dropped to his knees and he rocked forwards and backwards making crooning noises. Trelawney watched him, listened, tried to make out what was being said, but all he could identify was the phrase 'not possible' repeated twice. He stood where he was, waiting for the spasm to pass.

Eventually it did so and he said, 'Time to go, Hall.'

Hall raised his head slowly, but stopped before his gaze met Trelawney's. There was a large red patch on his left cheek and the eye above it was beginning to close. He opened and shut his mouth several times before saying loudly, 'But it *is* happening, isn't it?' His shoulders were shaking.

Now was the time to tread lightly, very lightly, Trelawney

knew. 'He was hysterical when we picked them up,' Stirling had said, and his subsequent treatment appeared to have pushed him closer to the edge. On the edge was good, but over it, where his sudden changes of mood and erratic body movements gave every indication of toppling him, was useless.

'Yes, it's happening,' Trelawney told him, 'but you still have time to stop it.'

'Anyway,' Trelawney said, 'if Hall is to be believed, and I think he is, we've killed the two senior men in his outfit... What?... Oh quite. Very restrained of you. It puts us back to square one, if we ever left it, but let me give you the list. There's a possible lead.' He settled the telephone hand-set between ear and shoulder, folded his arms and began to talk rapidly.

'From the Audi first. Nathaniel Samms, dead. He was the group's planner. John Hall, communications. Jurgen Frankel, German, car handler. According to Hall he once stated that he had worked for the Baader-Meinhof lot as a getaway driver. Alfred Harper and Joseph Coleman, hard boys. All right so far?'

'Keep going. You're on tape,' Rafferty's voice said in his ear.

'Okay. From Wilton Crescent, James Wakefield, dead. Equal and opposite to Samms. He led – well, what we'd call field operations. Patrick Boyd, Irish. Explosives specialist. Once again according to Hall there's a Provisional IRA connection in Boyd's case.'

'So where's the lead?'

'Not amongst that lot,' Trelawney said. 'Hall saw another man at the Islington house on two occasions. Mediterranean type he says. He never heard him speak. Samms and Wakefield talked to him in a closed room both times, but on the second visit he heard Samms say, "Have a seat, Basher," before the door shut. The name stuck in Hall's mind because it sounded too odd to be a real one and the man didn't look the type or size to have earned it as a nickname. My...'

He stopped talking when Rafferty interrupted with, 'I'm

ahead of you, Al, and it's a dead-end. The river police pulled Beshir Mahmoud's body out of the Thames early this morning. It was announced on the nine a.m. news on Radio Three.'

Trelawney unfolded his arms, took the telephone in his hand, looked at it, then held it up to his face.

'Why, Raff?'

'Why what?'

'Why was it announced on the radio? Pulling a corpse out of the river isn't exactly national news.'

'It is when it's nailed to a raft with "Died of incompetence" painted on it. God knows how many people saw it from the bridges before the police launch got there.'

'Nice people we're dealing with,' Trelawney said.

There was bitterness in Rafferty's voice when he replied, 'Yeah. Perhaps we should ask them to stand in for *us*.' There was tiredness in it too and Trelawney wondered if Rafferty had slept at all since leaving Scotland some fifty hours before.

Brusquely he said, 'Perhaps we should find out who they are! Look, Raff, get an interrogation team down here right away. They don't need to know anything about the Barry situation. All they have to do is take these people apart bolt by bolt to find out what's inside. None of us down here is trained to do that. I don't think they'll find anything because Mahmoud must have been the cut-out, but we have to be certain.'

Rafferty made no comment and Trelawney went on, 'Send our tame doctor too. The German called Frankel was shot through the wrist when he tried to pull a gun on somebody. It looks a mess. In addition to that Hall seems to be having some sort of nervous breakdown. Next, Osaragi will need camp-beds and bedding, plus a lot of food he can't very well buy locally without raising eyebrows.'

Trelawney began to massage his temples with a circular motion of finger and thumb with his free hand, but did not pause in what he was saying.

'I'm leaving the people under training down here to help out as guards, cooks, whatever, but I'm sending Peter Geddes, Reid and Stirling back to you. I'll follow. Oh, another thing. Would you send Osaragi a note stating that he is in sole charge here regardless of the rank of any officers visiting from Thayer Street? He's maintained the Min of Ag and Fish front for years and I don't want the local pub full of a lot of . . .'

Quiet laughter on the line stemmed the flow of words, then Rafferty said, 'All that is "Roger". Likewise "Wilco", except for Osaragi's authority. Write that yourself before you leave. You *are* the Acting Deputy Director.'

'Oh. Am I?'

'Well, I can't think of anybody else and you're making all the appropriate noises. And Al?'

'Yes?'

'Thanks. I went a bit dopey on you back there. Getting old.'

Rafferty saved Trelawney the need to reply by adding, 'You've only boobed over one thing. All you've said should have been told to Jane, not me. Try to get used to the idea, will you?'

Twenty minutes later the 'Ground-Air Crop Sprayers Ltd' van rattled over the cattle grid again. Trelawney turned right and began the return journey to London.

CHAPTER SIXTEEN

For the fourth time since he had opened the door to her Dr Williams glanced sideways at the tall, extravagantly good-looking girl, admitting to himself that her beauty made him nervous.

'It's all right to look,' she told him. 'Everybody does.'

The matter-of-fact tone flustered him further. He groped for, then thankfully remembered the opening lines he had been given and spoke them.

'You have three things to tell me. What are they?'

'27 May 1949. Car registration number LNQ 47T. Name Elizabeth Fields,' Fiona Langley said.

The details were the same as those given him over the phone with his instructions. He nodded, wondering if the first was her date of birth, then decided that, considering the source, all three were meaningless.

'Please lie down, Miss Fields. I'm going to give you an injection, but don't worry about it. Only something to make you feel relaxed.'

'Just being with you makes me feel wonderfully relaxed, darling,' she said, pushed her sleeve above her elbow and lay down on the examination table.

'Get your carcass in here, would you, Al?'

Rafferty released the key on his desk-speaker and sat staring at the tape-recorder on the table beside him. 'Dye me,' he said. 'Die me, for God's sake? Doh, ray, mee, fah, so, lah, tee, bloody-doh.' Then he lay back in his chair as Trelawney walked into the room.

'Sit down and listen,' he told him. 'I'm going to play a short piece of tape to you, but first I'll give you the scenario. Man screws girl. Man falls asleep. Girl lies awake contemplating the ceiling. Man talks in his sleep. Girl doesn't understand what he's saying and can't remember what it was. Girl is sent by me to Dr Williams who dredges some of the man's postcoital maunderings out of her subconscious under drugs or hypnosis or whatever he uses. The words are on this tape. I've cut out most of the English chit-chat between girl and doctor and left myself with this jumble.'

Rafferty reached towards the recorder, halted the movement of his arm and added, 'I was about to send it to a linguistic analyst when I made the brilliant deduction that as the man was a Pole he might be talking Polish. It being alleged that you are conversant with that language I'm going to try it out on you first. Okay?'

Trelawney told him it was and Rafferty switched on the tape-recorder.

The girl's voice was sleepy. 'Dye me. Does that mean paint me pretty?'

A gently reproving male voice. 'Now, now, Miss Fields. Just keep remembering.'

'All right. Dye me oots – ootsal – no, more like a "W". Ootsaworvatch. Something else. Pash. P-peeairsh. That's it! Dye me peeairsh ootsaworvatch.'

Rafferty stopped the tape.

'Mean anything?'

'Oh yes,' Trelawney said. 'Bed talk and part of a Polish poem. *Daj me piers ucalowac*. Give me your breast to kiss.'

'Oh, great. Never mind, here's the next bit.'

The tape started again with the girl's voice. 'Orangey.'

'What was orangey, Miss Fields?'

'Orangey. What? No, no. Nothing *was* orangey. Only orangey by itself. Or it might have been horangey, but that doesn't make any sense.'

'Never mind the sense. Keep giving me the sounds.'

Rafferty raised an eyebrow, but Trelawney shook his head.

'I think it was horangey. He said it several times.'

'Very well. Let's go on.'

'Once he said something like "Chebber metch yakish...", oh, it's so difficult!'

'Keep trying.'

'Chebber yakish... No, that's wrong. Chebber metch – chebber mietch yakish to sell v... ver jitsu. Ju-jitsu. Judo. Karate.'

'Now you're making it up, Miss Fields. Did he say all that?'

'No. Jitsu. Jichoo. Something. I'm so slee . . .'

The recorder clicked off.

'Anything, Al?'

'Play it again, will you?'

Rafferty did so, watching Trelawney scribbling on a pad, saw him frown, then nod.

'*Trzeba miec jakis cel w zyciu.* It means that it's necessary to have some aim in life.'

'Oh it does, does it. Bloody marvellous. So that's it. Williams couldn't get her to recall anything else and that leaves us nothing but the fruit. Can you kick that around a bit?'

'Orangey?'

'Yes, or horangey.'

Trelawney sat silently for over three minutes before saying, 'The "H" could be "CH" like in the Scottish word "loch". That would make the beginning "Chor". Then there's a Polish accented "a" sounding like the French "en".' He fell silent again, his eyes moving searchingly, then he went on, 'There's a word *choragiew* meaning flag. *Chorazy* makes a noise something like horangey, but I've never heard of it. Hang on, I'll get a dictionary.'

A minute later Trelawney came back carrying an open book.

'I might have taken a guess at that,' he said. '*Chorazy* is a standard-bearer,' and just caught Rafferty's whispered, 'Is it, by Christ?'

'Mean something to you, Raff?'

'I think so,' Rafferty said. 'I think it means that this operation has as much to do with the Trades' Unions as Barry's dog.' He reached for the telephone.

'Sue, you're the linguist around here. Remind me, what's the German for "the standard-bearer"?'

'*Der Bannertrager*, sir,' Sue Mitchell's voice told him.

'So it is. Thank you.'

Rafferty replaced the receiver as carefully as if it were the finest porcelain, then muttered, '*Der Bannertrager, Der Bannertrager.*'

'Didn't they call Hitler that?'

'What? Oh, did they, Al? Yes, I think you're right, but nowadays the soubriquet belongs to a man called Geoffrey... Geoffrey something. What the hell's his name? Geoffrey... no, Jefferies. Something Jefferies. Francis... Frederick. That's it! Let's go and talk to that bloody machine downstairs.'

'Was that Langley's voice?'

'Yes. Come on.'

Trelawney followed Rafferty into Records Section on the floor below. They crossed the long, narrow room with its rows of filing cabinets, its group of four small television screens with print-out machines below them and came to the computer room door in the far wall. Rafferty opened it.

He said, 'Hello, Mike, Harry.'

The two men said, 'Hello, sir,' in unison.

'Harry, go and buy yourself a pint of beer, or a poached egg or something, will you?'

The younger man smiled, left the room and closed the door behind him.

'Mike, let's see what we've got on a man called Jefferies. J-E-F-F-E-R-I-E-S. Initial "F" for Frederick.'

Michael Glendinning, the Head of Records, nodded and stabbed at the keyboard below the only television screen in the room. In the same second that his fingers stopped moving a list of names appeared in red on the black glass. It read –

'Jeferies A F
Jefferies F
Jefferies L F de B
Jefferies P F
Jefferiss G F
Jefferys F K'

Rafferty frowned at it, then at Glendinning. 'Has this thing lost its fan-belt or whatever else it considers essential to its well-being? I want information on a man, not bits out of the telephone directory.'

'It doesn't trust your memory or your spelling, sir,' Glendinning told him solemnly, then laughed. 'Actually, it's programmed to search for similar sounding names where the same initial occurs, just in case.'

'Bloody clever,' Rafferty said, 'but if it's finished showing off I'd like "Jefferies F" as I said.'

Glendinning depressed two keys and the list vanished to be replaced by 'Jefferies Frederick Born 1919 Avoca Co Wicklow Eire'.

'Is that all it knows?'

'It's just identifying the subject. It might not be the one you want.'

'All right. Ask it if it can provide a descriptive print-out.'

The word 'Affirmative' glowed on the screen.

'All right,' Rafferty said again. 'Set it going, but don't read it, Mike.'

Glendinning glanced at him. 'Would you like to operate it yourself, Mr Rafferty? I could make myself scarce. All you have to do is . . .'

He stopped at the shake of Rafferty's head.

'No thanks. All I ever get out of it is "Code invalid". I don't think it likes me.'

Rafferty stood, listening to the furious clatter, watching the lengthening rectangular tongue of paper growing from the machine. Against the wall, Glendinning sat apparently absorbed by the lines on the palms of his hands. The clattering stopped abruptly to be followed by a short ripping sound as Rafferty tore the strip free.

He read the typed words quickly and asked, 'Can you get me a picture of him?'

'On this screen if you like, Mr Rafferty. I just . . .'

'Don't bother. Bring me up a print – yourself.' He looked at Glendinning. 'And Mike, you've never heard of Frederick Jefferies.'

'Who, sir?'

Rafferty nodded and left with Trelawney at his heels.

CHAPTER SEVENTEEN

'You've got your important face on,' Jane said. 'Are we on to something?'

Trelawney didn't smile.

'I'm not sure yet but, if we are, I don't like it very much. In a pretty direct way this came out of your having Fiona Langley sent to Dr Williams.'

He put the computer plain-language print-out in front of her, walked round the desk and looked at it over her shoulder. It read:

Jefferies Frederick Born 1919 Avoca Co Wicklow Eire
Graduated BA 1942 Trinity College Dublin Eire
PhD 1948 University of Gottingen Lower Saxony Federal Republic of Germany
Main Disciplines Advanced Mathematics – Quantum Theory – Nuclear Physics

Granted US Citizenship 1969
Chair of Theoretical Physics University of Arizona Tucson Arizona USA
Visiting Lecturer in Mathematics Universities of Gottingen Lower Saxony Federal Republic of Germany and Durham England

No recorded political affiliations but possibility appellation German words Der Bannertrager end German words given to subject by Baader-Meinhof sympathizing element Gottingen students see SIS report quote Melody unquote June 23 1976 Reason not established
Permanent address rooms on Campus University of Arizona Tucson Arizona USA

'It wants us to be quite clear about the addresses, doesn't it?' Jane said. 'Have we got the "Melody" file?'

'Yes, but there's only a few lines on Jefferies. His name and *Der Bannertrager* occurring during the same conversation in a café the students use. There's no definite link because the reporting agent could only hear snatches of the talk. The single significant thing is that Jefferies was mentioned three times, *Der Bannertrager* four and the writer feels that the same person *may* have been being referred to.'

'Isn't it also significant . . . No, it isn't.'

Trelawney walked to a chair, sat down and asked, 'What were you going to say?'

'Something silly, darling. That it was odd for German students to be talking about some American professor at all, but why shouldn't they? He's a visiting lect . . . was the conversation political?'

His wife's change of course was so sudden that Trelawney blinked.

'In part, yes, from what the writer could hear.'

'Then it may still be odd. Does Raff know about this?'

'Yes. He dug it up.'

'Then let's have him along, shall we?'

Trelawney shook his head. 'It'll have to wait. He's out. Told me he had a bone to pick with Leo Volchak.'

'Did he now,' Jane said. 'That's very interesting indeed.'

Rafferty boarded the last coach of a west-bound Circle Line tube at Baker Street. It was almost empty and he sat down beside the glass partition by the double doors. The man who joined the train at Edgware Road took the seat next to him. He was middle-aged, slightly built for a Russian and had no trace of Mongol ancestry in his features.

'This is not a good place,' Volchak said.

Rafferty nodded his agreement. 'I know. I've never been particularly fond of the Edgware Road either.'

'I mean this train. Please do not joke with me.'

'It has its own form of privacy,' Rafferty told him. 'You know that as well as I. Would you rather be seen with me in a car, or milling around with all those security boys in St James's Park carrying copies of *The Times* opened at page seven?'

Volchak hesitated only for a moment before saying, 'You are right. I am a little nervous perhaps.'

'Oh come on, Leo,' Rafferty said. 'Don't *you* start in on the British understatement bit. You are not a little nervous, you are bloody frightened and what is more important Moscow is bloody frightened too. Nothing else explains your mistake in telephoning me seventeen minutes before the first news release of my Director's murder and nothing else explains your presence here. It isn't usual for Russian citizens to come running just because I snap my fingers. You were ordered to call me the day before yesterday and you were ordered to meet me now.'

'What you say is correct in each detail.'

'Great. So tell me all about it.'

'I do not know what knowledge you have of this matter, Mr Rafferty.'

Rafferty said, 'Don't let that worry you. I'll tell you when I get bored.'

Volchak's shrug indicated both his acceptance of the situation and dislike of the position in which he found himself.

'This conspiracy, Mr Rafferty, is one of major proportions. My government cannot stand by and permit it to come about. Consequently I am instructed to give you our assessment of it in case this should supplement your own information. I trust that this will be satisfactory.'

'Eminently.'

'Very well. At first we were unsure of the target. Indeed our information in that regard changed between the time that I telephoned your office and you returned my call. For that reason I could say little. You understand?'

'Yes.'

'There were several possibilities,' Volchak began, then stopped talking and opened a newspaper as people flooded on to the train at Paddington. Not until the crowd thinned at Kensington High Street did he turn to Rafferty again.

'For example, South Africa, Israel. Countries in the imperialist bloc where oppression exists. In the hands of freedom fighters in such places who knows . . .' Volchak left the sentence unfinished, then went on, 'Had you not contacted me today as you did, I was to approach you and inform you that the Soviet Government cannot in all conscience remain uncaring while a terrorist attack with nuclear weapons is carried out on London.'

He finally got around to it, Rafferty thought. Diplomatically too. Freedom fighters in Africa and the Middle East, terrorists in England.

'You're full up to the ears with crap, Leo,' he said. 'The word "conscience" was struck from the Russian dictionary during the Stalin purges. What are you trying to sell me?'

Until then the dead weight of the heavy, guttural voice coming so incongruously from Volchak's slim body had flattened any trace of feeling. Now there was audible tension in his words.

'To be irrelevant, Mr Rafferty, it is not necessary to be offensive. I dislike your manner.'

'And I, on the other hand, admire your command of the English language, but you must learn to apply your aphorisms correctly. There was nothing irrelevant in what I said. You are a representative of a government which has given terrorism a bad name, so don't talk to me about caring. Point your goddam rockets away from us and pull your troops out of other people's countries.'

Tapping Volchak's knee with a finger Rafferty went on, 'If you like we'll speak in Russian. That may make it easier for you to recognize the difference between the Kremlin being bloody frightened, which you have admitted to, and its developing a moral sense of responsibility to others as you now claim. Or is there a connection I've missed?'

Not accepting the invitation Volchak replied sharply in English, 'You are a very difficult man to talk to!'

Rafferty watched him carefully for several seconds, wondering if he had yet injected sufficient irritability and disorder into the conversation to destroy the symmetry of whatever statement Volchak had been instructed to make. The whiteness around the mouth indicated that he had and he decided it was time to probe.

'You're not all that interesting to listen to,' he said. 'As far as I can make out, you're postulating an atomic explosion, maybe explosions, in London. The prospect of such an occurrence either dismays your government on humanitarian grounds or reduces the Red Army to a state of dithering panic in case we assume you to be responsible and retaliate. I'm not sure which you mean, but neither makes any sense. You are neither fond of nor frightened by the British. Why should you be?'

The train drew into Gloucester Road station and both sat unspeaking in the comparative quiet. When it resumed its racketing progress through the next length of tunnel Volchak broke the silence between them.

'You are not a student of human nature, Mr Rafferty. In such circumstances we *would* be frightened of the British. With your capital city gone, and with it your government, there would be an automatic military take-over. Your bomber force is obsolescent, but a few, a very few would penetrate. It has always been so. And do not pretend to me that your submarine captains, after all these years, have not found a way to launch their own missiles without the nominal control of American settings and keys. This is too absurd to believe. So, Mr Rafferty, a relative pin-prick to the Soviet Union and its allies, but a pin-prick that would leave more dead Russians than the millions of my countrymen killed in the Great Patriotic War against Fascist Germany.'

Volchak grasped Rafferty's arm.

'What the United States would do is open to question. Perhaps, sanely, they would do nothing. About what your young military men, deprived of their leadership, would do there is no question at all. *That* is human nature. That we should reduce these islands to a radio-active desert would be no consolation to us. We do not want that pin-prick!'

Rafferty said, 'May I have my arm back, please?'

The Russian released it and relaxed, waiting, but Rafferty did not speak.

'Have you nothing to say?'

'Oh! Is it my turn? I got carried away listening to your scenario for World War Three. Yes, I have quite a lot to say. Firstly, the man you should be talking to if you want to avoid atomic acupuncture is a certain Frederick Jefferies, not me. If he succeeds I won't be here to help.'

The tension which had been growing in Rafferty eased at the near-comic look of relief on Volchak's face and vanished altogether at his next words.

'We progress at last, Mr Rafferty. I was beginning to think that I was talking to an ignorant fool.'

Jane Trelawney's voice came to Rafferty first. 'Fiona Langley slept with Dyboski for a considerable time. She may have heard things she doesn't remember now. I think Dr Williams should try to jog her memory.' Trelawney's voice followed. 'I might have taken a guess at that. *Chorazy* is a standard-bearer.' Next memories, his own vague memories of 'standard-bearer' in yet another tongue which had brought back the four-year-old 'Melody' file to his mind. A spore formed in the brain of a beautiful woman had germinated into an idea and now the idea had been shown to be a fact.

'You are,' Rafferty said. 'I don't even know why he is known as "*Der Bannertrager*".'

Volchak laughed. 'Why should you? It is of no importance. He is so named because the Sedona Centrifuge Construction Corporation is half-way up the mountain between that town and the city of Flagstaff. Your Frederick Jefferies owns it.'

Another station came and was left behind. Rafferty supposed it was South Kensington, but didn't look to see. He was frowning at Volchak to prevent any sign of elation appearing in his face. Volchak stared back at him curiously.

'You do not believe me?'

'Believe you? It's the corniest thing I ever heard. Flagstaff! Standard-bearer! As they used to say in my comparative youth "you've got to be joking". It's a basic rule in this business, as you ought to know, that a code name must never refer to its subject however obliquely. With a label like that I'd be frightened to set up a secret candy-floss factory at the North Pole in case somebody checked to see if there was a flag on it.'

It was Volchak's turn to frown. His was puzzled.

'But I assure you that's where the factory is. I thought perhaps you must know this.'

Rafferty said, 'I'm sorry. We've got our wires crossed. I know about the factory. I just can't believe in such a transparent code name.'

'Oh, now I understand. It is not a code name. It is a name given him by some stupid students who would like to be customers for his products.'

'The Baader-Meinhof lot at Gottingen?'

'Exactly. You have done your research well.'

'We have to,' Rafferty told him. 'There's a lot less room to stick pins in our map than yours.'

During those parts of the next half hour when speech between them was safe Rafferty walked a frayed mental tightrope woven of ignorance, inspired guesswork, crumbs of knowledge, sarcasm and charm. He mixed the last four ingredients carefully, the rope held and he kept his balance. What he learned amounted to little more than supporting evidence for the existence of the Arizona factory and its main function, but when the train doors hissed shut at Moorgate he had reached a conclusion. If nuclear devices were being assembled at the plant, none had yet left it. The Russian had not so much as touched on the possibility.

Was there anything to hang a time factor on? The killing of Havelock-Templeton could be taken to indicate that matters were coming to a head, or could it? They had taken a long time finding him after Fiona Langley had disposed of Dyboski. On the other hand the wiring of her flat pointed to a lengthy . . .

Volchak's voice broke in on his thoughts.

'I trust I have been of help, Rafferty.' He had stopped calling him 'Mister' after some particularly derisory remark.

'No, I don't think you have, Leo, but it's the thought that counts, isn't it? What do your people reckon to be the date of the first shipment? Ours put it at nine weeks.'

Rafferty glanced up at the row of advertising cards above the windows opposite him wondering what had made him pick on that particular number. The cards were blurring, their print fuzzy. One capital letter 'R' became two, inaccurately superimposed, separating from each other like an amoeba undergoing binary fission. Fission, fusion, Los

Alamos. No, not Los Alamos. That was New Mexico. That was the first time. The first time what? Something about Arizona. Sudden faintness. Why? No sleep since ... Watch it, you wet bastard!

He bent forward quickly, head down by his knees, fumbling with a shoe-lace.

'... think six at the outside.'

Head clearing. Re-tie shoe-lace carefully. Sit upright.

'Sorry. What did you say?'

'We think you have a maximum of six weeks,' Volchak said. 'They have hastened production since you eliminated Dyboski and may do so again if it is possible. The disappearance of their entire London cell has alarmed them.'

The words blew the last traces of mist from Rafferty's tired mind. He had already learned the source, information garnered, he supposed, by KGB networks in the States. Information Volchak had been authorized to give him anyway. Now the needling, the condescension, looked to be paying dividends. Off balance, Volchak had put a foot wrong and that mis-step might reveal his British connections, the possible origin of his knowledge of the target.

'Who,' Rafferty said, 'is Dyboski? And what do *you* know about a London cell?'

His face wooden Volchak replied, 'I have told you all you need. Now, at the next stop, I go.'

Rafferty shook his head. 'Now, at the next stop, you don't go. You sit right there until I hear what I want to hear from you. We haven't been once round the Circle Line yet and I'm quite prepared to make six laps.'

'You would detain a Soviet diplomat by force?'

'Oh hell,' Rafferty said. 'First it's aphorisms, now it's euphemisms. I think it's time we stirred you KGB boys around again. There's such a thing as overstaying your welcome, you know.'

'I have no connection with the KGB! I'm the ...'

'Skip it, Leo. You've just bought yourself a one-way ticket back to Mother Russia. Bunin goes with you.'

'Bunin? Who is this Bunin?'

'That's my line,' Rafferty told him. 'But as it's such a

forgettable name and as you can't have seen him for at least twenty minutes before you got on this train I'll refresh your memory. I'm referring to Viktor Aleksandrovich Bunin, the man you front for as the KGB's London Station head. He's on your Embassy list as Igor Sholokov. I forget the imaginary patronymic.'

The next stop came and went, marked only by the changing of a handful of passengers and the silence of the two men, then, 'I'm waiting, Leo.'

'You will continue to do so, Rafferty. Your cards are thrown away. As a result of what you have now said to me, Bunin and I automatically will be withdrawn. There is no longer a lever to your hand.'

There was some quotation. Something about the manner of your going, or his going, or ... or what? Nothing so becomes a man ... matter if you win or lose but how you play the ... *Patrick Rafferty*! Silly. So very silly. Tired and a bit old, that's all. Get on with it!

'You have a choice,' he said. 'You can go with your face dripping egg for having blown Bunin's cover. I'll arrange it so that they'll believe that and they won't thank you for it, or you can go with honour. I can arrange that too. They might even give you that medal that allows you to travel free on public transport.'

'You are proposing a trade?'

'Yes. I want the names of the people here you have been in contact with over this – er, conspiracy you called it.'

'And in return?'

'The identity of a man working for the Chinese who has penetrated Moscow Centre at a senior level.'

'I find that most difficult to refuse.'

'Then don't try.'

'How do I know it is genuine information?'

Rafferty shrugged, but didn't say anything and the Russian nodded as though he had been given a guarantee.

'The Pole Dyboski,' Volchak said. 'The chief co-ordinator. Whiteoaks he called himself here. He wanted our help. When we knew what for it was refused.'

'The Trades' Unionist?'

Volchak shrugged in his turn. 'Not really. It is their cover only and gives them ease of access. Most countries find difficulty in refusing entry to members of the International Trades' Union Movement.'

'Next.'

'The Libyan Mahmoud. Beshir Mahmoud. You will know that he was taken from the River Thames today.'

'Next.'

'There is no next, Rafferty. That is all.'

'I see. How very fortunate for you that they're both dead. What about this London cell you mentioned?'

'I know only that it has vanished. This was the last thing Mahmoud told us. The papers mention a gang kidnapping in Islington. Perhaps this was how you did it. Perhaps what happened to Dyboski will happen to them.'

Rafferty looked at him without expression and said, 'Enver Skendi, Russo-Albanian, age sixty, height one point seventy-eight metres, weight seventy kilogrammes, hair grey, eyes brown, obvious false teeth. I don't know what he calls himself in Moscow, but copies of his prints are in here.'

Dropping an envelope on to Volchak's knees he got up and stood by the doors. When they opened at King's Cross he got out and walked towards the exit. He didn't look back.

'That's about it, apart from the technical side,' Rafferty said. 'Most of that went in one ear and out of my nose.'

'Just give me his words, Raff. We'll edit the tape afterwards and somebody can tell us what it all means.'

'Well, it was an accumulation of thefts. Some in Colorado, some from the Lake Athabaska area in Canada, even, he thought, a consignment from as far away as – what the hell's the name of that place south of the Sahara nowadays? Used to be called . . .'

Rafferty stopped talking and squinted at Jane Trelawney, then asked, 'Haven't I said all this?'

'Yes, Raff. Headache?'

'Mmm.'

She went out into the passage, came back with a plastic cup filled from the water-cooler and set it down in front of him with four aspirins from her handbag. While he swallowed them she watched him gravely, feeling the first stirrings of anger inside her. This wasn't Rafferty at all. If anybody in the Department had a higher recall capability than her own it was he and tiredness was no excuse for his disjointed report because he had no right and no reason to allow himself to be tired.

Her thoughts about him during the early hours of the morning came back to her. They explained a lot, but not what he had been doing alone in his office all that time. Had it been the same the night before? It simply was not logical to sit sifting facts, probabilities, possibilities, when there were too few to cover the wires of the sieve, so few that they could be lined up and counted.

'Thanks. Where was I?' Rafferty said.

The anger died leaving only concern.

'You were going to give me the technical bits.'

'Shaky. Very shaky. Uraninite? Uranate? Or was it diuranate? Some damned uranium ore they'd knocked off. It's no use, Jane. It'll come back to me when I can think about it for a while. It's not so important.'

'It will be, Raff, when we can operate in the open again, get an analysis team on to all this and start asking questions of other people. There's the possibility of collusion, rather than straight theft, which might point to who . . .'

Rafferty raised his hands in surrender. 'I know, I loused it up. Spent too much time giving him the *suppressio veri* routine to – is that the right tag?'

'I expect you mean *suggestio falsi*.'

'That's the one. I didn't have any truth to suppress, did I? But I did suggest quite falsely that I possessed a sweeping knowledge of centrifuges. You should have heard me on the separation of U 238 from U 235 for the production of plutonium. Read about it in the *Reader's Digest* at the barber's one day.' He yawned hugely and the involuntary action made his eyes water. Wiping the moisture away with his finger tips he went on, 'I can't imagine why I thought it necessary to make him think we knew something. He was going to tell me anyway. Oh well.'

Rafferty pushed himself out of his chair and yawned again.

'One more thing,' Jane said. 'Did you believe Volchak when he told you Dyboski and Mahmoud were his only contacts here?'

'No, he was lying. That's why I put the finger on Skendi instead of Stasov. Let them sort that out.'

'Sneaky.'

He nodded, then asked, 'Have the interrogation boys come up with anything from Hampshire yet?'

'Give them a chance. They only left here at noon.'

'Oh, of course,' he said. 'That was today, wasn't it?'

When Rafferty had gone Jane sat for a moment staring at the place where he had been, then got up and left her office, moving along the passageway with her preoccupied fashion model stalk. She stopped at an open door, went in and shut the door behind her. Rafferty's secretary looked up from her desk and smiled.

'Hello, Liz. Can you spare a minute? I want to talk to you about Mr Rafferty.'

'It's all right, Mrs Trelawney. I've noticed and it'll be taken care of.'

'Are you sure?'

'Quite sure. Don't worry,' Liz said and smiled again.

Jane walked back to her room vaguely embarrassed at the formality with which she had thanked Liz, as though the girl had offered to make canapés for a cocktail party to which she was not invited. Angrily she pushed the memory aside. The real embarrassment lay with Rafferty. The slick talk, unfunny, mostly unnecessary. His recall hadn't failed him there as it had over the technical aspects. The conclusions he had reached both about the present availability of the weapons and Volchak's honesty were based on nothing that he could explain. He had been handed the key and dropped it. Now someone else would have to pick it up and turn it and there was no question at all of who that someone would be.

CHAPTER EIGHTEEN

'I always said that killing the man with the long name was a mistake. Nobody would listen to me and look where it's landed us.'

The speaker was a very thin middle-aged woman with blue-rinsed grey hair, expensive, uninteresting clothes and an accent which could have originated at some point in the Atlantic mid-way between Eire and the eastern seaboard of the United States.

An elderly Japanese sitting near her smiled, his expression seeming to convey both agreement and encouragement. He hadn't understood all her words, but was too polite to say so.

'There! At least Dr Hatoyama sees my point of view,' the woman said.

At a window of the Ritz suite a stoop-shouldered, bald man stood watching the traffic moving along Piccadilly. He looked like an impoverished clerk who had long ago resigned himself to failure, but the impression was misleading. When he spoke, his English resembled that of a British actor playing the role of an officer in the Waffen SS.

'What you have *always* said, Mrs McDowell, is hardly of interest to us in that context. What is done is done and I had my own excellent reasons for ordering that execution.'

'Such as, Herr Gesner?'

He turned and looked at her then, the sunlight glinting on his bald head.

'When it was proved beyond doubt that the woman who killed Dyboski was a member of the man's staff I felt it necessary to establish what sort of person we were up against and who was in his confidence. Infiltration was achieved quite simply by means of money and certain sexual overtures from one of our people.'

Primly Mrs McDowell said, 'I'm more interested in their outcome than your methods, Herr Gesner. You made an inside contact. Then what?'

'As you wish. I learned from my informant that this Havelock-Templeton was possibly acting on his own initiative. As it would be difficult, if not impossible, for him to have obtained authority in this country for what he had done, I upgraded the possibility to a probability and had him eliminated. That left the woman. To increase the chances of establishing if she knew why she had been ordered to kill and if she had been assigned other targets by her late superior I set watch on her flat.'

'Sure you did *and* lost your entire London goon squad as a result. I told you the whole thing was a mistake. Who snatched those boys and what will they have had beaten out of them by now?'

Gesner pursed his lips, walked to a chair and sat down.

'Obviously the security people have them,' he said. 'I don't know how the two traps were set, but it's of little importance. They have been replaced by the Birmingham cell now and anything they may have been persuaded to talk about cannot harm us because they had no knowledge of our objective.'

Mrs McDowell let her eyes stray around the room. They came to rest on the Japanese. He was asleep. She looked back at Gesner.

'That guy spooks me. Do we need him at these meetings?'

'No, Mrs McDowell, but this is his suite and it provides a useful meeting place for us on this brief visit. He is our expert on radiation, fall-out and . . .'

'Okay, okay. I know what he is. Tell me about this Mahmoud thing. He was your man, wasn't he?'

'An entirely administrative matter,' Gesner said. 'You need not concern yourself with it.'

Mrs McDowell took a compact from her handbag, examined her face in its mirror and began teasing strands of hair into place.

'What I need or need not concern myself with is my affair,' she told him. 'It might be an idea if you remembered that you're talking to a sizeable slice of your assets. I like to protect my investments and when I see photographs of somebody on my payroll crucified on a goddam raft in all the goddam

British papers I like to know how come he got that way. Let's hear about it, buster.'

Her voice had been mild, but he jumped when she snapped the compact shut.

'Very well. Beshir Mahmoud was guilty of greatly misplaced initiative. Upon the disappearance of our London cell and of Dyboski's murderess he tried to locate the home address of another of the security organization's operatives, an attempt on whose life by car bomb had miscarried. No doubt his intentions were good, but he was unaware of two things. First, all their addresses were available to me through my contact, so his efforts were wasted. Second, in view of our setbacks I had decided to adopt as low a profile as possible.'

'Let me see if I have this straight,' Mrs McDowell said. 'You torture the poor little man and then kill him for trying to find somebody's address. Next, you nail him to a raft and sail him down the river for a million people to see *to maintain a low profile*. That's just great. I wonder what you'll dream up for an encore.'

The German pursed his lips again before saying, 'My dear lady, if you will kindly permit me to finish. Mahmoud tried to follow the wife of this operative to their home. She – er, I believe "made a switch" is the term and became the pursuer instead of the pursued. From the mark behind his ear she probably struck him down with the heel of her shoe, but that is conjecture. What is not conjecture is that she removed his wallet while he was unconscious. His identity was, thereafter, known to the authorities and that placed our entire operation in jeopardy.'

'He knew things?'

'Oh indeed. He was the link, the cut-out, between the cells and the executive. Consequently, he knew the location of our properties. As a precaution we have now abandoned these until they are required for placing the bombs. But what was infinitely worse was that he could identify me and if they took me . . .' He left the sentence unfinished.

'You're beginning to make sense, Herr Gesner, but why the Viking funeral bit?'

'Justice, Mrs McDowell. Justice which must be seen to be

done. The rules under which we work stipulate that anyone who puts a colleague at risk dies unpleasantly. Mahmoud had made himself a potential source of danger to the whole organization and was dealt with accordingly. The point will not have been lost on others and the pattern fits that of gang warfare adopted by the press.'

'It figures,' the woman said and stood up. 'I have a plane to catch. You going back to Germany?'

'Yes.'

'Stand by to return here at short notice. Jefferies will be shipping out his first package ahead of schedule.'

Frowning, Gesner said, 'That is most unwise. I have much to attend to at Kassel. We have planned with precision and it is essential that we . . .'

'Hold it,' she broke in. 'You don't get precision out of idealistic geniuses. He just wants to set the world to rights the way he sees it. It's up to you to take up the slack. That's what you're in this thing for, so do your job. You're the organization man.'

'But . . .'

'Don't you "but" me, buster. You've had it your own way in committee as far as priorities are concerned. You don't like the British too well because their goddam air force chewed up your goddam Luftwaffe and set you on the slippery slope. You'd like to see the Jews to hell and gone off the West Bank of the River Jordan. In fact, you'd like to see the Jews to hell and gone, period. So, top of the list you get the London target with the Tel Aviv target to follow. What are you griping about? *Your* reasons are forty years out of date already, so what's so bad about catching up a week or two?'

They looked at each other in silence for a long moment before Gesner asked stiffly, 'May one enquire what are *your* reasons for partaking in these ventures, Mrs McDowell?'

'Money, Herr Gesner,' she told him. 'Just that. When the host nations have done what we tell them to do, their troubles aren't over. Before we let them off the hook they have to dig into their bullion vaults. Boy, do they have to dig and we have five of them listed for digging.'

He watched her leave the suite, hating her and resenting

the power the money she already had gave her. Although it represented less than a fifth of the budget it was a sum they could not manage without. Not accompanying her to the door gave him some satisfaction. Having withheld from her knowledge of the link he had forged within Whitehall itself gave him more. That would remain his own secret power source.

CHAPTER NINETEEN

To Rafferty his secretary looked neatly put together, despite a little too much soft blonde hair around a nicely arranged face which varied between fairly pretty and pretty depending on her expression. Her best features were a well-formed, determined mouth and calm hazel eyes. At the moment she looked only fairly pretty because the hazel eyes were angry.

'What are you doing here, Liz? I sent you home at seven.'

'I went home at seven,' she said. 'At eight I telephoned your flat to see if you had done what *I* told *you* to do. You weren't there and here I am.'

'So I see. Can I do anything for you?'

'Yes, do as I said. This is the third night, Mr Rafferty. You aren't helping yourself or us by behaving like this. If you've slept anywhere since Monday night, which I doubt, it's been in that chair. That's no use and – and your shirt's *awfully* dirty!'

The tone of the final statement had obviously clinched the matter for her. He started to smile then experienced a violent reversal of feeling.

'Oh shit!' he said and flung the ball-point pen he was holding at the wall to his left. It struck blunt end on, but still tore an inch-long gash in the surface.

She moved to his desk, stacking files and papers while he watched her without protest. When they were all in the safe she closed the door, spun the dial and turned to face him, eyebrows raised enquiringly. Seconds later Rafferty was walking along the passage beside her.

Outside the building she turned south with him.

'Now where are you going?' he asked. 'You live off Regent's Park.'

'I'm going to see that you don't sneak back to the office. Here, you can carry this.'

'What is it?'

'Some proper food and a bottle of wine. I'm tired of bringing you cheese rolls.'

Rafferty lay back on his bed watching her undress.

'I've always kept anything like this away from the office,' he said.

'We're not at the office. The carpet's a different colour.'

'I'm glad you wear stockings. Much more glamorous than tights.'

'The personal opinion poll I conducted indicated that that would be your preference,' she said. 'Now be quiet and lie absolutely still.'

Her love-making was gentle, practised and, he guessed, with little thought of self. When he fell asleep in her arms he lay without moving for five hours until a shaft of early morning light touched his face through a small gap in the curtains. He awoke with a start.

As gently as before she put him to sleep again.

At his home in Gottingen the bald man got up from the breakfast table to answer the telephone. '*Hier ist Heinrich Gesner*,' he said, then listened without interruption for nearly three minutes.

When he spoke again it was in English. 'It all sounds very dramatic, but no, it is of no concern to us. I congratulate you however. Please continue to report everything. Even this strange affair. Who knows? A connection may emerge.' It annoyed him to find that his hand was shaking enough to clatter the receiver when he replaced it.

Almost immediately he picked it up again, dialled a long series of numbers and, seconds later, a sleepy voice in Grand Rapids, Michigan said, 'Who is it?'

'Gesner, Mrs McDowell. It is very early with you. I am sorry, but this is vital. Yesterday I mentioned in passing a man whose wife is adept with a high-heeled shoe. That man left London this morning for a holiday in the south-western United States.'

He talked for longer than his caller from London had done, searching, in a language which was not his own, for words which would be understood only by the woman he was talking to.

Finally, 'Yes,' he said. 'Sunday night, but I recommend that you take action as soon as possible.'

The receiver rattled on its rest again when he rang off.

Rafferty arrived at the Thayer Street offices at 11.25 a.m. and went straight to Jane Trelawney's room.

'Hello, Raff. You look a different person!'

'Do I? I certainly feel it. In fact I feel better than at any time since I collected Barry from Dorset. How's he, by the way?'

'Smouldering.'

He grinned and she thought how nice it was to see him do that again.

'Right,' Rafferty said. 'Let's have Al in and get this thing moving. We've got something to chew on now.'

'He's gone, Raff.'

'Gone? Where is he?'

'Somewhere over the Atlantic.'

He stood looking down at her thoughtfully, no longer amused. She looked calmly back at him.

'That was rather high-handed of you, Jane.'

'My dear,' she said, 'you gave me this operation to control and I shall control it until you order otherwise. If you don't like my methods you can always take over yourself and put me back on field work.'

'Did your methods include putting *me* into bed with a girl?'

Jane Trelawney's wide mouth twitched upwards at one corner, but she caught the smile and stifled it.

'*A* girl. How gallant of you to protect her name. But to answer your question, yes, the idea did cross my mind, but Liz had thought of it before me. Are you all overcome with remorse?'

'Not so you'd notice. I got the impression that I wouldn't have been given any say in the matter, so I didn't try to argue.'

'Good. Now why don't you sit down and I'll tell you what I've done so far?'

'If you please,' Rafferty said and folded his lanky frame into a chair. He had just learned, as Trelawney had discovered years before, that it was as easy to be angry with this woman as with anyone else, but that to sustain the condition was next to impossible.

'Do you remember Robert Purvis?' she asked him.

'Yes, I do. Bogota "Resident" until a year ago when we moved him to Washington. What about him?'

'When you had told me about your meeting with Volchak I called him, strict hush of course, and asked him to check on the Sedona centrifuge plant.' She picked up a sheet of paper, glanced at it and put it down again unread. 'It's a perfectly genuine registered company manufacturing all sorts of centrifuges. Small ones for blood samples, cream separators and so on. They also have a contract with the US Atomic Energy Commission for the supply of the big ones you were talking about.'

'Could be very good cover,' Rafferty said. 'They might have built a pre-production model and kept it running.'

'That's what Al and I thought, so we spent some time in the library boning up on the subject. As it isn't exactly the Department's line of country our publications on nuclear physics aren't all that hot off the press and there may have been a lot of changes, but this is what we found out.'

She steepled her fingers and stared at them with very wide eyes.

'First, making plutonium isn't just a matter of separating U 238 from U 235. You need an atomic pile. In the reaction U 238 absorbs neutrons from U 235 to form another isotope, U 239. This emits a beta particle and turns into another radio-active element called neptunium 239. This in turn, discharges another...'

'Hold it, pretty lady! You've lost me and who said anything about plutonium anyway?'

Still staring at the tips of her fingers, 'You did, yesterday. You weren't being quite as precise as usual and it put me off track for a bit.'

She turned her gaze on to him and said, 'Then it occurred to me that if obtaining uranium 235 was a simple centrifuge operation, that was all that was needed. Forget plutonium. You can make a very horrid bang with U 235. It was the basis of the first atom bomb. Probably it's all much more complicated than that, but . . .'

Jane fell silent and contemplated her fingers again.

'So you concluded what?'

'So we concluded that as we couldn't do any of the obvious things like picking up a telephone and asking somebody, or informing the government, or dropping round at the American Embassy because that would have been as good as informing the government, all that was left was for Al to go and look.'

'And when he's looked?'

'That depends on what he finds.'

Rafferty moved restlessly in his chair, then got up, walked to the window and jack-knifed into a sitting position on the sill, arms around his knees. He liked sitting on window-sills.

'If I know Al he'll probably find some way of blowing it up,' he said. 'Great chap for blowing things up is Al.'

Jane moved her head in an affirmative gesture, but didn't speak.

For countable seconds there was silence. It was broken by Rafferty.

'I didn't much like that nod of yours, Jane. What else have you cooked up between you?'

'Purvis is sending a consignment of Young's boxes of tricks to Phoenix by private jet for Al to collect on arrival,' she told him, then added quickly, 'No, Raff! Hear me out. I know there is an agreement between the States and ourselves that we will not carry out clandestine operations on each other's territory. I know Al has no right to be over there with explosives and firearms in his possession. I know he has no right to be there at all on a visa forged by Documentation Section. I also know that you were right when you told Al that this business could mean the end of the Department in its present form.'

She took cigarettes from her bag, lit one and tossed the packet to Rafferty. He said, 'Thanks,' helped himself, then reached out and placed the packet carefully on the corner of her desk as if afraid of breaking her concentration.

'Obviously we are accountable to the government,' she went on, 'but we must be permitted to operate on a long rein because any rigidly imposed accountability would emasculate the organization hopelessly. The Prime Minister said as much about the security services in general in the House recently.' Jane smiled briefly before adding, 'Don't worry, I'm not going to make a speech. I just want to know if I have a correct understanding of your thinking.'

'Perfectly correct.'

'Very well. So much for our hopes for the Department and its future. Now the other side. There are three of us in England, you, Al, me, who think we know what's at stake. There is also an unknown number of Russians here and at home with the same information. If Volchak is to be believed, they're nervous and if we don't act on what they've told us they're going to tell somebody else here who will. Do you think that's right?'

'Yes,' Rafferty said. 'I do. They won't have wanted to approach the Americans because that would reveal to some degree how extensive their networks over there are, so they came to us.'

Ash from his cigarette fell on to the carpet and he stretched a leg down to scuff it with his shoe before saying, 'I wonder why *us* in particular.'

'KGB mentality? They think we run the country? No, that's silly. Perhaps they think we would never acknowledge a Russian tip-off. Just claim the credit for ourselves and leave them in the clear.'

Rafferty said, 'Hmm. Could be. In any event they'll go government to government if we aren't seen to do something pretty soon.'

'We will be,' Jane said. 'According to Purvis the factory is on a five-day week.'

'Yes?'

'Today's Friday. If everything goes well that factory will be the busiest place in Arizona on Sunday night. If . . .'

Rafferty started to say something, but she talked him down.

'If it doesn't, I have promised Al that you will put the whole thing to the Prime Minister not later than noon today week. I have also promised him that if you refuse I shall do it myself and before you start thinking about restraining me physically you might as well know that . . .'

Abruptly Rafferty swung his legs to the ground, mashed his cigarette in the desk ashtray and said, 'I might as well know that you've left copies of a letter with various people to be delivered to the PM unless they hear from you before noon next Friday. Take your gun out of my ear, honey. I happen to agree with you.'

For the first time in his life Rafferty saw the face which bewitched him by day, and intruded more often than was comfortable for him in his dreams, crumple. Accustomed as he had become to its serenity, serenity which would have been almost inhuman but for the laughter underlying it, the sight shocked him. So, when she spoke, did the unsteadiness of her voice, a voice he had grown to think of as God-given for calming excited agents. He looked away from her.

'I'm so glad, Raff. I – I – Even if it spread no further than London – the millions – suppose somehow the Department survived, it can't be balanced against that. You must see . . .' Then in a sudden rush of words, 'If you leave us out of it altogether Whitehall still has a very large Intelligence machine. Then there's the armed forces. They aren't massive any more, but they're razor-sharp. We have allies too. Good ones. If we're to fight this bunch of madmen we can't ignore all that help. We can't play at being "The Three Musketeers" when the whole . . .'

He turned back to her and placed a hand over one of her tightly clenched fists.

'I know, Jane,' he said. 'I *know*. I've *told* you I agree with you. Now you tell me what that husband of yours thinks he's going to do. Will there be an atomic explosion in Arizona, or will simply burning the factory down satisfy him?'

Snatching her hand away she said, 'Don't you dare joke about . . .' then stopped in mid-sentence and touched his fingers with her own.

'Sorry, Raff. End of hysterics. Considering the situation

which may develop what I was thinking about was entirely selfish and just a tiny bit out of proportion.' Her voice was perfectly calm again.

'Tell me.'

'Yes, all right. When Al's on this sort of job he's remarkably difficult to stop. If somebody tries to get in his way – well, I was wondering if Arizona is one of the States which still retains the death penalty. Silly, isn't it? He could have died a hundred times behind the "curtain" or some other rotten place. I'd have found that easier to bear than – oh, by the way, if you know the answer don't tell me. Now, you asked what he was going to do.'

'Yes.'

'He's going in through Phoenix, as I said, because it's a long way from Flagstaff. After the car bomb attempt on him at Professor Morris's place he knows he's been fingered, so he's approaching the target area from a point they aren't likely to be watching.'

As though they were no part of her, her hands made some unnecessary rearrangement of the objects on the desk while her eyes held Rafferty's.

'Naturally,' she said, 'what he does will depend on what he finds when he gets there, but the provisional plan is to set Young's charges wherever they'll produce the most spectacular results without hurting anybody. At least, I hope nobody gets hurt. That's why we picked Sunday. All we want to do is to bring the Fire Department and the police and the FBI running. The press too of course. Then an anonymous phone call to the FBI and the newspapers. After all the commotion I don't think they'll treat the call as a hoax, or just carry out a perfunctory search. I think they'll take the place apart piece by piece.'

'I like the sound of that,' Rafferty said. 'Nice and methodical. Al vaporizing it in a millionth of a second might be considered impetuous.'

Neither of them smiled.

CHAPTER TWENTY

The menu began 'Open-face Rubin corned beef lovin'ly thin-sliced & tenderly piled high, blanketed with steamin' hot sauerkraut, gently laid on fresh rye bread, smothered with delicious Swiss cheese & warmly placed under the broiler. If we're busy, delete all the adjectives and adverbs – $3.25.'

Trelawney smiled and read on, learning about Taco Salad which was claimed to be great for dieters and a Tiajuana Torpedo which, from its contents, definitely was not. Just as he finished reading that 'Yer waitress will be happy (we told her so) to split yer order any whichway' a girl's voice said 'Howdy!' It came out in a controlled bellow and he looked up to his left.

Tall in Stetson and cowboy boots, wide-hipped, big-boned, she had the glowing prettiness of her nineteen years and perfect physical condition. Her expression seemed to be telling him that he was the nicest thing she had seen all day.

'I'm fine. And how are you?'

'Right on!' The same happy bellow. 'Say! You British?'

'Yes, I am.'

'Wow! That's great!' A flash of well-formed, very white teeth. 'Wait till I tell my dad. He was over there with the Eighth Air Force and he says . . . Hey, you don't want to hear about my dad. What's it gonna be? Don't have the fried chicken. It's kinda stringy. We're sending the whole consignment back.'

Trelawney ordered, grinned and added, 'Some of the 999 Island dressing with the salad, please. What happened to the last island?'

Another flash of teeth. 'Went down in a hurricane. Crazy menu, isn't it?'

He watched her walk away, her nearly successful coltish attempts to control her high-heeled boots proof that she belonged on a tennis court in sneakers. So friendly, he thought. Just a college kid earning some money for herself out of school and better at what she was doing than the majority of women who made their living as waitresses at home in England. It occurred to him that if Jane and he had had a daughter she would have been about this girl's age now. That would have been nice and if she'd been a duplicate that would have been all right too.

For a moment he felt almost jealous of the unknown American who had been in the Eighth Air Force, then his leg touched the brief-case Purvis had had waiting for him at Phoenix's Sky Harbor airport. It contained twelve of Young's compact explosive devices and brought him sharply back to the present.

The restaurant hadn't yet filled up, or perhaps the rush was over, and he had selected a table by the window from where he could watch his rented car. It was parked close to the main door in the full glare of an overhead arc-light and he doubted anyone would dare tamper with it. Not that he expected trouble yet. He had driven south out of Phoenix for several miles in the direction of Tucson before doubling back through the city. He had not been followed then, or on the turn-off to this little town called Cave Creek. Why should he be? The car was just another Buick with 'Grand Canyon State' on its licence plate. But still he watched it.

'Dad says you Britishers don't care too much for all the stuff on the side we like to eat here, so I told the kitchen to go easy. I hope that's okay. Plenty more if you want.'

Trelawney looked at the large meal she was transferring from her tray to his table, then up at her.

'Thank your father from me, will you? I just might make this lot. With the whole works I'd have gone down without a trace, like that island.'

She giggled and said, 'Anything you want, just yell. You hear?'

It was twenty hours since he had boarded the Air India 747 at London's Heathrow early that morning or, more accurately, the morning before, but he wasn't tired. Sleep had claimed him for most of the flight to Kennedy and he had even managed to doze occasionally on the American Airlines plane which had carried him diagonally across the States to the capital city of Arizona. What had *it* been? A DC 10? It didn't matter what it had been. What did matter was that he had crossed seven time zones and where he now sat eating steak and salad it was still only eight in the evening of the same Friday on which he had left London.

He looked at his car again, then at the girl laughing with a couple dining four tables away and began to examine very carefully the idea which had formed in his mind.

Immediately, because self-deception was not part of his character, he admitted to himself that it had been born of emotion. His parting from Jane that morning had been more emotional than any that had gone before by virtue of its abruptness. A budding actress before Barry had persuaded her to join the Department she had, from some recess in her memory, recalled the old theatrical superstition against wishing anybody luck on opening night. Pale-faced, 'Break a leg,' she had said and walked away without kissing him.

Existence of emotion noted, but idea not invalidated.

Emotion flows over into untypical wish for a daughter because a pleasant American child behaves like a pleasant American child. Noted and irrelevant.

Because of their shared occupation there had never been any question of Jane bearing children. Living from day to day, the only course open to them, they were happy in each other.

Not only this girl had been welcoming. The immigration official at Kennedy airport, 'Enjoy your stay, Mr Armitage,' and the Customs man's smile and his hand gesturing him through with no baggage search. So different from the Home Office mutes who guarded Britain's gateways with cold, blank eyes and the Customs officers who used cynical officiousness as an antidote to boredom.

To emotion add deeply ingrained antipathy to petty bureaucrats. Totally irrelevant. Ignore.

Trelawney stabbed his fork impatiently into a piece of steak, then paused with it half-way to his mouth.

Don't ignore. Re-phrase. To emotion add marked preference for courteous officialdom. Better. The piece of steak completed its journey.

Emotionally he wanted this job quickly done so that he could take himself and his trade away to some other country where living a lie didn't matter to him. Why it mattered here he was unsure, but matter it did and that too, he recognized, was totally irrelevant. Nevertheless, he was glad of a valid reason for departing from an agreed plan which would have extended the life of the lie.

'Enjoy your stay, Mr Armitage.' Officialdom could be courteous, but that didn't make it inefficient. The eyes, cold or friendly, were still there. He let his imagination build a picture of two faceless men in a featureless office somewhere at Kennedy airport.

'Harry, something's been bugging me all day. That big Limey with the busted nose – there, off this Air India flight – I know him from someplace. Evens is as far as I go, but I'm betting his name ain't Armitage. What did he give as his address?'

'He didn't. Just touring around.'

'Okay. Let's have the car hire outfits checked and all outgoing flights from here, La Guardia and Newark. And put this description on the telex. Ready?'

'Yeah. Go ahead.'

The chances of such a conversation taking place were not necessarily low. He was known to various members of the American security services some of whom were personal friends and, for his size alone, he was noticeable. So the telex message could be sent, could already have been sent. Either way he guessed that fifteen minutes after its transmission they would know with reasonable certainty that a British agent named Trelawney, travelling on a false passport, was somewhere in Arizona with the Buick parked outside the window. Transgression of the law apart, they would be extremely interested to know why.

Both Jane and he had been aware of the risk, accepting it because they had no alternative, because, with their self-imposed restrictions, there was nobody else. Rafferty she had adjudged to be under strain and unusable for that reason.

Even had he not been, his absence would have been difficult to explain to the Minister.

There had also been no alternative to the false passport. The use of his own name would have attracted immediate attention and polite offers of help with whatever it was he wanted.

So James Philip Armitage had come to the States as a tourist with an interesting schedule – one day in transit, another day resting and recovering from jet-lag to minimize errors of judgement, a third for reconnaissance of the target he would hit in the early hours of Monday morning, or the last of Sunday night.

But James Philip Armitage was not tired because he had slept his way across the Atlantic. With a disrupted sleep pattern over recent days, and frequently throughout his life, there were no symptoms of jet-lag. Finally, given the possibility that every police patrol car was now his enemy, he doubted the wisdom of the exposure reconnaissance would entail. Glad to have a practical as well as an emotional reason for prompt action he waved at the girl and mimed writing out a bill.

When he had paid what he owed, 'Have a nice evening now,' she said.

'You too,' Trelawney told her and walked out to blow up a factory.

When Trelawney was unlocking the Buick under the arc-light outside the restaurant his wife was lying on their bed staring crossly through the open window at the sunlight playing on the roofs of the houses opposite. Dawn had come to London some time before and she had watched it do so just as she had watched the silhouettes of the buildings against the night glow of the city for several sleepless hours.

She was cross because she hadn't slept and she hadn't slept because she was cross, which was infuriating. The sheet had tangled itself around her feet and she reached for it, pulling it up to her chin, holding it there with both hands, thinking of all the things she was cross about.

Patrick Rafferty, of all people, allowing himself to get in

such a state! No, that was ridiculous. The reason for it she understood perfectly and, thanks to Liz, the phase was over, but if men didn't have these weak spots how much simpler... The thought died, unfinished, leaving her angrier still because she had broken down in front of Rafferty. Stupid bitch! Did it matter? Of course it mattered! But only to her, so it didn't matter. Forget it and don't do it again!

Then there was the failure of the interrogation people to come up with anything. Not their fault. What could they be expected to produce at 'The Abattoir', talking and listening for hour after hour with virtually no idea what questions they were supposed to be seeking answers to, apart from who else in the country was in the organization? A lot had been learnt since Al had asked for them to be sent down, but they'd been told none of it because Raff believed that the risk of a leak through them, or one of them, was unacceptably high. Through *them*? The Russians could blow the whistle on the Department any time they felt like it and they'd feel like it as soon as they discovered that Raff had misled them over the traitor in Moscow Centre. And they would discover it. To use a standard confusion ploy at such a time! Really! That had to be put right before Volchak and Bunin left the country. Volchak might even be persuaded to say more in return for an honest trade. Perhaps she should see to that herself.

Her last thought put a positive end to the night for Jane. She looked at her watch and compared its reading with the alarm clock beside her. Both told her that it was fourteen minutes past five. Muttering something unintelligible she threw the sheet aside, swung off the bed and began walking up and down the room. Despite her long legs Trelawney's pyjamas, which she liked to wear when he was away, made her look small.

Perhaps she should see to that herself! As if it wasn't enough to be running two agents, one her superior, the other her husband, with no Director to whom she could appeal or from whom she could seek guidance. With Al in the States there wasn't even anyone she could talk things over with except Raff and he, with his self-confessed inability to control the destinies of those below him in rank which meant everybody in the Department, was more hindrance than help. To a degree he was still abiding by the rules he himself had formulated in allowing her freedom of action, but when she approached an area he considered too sensitive he would fall back on his rank and veto the move.

The sleeves of Trelawney's pyjama jacket kept sliding down and covering her hands. She pushed them up over her elbows and went into the kitchen to make coffee. With her second cup she lit a cigarette and began thinking about Julian Havelock-Templeton. He was the real culprit and for a moment she toyed with the idea that he had been bent. No, his death absolved him from that at least, but it had been insane of him, criminally insane, to have confided in nobody, not even his second-in-command. Professor Morris had told Al that the late Director was more inclined than most to act on his own initiative and Admiral Bembridge, when Raff had contacted him on a secure line, had added the opinion that he was obsessed by secrecy. Well, that fitted the facts and got her nowhere. If only they could break that numbers code. He must have left *something* on record, some key. No *must* about it she reminded herself and frowned at her cigarette.

Jane started to make breakfast, then abandoned the task. It was still very early and it could wait until she had showered and dressed. She returned to the bedroom and took off Trelawney's pyjamas, thankful that there were two days to go before he would be in any danger, wishing she could be certain that the Arizona plant was the only target they should be aiming at.

Less than thirty minutes later she telephoned for a car to take her to Thayer Street, her irritability replaced by a cold resolve that there would be no more half-measures, no more scruples and no more talk, in the way Rafferty meant it, of sensitive areas.

CHAPTER TWENTY-ONE

When he turned north on Interstate Highway 17 Trelawney accelerated to 57 mph, pressed the 'cruise' button on the end of the indicator arm and took his feet off the pedals. The Buick's speed dropped to fifty-five and stayed there. Gradients, up or down, made no difference. The big engine held the speedometer needle precisely on the nationwide legal limit. He thought it was the most boring form of locomotion he had ever experienced and wished he was driving the Lotus on a motorway at home.

Suddenly fed up after only three miles he put his foot back on the accelerator and the dashboard squawked angrily at him when his speed passed fifty-eight.

Trelawney sighed, then said aloud, 'You're absolutely right. We don't need the police just now, do we?' He went back to 'cruise', thankful that he had only one hundred miles to travel and began to think about what he was going to do when he got there. A minute later he stopped doing it because it was so pointless.

Beyond the turn-off to somewhere called Black Canyon City he brought the car to a halt on the sandy verge and began to dismantle the automatic Purvis had put into the brief-case with Young's cassette-sized bombs. With the gun stripped down to its major components, he got out and threw the individual pieces in various directions as far as he could into the desert. He did the same with the shells from the three clips of ammunition, then returned to the car and drove on, intrigued by the mixture of Anglo-Saxon, Spanish and Mexican place-names. Bumble Bee, he liked that one, Cordes Junction, Camp Verde and, as he branched left for Sedona, a sign pointing the way to Montezuma Castle. Surprised by the last he shook his head, prepared to bet that Montezuma had never been near the place.

Then, 'Don't be so damned literal,' he told himself and the car.

He was surprised too by the scarcity of road traffic. Outside the towns, he had seen fewer than thirty vehicles travelling in either direction since he had left the restaurant where he had dined. Idly he wondered if the oil crisis was biting at last. It was only when he drove in to Sedona that his mood of detachment vanished. Close now. Time to re-run the information stored in his head.

He left Sedona on Highway 89A, as Purvis's cipher to London had said he should, a few minutes after midnight, his headlights illuminating the tops of large trees almost at road level to his right. That checked. They were growing out of the dark void of Oak Creek alongside which the road ran. A bridge, name forgotten, 1.5 miles out of town. Again check. What next, Purvis? Oh, yes. Another, called Oak Creek Bridge, six miles on which would place the watercourse on his left, then a run to the switchbacks snaking up the mountainside to a place named Lookout Point six and a half thousand feet up with Flagstaff beyond it.

'Much of Oak Creek Canyon visible from Lookout Point,' the coded telex had said, 'but factory which understood to be west of road probably hidden behind mountain spur for environmental reasons as this area and Sedona vicinity both of great scenic beauty.'

Waste of cipher groups, Purvis. Hardly seen a thing except road and no interest in tourist blurb anyway. No, that was unfair. A perfectly relevant comment and particularly so as one of the reasons for being there after dark was to pick up the loom of lights above a fold in the ground. And lights there would be, weekend or not, for security and for the maintenance teams. But how many? How strong? Would they be lost against the glare of Sedona? If . . .

'If nothing,' Trelawney said. 'Just go and see.'

There was no need to go and see, no need to travel as far as Lookout Point. Some ten minutes after crossing the second bridge the Buick's beams picked out the words 'Sedona Centrifuge Construction Corporation Inc' on a sign pointing to an access driveway to his left. Three-quarters of a mile further on he found a place where he could pull off the rock-bordered road.

He got out of the car and stretched his back, then gave a convulsive shudder. Frightened? No, not yet. That would come later. It was cold up here at night. A lot colder than the oppressive heat of Phoenix. Colder than the controlled atmosphere in the car. What to do with the car? Run it in amongst the small group of pines ahead? No sense in that. Partial concealment would arouse curiosity. Leave it where it is with the bonnet open. When had he last done that? At Hyde Park Corner of course, when he had abandoned the Lotus to follow Barry all that time ago.

Trelawney grunted, impatient with himself. All that time ago had been not quite four days. He raised the bonnet, took a pair of pliers from the tool-kit in the boot and, brief-case in hand, walked towards the bluff forming the wall of the lay-by provided by nature at the roadside.

It was an easy climb, twenty feet of fissured rock at roughly the same number of degrees from the vertical, but the brief-case was a nuisance and, half-way up, he tied it to his belt with a handkerchief. At the top he saw the loom of the lights immediately, the lights themselves hidden, as Purvis had suggested, by a pine-covered ridge. He began to walk towards them.

At seventeen minutes past one he lowered himself to the ground and lay looking down on the factory. Roughly L-shaped because of lie of land – area six to eight acres – lighting intermittent except for arcs on each upright of perimeter fence – movement slight – one unladen fork-lift truck travelling east on far side of compound – four men grouped by door of trailer on near side one holding mug – probably mobile cafeteria – one man visible through window of gate-house on access driveway – no dogs in sight.

He crawled back the way he had come thinking about rattlesnakes, knowing that Arizona had its full share of them, hoping they preferred desert to mountain or had the sense to retire to their holes at night. When he was far enough below the ridge he stood up and began walking again, circling round to approach from the other side. The pines grew to within fifty feet of the wire there and it was a long way from the cafeteria where constant traffic could be expected.

To reach his departure point at the edge of the trees took him only eleven minutes and he crouched in their shadow looking across the brightly lit expanse between himself and the wire. No movement, but he could hear the faint sound of voices and, more clearly, the clang of metal on metal coming from one of a row of large windowless structures made of some aluminium alloy. Then he noticed the pile of empty oil drums fifty yards to his right. They had to be empty from the casual way they had been stacked. Four or five had fallen against the wire and that was very interesting. He could use the pile as cover and go in screened by it in the knowledge that the fence, at least up to the sixth strand, was not electrified. Seconds later he was kneeling by it, panting a little from his sudden sprint, working at the wire with the pliers from the car.

It was tough, the wire, and the pliers not as heavy as he would have wished, but the strands parted one after the other, five close to the upright, four sunk into the concrete strip embedded in the ground. No shock, no siren, no clanging bells. When he pushed, a triangular section of fencing moved away from him and he crawled through the gap left by it wondering if he had set off some silent alarm in the gatehouse, or alerted the local police.

The first four of Young's bombs clicked magnetically on to the petrol tanks of three large articulated trucks and a Shell road tanker standing side by side in a transport area. 'Only two dials, Mr Trelawney sir. Left, minutes. Right, hours. If you want to throw it at something, turn either one anti-clockwise and it'll go off on impact, but do throw it a long way, Mr Trelawney.'

Ninety minutes to detonation should be about right he thought and reached out to make the first setting. His hand stopped its movement before it touched the dial.

'You bloody, bloody fool!' he whispered furiously to himself, grasped the bomb in both hands and jerked it off the tank, then did the same with the other three. The effort it took to break the magnetic coupling was considerable and when all four were back in the brief-case his hands were trembling but not, he knew, from exertion. He shook his head fiercely to clear it of the grim picture of blazing buildings and screaming people in Flagstaff or Sedona. His hands steadied and he looked around him for something that would not move out of the factory.

Transport needed fuel, so where were the storage tanks? Underground obviously, but there had to be filling connections and dispensing pumps on the surface. He saw the pumps, one for petrol, one for diesel, just beyond the third truck at the same moment as the sound of footsteps reached him. Dropping flat he pulled himself and the brief-case under the road tanker. The footsteps were quiet, purposeful, and he wondered if it would not have been wiser to have stayed on his feet.

'You pulling out?'

'Nope. Gotta leak in the air-brake system someplace back here.' That was a long speech to make and hope to sound American. He found himself holding his breath.

'Uh-huh.'

The footsteps, still quiet, still purposeful, didn't falter and Trelawney let his breath out slowly, watching the feet themselves recede.

The filling points and inspection covers for the storage tanks were locked, so he attached a bomb to the base of each of the pumps and set the dials – Hours 1, Minutes 30 – then knelt, looking, listening. No movement. Sounds as before.

Staying as far as he could from the brightly lit fence, keeping to whatever shadow there was, he made his way to a wired section surrounding six big gas containers, widely separated. The gate was chained and padlocked. To climb the fence would be easy and very foolish. 'No, Mr Trelawney. No way will they go off if you drop them. Not unless you've turned a knob anti-clockwise like I told you.' Glad of Young's assurance he twisted the dials on six bombs to Hours 1, Minutes 25, and lobbed them in succession over the wire. Each fell within a foot or two of the individual container he had aimed at. Unmarked as they were, there was no way of telling what they held, if they held anything. Their gauges he could see, but not what they read. Then he remembered the padlocked gate. They held something. Butane probably.

Four bombs left. What now? Buildings large or small were

out. People could be inside, could *go* inside at the wrong time. But then he could make them come out again, couldn't he? Yes, he could help them that much.

Satisfied, he approached one of the smaller structures, a store of some kind from what he could see through the dark windows. Wooden crates. Wooden crates of what? Might or might not burn. No matter. Time running out. No magnetic attraction from alloy wall. Tear plastic strip from back and watch adhesive welling out. Stick in place and set Hours 1, Minutes 19, on dials.

A similar building, windows shuttered, no apparent lights inside.

'Hold the damn thing steady, Joe, for crissake!'

'All right, all righty. But hurry. It's heavy!'

Trelawney crept away.

Another wired enclosure with 'Danger' signs on it and a bulky, ten-foot electrical installation inside. Transformer? Circuit-breaker? He didn't know what it was, but something would happen when it went up. Hours 1, Minutes 12, lob.

He left the way he had come, pulled the triangle of fencing into place after him and ran for the pines. Nobody saw him go.

There were still two devices left. He timed them to go off five minutes before the rest, put them back in the brief-case and pushed it out of sight into a crevice in an outcrop of rock. That, he thought, would bring them running out of harm's way.

Ape-like, finger tips touching the ground, he went quickly up the steep slope through the trees. Just before he reached the crest a man's voice said, 'And just what the hell do you think you're doing?'

'Looking for a dime I dropped,' Trelawney replied and stood slowly upright.

There were three of them, two standing motionless ahead and to the right, another moving in from the left. He placed himself with a tree at his back and waited.

It was a little after 6.30 a.m. when Jane Trelawney walked into Barry's old room on the fourth floor of the Thayer Street building. He was asleep on the sofa in the secretary's office adjoining it. She shook him gently by the shoulder.

'Good morning, Charles. How are you?'

He opened his eyes, blinked sleepily and said, '"Morning, my dear. Since you ask, I'm unconvinced of the need for this incarceration and extremely bored. Apart from that I suppose I'm all right.'

'Isn't Sue Mitchell looking after you properly?'

'Oh yes. She's a nice enough child, but I want to go home.'

'So you shall in a few days. Now tell me something. In your opinion how secure is Fiona Langley?'

Barry blinked again and said, 'Who?'

'Come on now. I'm talking about the sexy sadist you employed some years ago as an eliminator.'

'You know about her?'

'Charles, that's fairly obvious from what I've said.'

'Yes, of course. Would you mind pulling that blind up? I can't see you properly.'

She did as he asked, turned and watched him lever himself upright against the end of the sofa.

'Until the time of my retirement she was as secure as anyone can be considered to be in this business,' Barry said. 'Naturally, I can't vouch for her now, but I expect she's the same.'

'What made her so?'

'The war and the fact that she must be partly mad, that is if it's possible to define madness.'

'The war?' Jane said. 'She's a bit young to have been affected by that. Was she born then?'

'Must have been about one when it ended,' Barry told her. 'Orphan. Brought up in some home or other. Had a pretty rotten childhood. I got her out of a Paris jail in – I think it was 1973. Exchanged her for a man the French wanted to execute more.'

'Why did you do that, Charles?'

'I needed someone with her talents who nobody in the Department knew about. Who not even the Minister knew about. As her interpretation of women's lib had been to hire herself out as a contract killer she had the necessary background.'

'And yet the French police caught her.'

Barry nodded. 'She was younger then and had never been trained. That was put right.'

'I see, but are you now telling me that she is secure simply because she is in your debt? You mentioned the war and madness a moment ago.'

'No, I'm not. She doesn't like me any more than I like her, which is not at all. The war robbed her of her parents. Mother killed by one of the last V2 rockets to fall on London. Father commanded his regiment and was beheaded by the Japanese during our advance through Burma. I knew him out there which was why I was able to make the connection when she was on trial in Paris. The name rang a bell.'

Barry fell silent and Jane stood patiently saying nothing, watching him twist his beard into a corkscrew shape. After a moment he began talking again.

'Never understood her motivation.' He paused, scowled and went on, 'Now they've got *me* using that word! Hate it. Almost as bad as the relationships they talk about today when they mean they're living together. Still, mustn't ramble. When she was grown she became actively and violently xenophobic. Why she did that is one of those chicken and egg questions. Was she avenging a mother she couldn't remember and a father she had never seen, or was the killer instinct there all the time? I think it was the latter and, if she goes in for rationalizations, she could have used the death of her parents as a peg to hang that instinct on. Anyway, she . . . er, I'm sorry, my dear. Lost track of what I was trying to say. It's a bit early in the morning for me.'

Jane sighed. 'She grew up to hate foreigners and, for whatever reason, you believe she saw them as a target. Do you mean all foreigners, or just the nationalities we had been fighting?'

'It began with our ex-enemies, but I weaned her away from that by pointing her at people, including our own, who had become a danger to national security. As far as I am aware she has never deviated from a task and never failed. Now, I hope

I've answered your question because I find the subject most distasteful. It makes me feel like Frankenstein. There are times when . . .'

'You didn't create her, you programmed a ready-made product and that's hardly the same thing,' Jane said and left him abruptly. She was in no mood to listen to a declaration of remorse.

Back in the passage she saw that Rafferty's door was open and felt thankful that he had come in early. The momentum she had built up was carrying her along and she wanted no checks to deprive her of it in case she faltered in her purpose.

'I want to talk to you, Raff.'

Rafferty glanced up from his desk to say, 'Then come on in,' but there was nobody there to say it to and no sound except the receding click of her heels. A frown, part puzzled, part amused, on his face he stood up and said softly, 'I think I've been summoned and that makes the second bird in thirty-six hours to order me around.' He walked slowly to her room, went in and closed the door.

'Ultimatum. It expires at eight a.m. precisely,' Jane said.

It occurred to him that he had never seen her expression so cold. Even the feather-light brush strokes of tiredness under the great eyes, instead of softening her gaze made it the more penetrating by contrast.

'Then you had better deliver it,' he told her.

'I intend to. There'll be no more pussyfooting around with the prisoners at 'The Abattoir'. I want information from them, I want it today and I want a free hand in getting it. If you don't agree, the copies of the letter I wrote leave for Downing Street in one hour and ten minutes.'

'I see.'

Her eyes flashed at him. 'I *see*? Aren't you going to say, "But this is blackmail"?'

'All right,' Rafferty said. 'But this is blackmail.'

His faint smile was not returned and he went on, 'You'll be glad to hear that I reached a similar conclusion last night. I'll go down there right away and lean on them a little. If that doesn't work we'll have to resort to narcotics.'

Looking, as he was, into the most fascinating eyes of any

woman he had ever seen had never before failed to give him pleasure, but the absence from those eyes of the gently amused compassion which he had thought always lived there made her seem like a stranger to him. It also made him feel uncomfortable.

'I said I wanted a free hand, Raff. The time for leaning on them, as you put it, is long gone. They'll have gathered their wits by now and neither of us is a trained interrogator. We don't have the skill to use Pentothal or sodium-Amytal or whatever, and we no longer have access to people who do.' She looked away from him, then back again. 'I'm sorry, but this has to be fast and vicious. It's very horrid I know, but we have no choice.'

'What do you have in mind?'

'I have Fiona Langley in mind. She was instrumental in breaking the man Hall with little more than her reputation. I'm going to let her demonstrate what she can do with him and the rest of them in person.'

'It's sick, Jane.'

'It is, isn't it?' she said, walked away from him and sat down behind her desk. 'So is an atomic explosion in a heavily populated area. So is Al's putting his life on the line to no purpose because we failed to anticipate the possibility of other danger points. So is the world and the job we do in it.'

'But there must be . . .'

'Raff!'

'Yes?'

For a moment she didn't speak, then, 'Oh, for heaven's sake don't stand there looking injured. Sit down and listen. You can't fight me over this and win, so what's the point of trying? I want to stay friends.'

He sat down without speaking.

'The trouble with you,' she said, 'is that you're too like Charles Barry and, if you think about it, that's quite a compliment. Perhaps you were born that way, perhaps you worked together for so long that some of him rubbed off on you, or it could have been the other way round. I don't know. But what I do know is that you are both incurable romantics. Do you remember how he always referred to women agents, even the opposition's, by their surnames so that he didn't have to think of them as women? How I was always called Trask before I married Al?'

'Of course I do.'

'Good. Do you also remember what they did to Paul Ellis in East Germany and Harry Carlson in Chile?'

'Do I score points for saying "yes"?'

'Do you remember, Raff?'

'I remember, Jane. What about it?'

'Just that what happened to them was so unbelievably, terrifyingly awful that what Fiona Langley did to Dyboski must have been like a good-night kiss. I'm not defending her, I'm reminding you that people, all people, will go to the most incredible lengths in the name of national security. Isn't it funny that *I* should have to remind *you* of that?'

'Hilarious.'

'Oh dear,' Jane said. 'You still aren't with me. Let me spell it out for you. You can't accept the fact that Dyboski was brutally killed by one of our women. No, that's wrong. You acknowledge the fact, but it revolts you to such an extent that you can't so much as contemplate employing her to do a vital job, even though you used her to frighten Hall on that first night.'

'That was a little different.'

She ignored the remark and went on, 'I understand that she's very good-looking. Is that right?'

'It is.'

'Well, that probably makes it worse for you. Do you want her?'

'Like I want a black-widow spider.'

'That's a relief,' she told him, 'but will you try to get it out of your head that the Department is in this straitjacket because of her? I fell into that trap to begin with when we thought all this was something to do with the Trades' Unions, but now we understand the full gravity of the situation her action, even if she doesn't know it, becomes justifiable. What does not and never will become justifiable is Julian Havelock-Templeton's idiocy in not telling you what was going on. Can you imagine you going to the Minister and saying, "I'm sorry about all this radio-activity. It seems that the man I recommended for a directorship in my place was an egomaniac"?'

Rafferty's head moved slowly back and forth in understanding and Jane felt some of the tension drain out of her.

Speaking more gently she added, 'Charles Barry told me this morning that she made him feel like Frankenstein, but he still had the guts to use her. So have you. Stop thinking about weird women. Think about weapons. She's the best we have for this particular purpose.'

'A couple of days ago,' Rafferty said, 'I felt it necessary to apologize to Al for talking emotionally. I do so now to you. A bit before that I told him that you were very wise. That was impertinent, but true. Your ultimatum is accepted.'

Relief and the stilted words tugged at her mouth, but she fought the smile down and watched him get to his feet.

'Jane?'

'Yes, Raff?'

'Would you really have pulled the plug on me at eight o'clock if I hadn't agreed?'

She replied obliquely, her desire to laugh gone.

'I'm fully aware that the continued existence of the Department is vital to the country. If you'd refused I was going to borrow some of her kinky clothes and do the job myself. I think you would have liked that even less.'

'Yes,' Rafferty said. 'I would have liked that even less.'

CHAPTER TWENTY-TWO

They had moved in close, facing him in a half circle five yards from him.

'Sounds kinda foreign to me.' The same voice, its owner a tall, thin man.

'You sound kinda foreign to me, so that makes us quits,' Trelawney said.

'Is that right? Well now, I'll tell you what we'll do. We'll take a walk back the way you came and discuss this over a cup of coffee. I like meeting new people.'

Trelawney shook his head. 'I don't. It makes me shy. Anyway, I have an appointment.'

'You sure do,' the man told him, then, 'Bring him along, Eddie.'

The dark figure to his left cracked his knuckle-joints, said, 'Sure thing,' and moved forward.

His jacket already loose on his shoulders Trelawney shrugged out of it and threw it at the man's head, hoping to envelop it, saw the head jerk aside, then backwards, a hand darting to the face. A corner of the material had flicked an eyeball Trelawney guessed and slashed at the underside of the nose with the edge of his hand. Eddie died instantly, the cartilage of the septum driven through the nasal cavity of the skull into the brain.

Trelawney whirled and leapt for the third man, the man who had not yet spoken, but in the dim light filtering through the trees from the fence now nearly two hundred yards away he didn't see the tree root and fell heavily, clumsily. He *did* see the toe of the shoe just before it struck his temple, but there was no time to do anything about it.

Consciousness stayed with him but, for a long second, awareness of what he was trying to do slipped away. The pain in his shoulder as his left arm was forced upwards behind him brought it back again. Jerking his knees under him he made from a near-impossible position the greatest single physical effort he could ever remember and reared to his feet, lifting the man straddling him.

'So okay,' a voice behind him said. 'So let's stand up if you want.' The arm lock increased in intensity and he could hear muscle fibre cracking under the strain. Head and vision still not quite clear. Who was behind him? Who in front? Did it matter?

'See what's with Eddie. I've got this bastard.'

Vision clearing now. The shorter one going to look at Eddie. It had been the thin one's voice behind.

'Jesus! Eddie's dead!'

'The hell you say!'

'He's dead for sure.'

The shorter one coming back, holding something, then the smashing concussion of a gun barrel against the side of his face and the taste of blood. Trelawney's head snapped to the left and immediately to the right again as it met the gun barrel coming back. His tongue felt the jagged edges of broken teeth and he spat out blood-stained fragments wondering why he was still conscious. Blows too high. Missed the angle of the jaw probably. Whatever the reason he was awake and painfully aware. Gun coming.

'Hold it! You'll knock his goddam head off. We have to know who he is and what he's doing.'

'Yeah, I guess we do at that.'

'Gimme the gun and use your knife. Prod him a little, like where it hurts, but don't kill him.'

One hand released his imprisoned wrist to accept the gun and Trelawney decided to faint. As he dropped his chin on to his chest and let his knees buckle, the focus of pain shifted from face to shoulder. It was excruciating, but he clenched his broken teeth and kept silent.

'Can't hold him. He's out.'

'Let him fall. I'll work on him on the ground.'

His arm released, Trelawney raised his head and launched himself forward, heard a startled curse and saw the silhouette of a raised arm. There was the merest flicker of light on steel at the end of the arm too and, in a detached way as though it had nothing to do with him, he experienced relief that the man should attempt anything as stupid as a downward stab.

He blocked the descending forearm with his own, sinking to absorb the momentum of the stroke, hearing in the same detached fashion a gasp driven from him as the impact was transmitted to his injured shoulder. Delayed shock from the blows it had received had control of his head but, years before, training had become instinct. Pressing upwards, he passed his right arm under the man's right armpit, grasped the hand holding the knife from behind and bore down with all the strength left in him.

The man screamed insanely while, his arm torn out of its socket, he somersaulted over Trelawney's back, a sound which cut off abruptly when his body struck a tree. Trelawney had the knife in his hand. Another man somewhere, wasn't there? He threw himself sideways and the gun butt struck him where the spine and pelvis meet instead of on the head. Feeling his arms fly outwards he assumed that he must be performing a swallow dive. The drop seemed very long before the water closed over him, but not at all unpleasant.

Lumpy. Something lumpy he was lying on. What? Think back. When they'd killed him he had tried to picture Jane's face, but had seen only Osaragi's normally expressionless features twisted by disappointment and Commando Sergeant Pender stiff with embarrassment. One of the best to come out of 'The Abattoir' Trelawney had been. Almost as good as Rafferty at his peak. It must have been awful for them seeing him act like a drunken tearaway in a bar brawl.

He tried to crawl off the lumpy thing, but his legs wouldn't work. Neither would his left arm. Silly! How could they work when he was dead? Then why could he move his right? Strange. Groping under his chest he examined the lump. It felt like a human head. 'You'll knock his goddam head off.' Who had said that? It wasn't *his* head. That was still where it had always been. He turned it slowly, experimentally, and saw lights, quite bright but distant, partially obscured by the trees growing down the slope.

In the softest of whispers, 'Howling Hades,' Trelawney said, then lay without movement for a quarter of a minute watching for any unusual activity at the factory site because he remembered that the man he was lying on had screamed. There was none, but he continued to lie where he was, letting segments of memory slot into position in his mind until the picture was almost complete. It was the best he could do. The whereabouts of the thin man was not on record.

Looking at his watch caused some discomfort. He had to grasp his left hand in his right and pull it in front of his face to see the luminous dial and that hurt his left shoulder. Fifty-two minutes until the warning explosion in the rock crevice. He hadn't been unconscious for long, but he must leave at once. The thin man could already have reached the gate-house.

Try legs again. Some reaction, but very feeble. Then roll.

His spine hadn't liked that, but it was good to be on level ground without the lump under his chest.

Reach out and feel for pulse in neck. Dead. Roll again to get face down, then force body into kneeling position with right arm. His spine didn't like that either, but he held the pose until the mist thinning in front of his eyes told him that his head had stopped complaining about it.

The thin man was dead too. No need to feel for a pulse. The haft of the knife was protruding from the lower abdomen, the blade embedded to the hilt where the involuntary reflex action of Trelawney's arm had driven it. A large area of the trousers was black with arterial blood. He pulled the knife out, wiped the handle clear of prints and closed the other man's fingers around it.

'Damned clever,' he said aloud. 'That'll confuse them for at least thirty seconds.' Then he crawled away on his hands and knees, searching for his jacket and a tree with a low enough hand-hold to grasp and haul himself upright. Almost upright.

Trelawney made his way back to the Buick stooping slightly, moving sometimes crab-wise, sometimes with a wobbling forward shuffle, his method of progress dictated by the demands of his legs. His back shrieked at him when he took an incautious step and sent lightning lancing across his buttocks and down his thighs. Something, he knew, had happened to the sciatic nerve and he muttered at it in child-like frustration. He fell twice and the world toppled and spun about him. When it steadied, regaining his feet was prolonged electrocution. Once he was violently sick.

The twenty-foot bluff was pleasantly simple. He slid down it, checking his rate of fall with his good arm and the descent hardly hurt him at all.

Flagstaff was only a few miles ahead and the time for detonation four minutes away when he slowed the car and made a U turn. It was not, he found, an easy thing to do with one hand. Parked at the roadside, he switched on the overhead light and looked at his face in the driving mirror. A chipmunk stared back at him. A chipmunk with its cheeks crammed with nuts if, he thought drearily, that was what chipmunks crammed their cheeks with. There was a discoloured swelling on his left temple and dried blood traced paths from both corners of his mouth over his jaw on to the collar of his shirt. He was also very dirty.

His handkerchief removed the blood and some of the grime from his face and neck, but there was nothing he could do about the swellings, the state of his clothes, his dangling arm or disobedient legs.

Very calmly he said, 'You must be the most conspicuous bastard in the State of Arizona.' He said it calmly because the fear for which there had been no time before had arrived.

No road traffic. Teeth beginning to ache. Thirty seconds to first detonation. Turn off ceiling light.

The fight in the woods had destroyed whatever chance he had had of retiring quietly from his area of operation. It had left him insufficient time to reach Flagstaff, turn in the Buick and take a flight to somewhere, because cars proceeding away from the vicinity of Sedona would inevitably be stopped as soon as the emergency forces were on the move. Two minutes, three, after the major blast? He didn't know and that was why the car was facing in the direction from which it had come. They'd pay little attention to vehicles travelling towards the disaster except, perhaps, to turn them back.

Initial detonation.

No flash, no sound, no vibration. Distance too far and land formation too effective a barrier, but the pair of bombs in the brief-case had gone off. Young had made them and what

Young made worked. Run and look, all of you! Run and look at the smoking crater in the pine wood! Look at the fallen trees! Get away from that factory! He found himself making futile urging motions with his right hand. Stopped doing it.

Lights in the driving mirror a long way back. Impossible to be them yet, unless it was a police patrol reacting to a radio alert. Start engine and drive off. Forty mph. Lights growing in intensity, but slowly. Two minutes. Close behind now, then an unmarked car overtaking sedately. Wait until well ahead. Pull into side and stop.

Trelawney began worrying about his appearance and physical condition again. But for them there would be nothing concrete to connect him with anything. But now! Would Mr Armitage kindly consider himself under arrest and listen while the officer read him his rights? Did foreigners have any rights to be read to them? Could Her Britannic Majesty's Ambassador to Washington find it convenient to call on the Secretary of State? The Secretary was curious about the actions of a British agent in Arizona. No doubt there was a simple explanation for them but, so far, it had escaped the Secretary. Oh, Jesus!

Quite suddenly his mood of gloom was swamped by a wave of self-contempt. The possibility he feared had been foreseen and accepted before he left London. The stakes were far too high for it to have been otherwise.

'Don't snivel,' he said and a bright flash lit up the sky to the south. It vanished at once to be replaced by a glow like a clear moon yet to rise above the ridge of mountains. When it reached him the sound resembled a very brief ripple of distant thunder and he knew that his attempts to achieve a simultaneous explosion of Young's ten devices had been reasonably accurate.

They appeared in his driving mirror very quickly. Two sets of headlights, a gap and then an indistinguishable number behind. He started driving again because that was what he would be expected to be doing, then steered off the road and parked when it would be obvious to him what the overtaking vehicles were.

The two police cars ripped past him in a blur of coloured lights, their sirens wailing as if in despair of keeping pace with them. Four fire appliances followed at almost the same frantic speed, then another police car and, finally, two ambulances. At the sight of those Trelawney winced, then reminded himself that their presence was standard operating procedure.

He followed slowly in the wake of the hurtling convoy for two miles, then pulled off the road yet again to let two heavy-duty rescue trucks go by. Even those big vehicles must, he thought, be doing close to 80 mph.

There were seven police cars parked at or near the access driveway to the factory, their sirens silent but their lights still flashing and radios producing staccato bursts of speech.

A big cop standing in the middle of the road made violent sweeping gestures with an arm as though trying to move the Buick by sheer physical force. His face was angry and Trelawney, with an empty road behind him, felt as though he was holding up a presidential motorcade. When he accelerated past the man he caught the words, 'Get your ass out of here, bud!' The glow of the fire was clear in the mirror as he drove on to Sedona.

In the centre of the town he turned into a parking lot fronting a motel. Ronde, La Ronde, Rondee, something like that. The neon letters kept merging and separating, merging and separating. There had been a lot of people in the pre-dawn streets staring at the fire on the mountain, some grave, some laughing and cheering official transport on its way, but there were no people here. He found a vacant slot at the far end of the area and drove into it, one side of the car against a wall.

Getting out was difficult. His feet didn't want to move and when he forced them to do so steel claws closed on the base of his spine. He got his left leg on to the ground by grasping his trousers above the knee with his good hand and placing it there. Then he turned his body cautiously and repeated the process with the other leg. Getting into the back and closing the door after him was harder still but, inch by inch, he managed it.

Face downwards on the floor between the front and back seats, it had to be face down so that he wouldn't snore, knees drawn forward under him, Trelawney wondered if it was possible to achieve a more uncomfortable position. Deciding that it was not, he had begun to hope that he was out of sight to a casual passer-by when he fell asleep.

Cramp woke him, cramp at the back of his thighs. He fought it by trying to anticipate and counteract the twisting drag of the muscles there. It didn't work very well and he felt the beginnings of panic because his shoulders were jammed between the front and back seats. Wrenching them free caused a momentary black-out, then he found himself sprawled on the upholstery sweating and panting shallowly. It was broad daylight and, his watch told him, eight minutes past ten. By the time he had crawled over into the driving seat it told him that it was quarter past. There were people about now and he hadn't dared get out of the car.

God, his clothes were in a mess. Blood on his shirt. His own. Blood on one trouser leg. The thin man's. Jacket split across the back. He could feel the slackness of it. That had happened sliding down the bluff he supposed. Dirt everywhere. It didn't matter. His head was clear now and he knew what he was going to try to do next. Deliberately he tore his right jacket pocket, leaving it to hang down from the stitching at the bottom. Rondes the name was. He drove out of the parking lot.

There was no need to search. The kind of bar he had hoped to find was almost directly across the main street from the motel. Stopping in front of it, he sat for a moment watching the column of smoke rising from the mountainside. It wasn't very impressive. They had obviously got the blaze of the night before well under control. Then moving with extreme care he levered himself out of the car on to the sidewalk thankful that beyond a curious glance or two nobody paid any attention to him as he limped unsteadily across it and into the saloon.

It was dark inside after the brilliant sunshine, except at the far end where a spotlight shone on the towering figure of a stuffed polar bear rearing on its hind-legs, but that only seemed to intensify the dimness of the rest of the big room. From behind the bar the only occupant stared at him.

'What in hell happened to you, mister?'

'Everything,' Trelawney said. 'I'd like to use your phone.' No need to worry about his accent. With his mouth so sore and his jaw so stiff there'd be trouble making himself understood in anybody's version of English. Just don't use British expressions.

'Why pick on my place? Looks like you should be in the hospital or telling the cops who done it.'

'Because I need a pay-phone. They don't have extensions for people to listen on. This is government business. Here.'

Trelawney put his hand to his right pocket, blinked, looked down at it and said, 'Oh shit! First my gun, now my badge.' The man behind the bar watched him warily while he went on, 'Listen, do something for me, will you? I'm a little shook up and this arm's bust or something. Get me the FBI Phoenix office. Please. It's very urgent.'

The magic initials worked their charm and the other's suspicions fell from him. He came out from behind the bar and hurried to the wall telephone.

'You got the number?'

'No. I'm from Albuquerque. It'll be in the book.'

'Sure, sure.'

Trelawney watched him flick over the pages, heard him muttering numbers to himself as he dialled.

'It is? Great. Get me the guy in charge, will you, honey? I've got one of your agents here and he's in pretty poor shape ...Yeah...Thanks.' A short pause then, 'Yeah? Okay, here's your boy.'

Trelawney took the proffered telephone and the man walked quickly away to the far end of the long bar.

Speaking quietly into the mouthpiece Trelawney said, 'I'll tell you this once only, so get it right. The Sedona dump was bombed because it's manufacturing illicit nuclear weapons for use against Israel. We'd like that stopped. You now have every reason for moving in your investigation teams and digging real deep. This message is no more a joke than last night's explosions. Act on it, you hear me? Act on it *now*.'

A male voice at the other end began to say something as he put down the receiver.

There was nothing kinky about Fiona Langley's clothes when she walked into the long sound-proofed shooting range at 'The Abattoir'. She looked as demure as it was possible for her to do in a simple, cream-coloured silk dress. Of the five men standing roped to empty gun racks at the far end only Hall reacted visibly to her arrival. He shuddered convulsively.

Sergeant Pender would have checked the number plate of her car from a distance she knew, but none of the staff would know who had driven it and nobody would come near the range until she drove away again. Those had been the orders from Thayer Street.

The big oblong block of fishmonger's ice she had asked for was lying in a plastic tray on the floor near the group of men and two single-bar electric fires with long leads stood against either wall. She moved slowly down the room and stopped in front of Hall.

'Hello, Mr Hall. It's been a long time, hasn't it? Can you wait another half hour or so? I shan't be needing you before then.'

Four of them were handcuffed, arms behind their backs, short lengths of rope securing them to the gun racks. The fifth had his elbows strapped together because of the bandage on his wrist where Reid had shot him. So that was Frankel, the one they had suggested she concentrate on first.

'Which one's the German?'

'*Ich bin* . . . I am a German,' Frankel said.

'How nice.'

She released him from the gun rack and pushed him towards the plastic tray with the ice in it.

'Up! Up, up, up! You don't want me to hurt your poor wrist, do you?'

He stepped up on to the ice cautiously, seeking a secure foothold. Standing behind him Fiona Langley took a coil of piano wire from her shoulder-bag. One end of the wire was formed into a noose. She held that in her left hand and threw the coil over a transverse steel beam above her head with her right. She heard a sharp intake of breath and thought that that would be Hall.

The noose around Frankel's neck was tight, but there were two inches of slack in the rest of the wire after she had tied the other end to a radiator set against the wall. He stood, white faced but steady, watching her fetch the electric fires, switch them on and place them three feet from the ice.

'It takes about twenty minutes,' she said. 'I've timed it. If you're lucky the ice may melt unevenly and you'll slip off sooner than that. Of course, if you'd like to end it quickly you know what to do.'

'I have nothing I can tell to you. Many times I have said this to your friends, *Fräulein*.'

'Oh, I know that. They're quite satisfied that you know nothing. I meant you could just step off the ice.'

'Why do you do this to me?' He still stood steadily, but there was a tremor in his voice.

'What a silly question,' Fiona Langley said. 'To hang you of course. When you are dead and the clock over there will tell you when that's likely to be, it will be poor Mr Hall's turn. He doesn't know anything worthwhile either, but by then the others will be glad to tell me what I want to know.'

'What is it you are wanting to know?'

'The answers to some questions I shall be asking the last three about nuclear bombs. Now, if you'll excuse me, I shall leave you. This form of execution is really very distressing to watch and I have to fetch Mr Hall's block of ice.'

She walked to the heavily padded door at the side of the range which protected Osaragi's office from the sound of firing.

'Tell her, you stupid Kraut bastard! She's the one that killed Whiteoaks and she'll do us both too! For pity's sake *tell* her!' Hall was on the brink of hysteria.

'*Fräulein, bitte* . . .' The rest of the sentence was cut off by the closing of the door, but she could still hear sounds through the peep-hole drilled through the wall. Words came clearly again when she pressed down the switch of the speaker on Osaragi's desk and she listened to Hall's frantic description of herself, her eyes fixed absently on the slowly revolving spools of a tape-recorder. He seemed unable to stop, pausing only to take in gulping breaths. When he began repeating himself an unknown voice shouted at him to shut up.

Pleas to Frankel to tell what he knew followed, some in unidentified voices, most in Hall's.

'Tell her about that Geoffrey somebody you drove for! The one at the German college!'

'Tell her what Mahmoud told you he had heard!'

They were shouting now.

'How am I to tell her when she is not here?' Then a spate of German too fast for her to catch anything but the fear in the words.

'Then tell me, you filthy sod! She's going to hang me next! Don't you understand? Tell me so I can tell her!'

'*Ja*, is good for you but I am already to hang! Why I tell you, bloody Hall?'

Ten minutes.

Fiona Langley crossed to the peep-hole and looked through it. The wire was stretching vertically upwards from Frankel's neck now, the slack gone from it. She went back to the desk, sat down and lit a cigarette.

It was hard to distinguish words with all of them shouting at once, Frankel in German. No matter. If he was saying anything important they'd isolate it from the tape.

A rapid diminution of sound, then, 'Hall's fucking fainted!'

'He'll dislocate his arms.'

'So what? He'll be dead in half an hour if this goes to schedule.'

'It's all right. Here he comes now. Woken himself up.'

'"All right's" a bloody funny expression to . . .'

'Shut up! All of you!' A voice of authority. Probably, she thought, the little wizened man who had stood up to Rafferty. 'Frankel ain't got much longer to go. We've got to get that woman back. You're shit scared of her, Hall. Know what her name is?'

'Fiona.' A dead, hopeless voice. 'The man with a handle to his name called her Fiona.'

'Right then. Shout it all together and keep on shouting it.'

It came blaring out of the speaker, 'Fiona! Fiona! Fiona!'

She turned the volume down, stubbed out her cigarette and went to the peep-hole. Frankel was on his toes, legs quivering, the wire biting into his neck.

Sixteen minutes.

The shouting wavered, died. She waited for one more minute before going back into the shooting range.

'Quick! Let him down! He'll talk.' The wizened man.

A hand flew to her mouth. 'Oh my God! Isn't it over? I can't stand to see . . .' Turning, she took a step back towards the office.

'He knows. He knows a lot.' The dead, hopeless voice again.

She looked at him and smiled.

'You'd better be awfully right, Mr Hall. I would hate to be you if you're wrong.'

It was nearly midnight when Fiona Langley reached the Kensington flat the Department had made available to her while her own was out of bounds. She walked into the living-room, glanced round and saw Jane Trelawney standing in the bedroom doorway with a gun in her hand.

'I suppose you *are* you,' Jane said.

'Yes. I'm Fiona Langley.'

'Incredible. I *was* warned, but you're startlingly good-looking.'

'Coming from you, Mrs Trelawney, that's quite something.'

Neither woman smiled.

'Would you like a drink?'

'I'd love some coffee,' Jane said and dropped the gun into her bag.

The other woman nodded. 'I'll get it.'

Jane watched her through the doorway to the kitchen. Same figure. Same walk. Even an echo of the same face when she squinted at it through almost closed eyes, but only the faintest of echoes. Remarkable.

'Did you have to . . . Are they . . . ?'

'No, I didn't have to and they're perfectly all right. Except for Frankel. His throat's going to be very sore for a few days, but he'll get over it. They behaved like lambs. The results are on the tapes in that bag. Do you want to listen to them or shall I give you a résumé?'

'A résumé, please.'

'Very well. I can't do any interpretation for you because I don't have enough of the background, but I can tell you what they said.'

'That'll be fine.'

They sat down facing each other, cups of coffee in their hands.

'Frankel,' Fiona Langley said. The name came out sharply as though she were a staff officer beginning a briefing with the word 'Objective'. 'Part-time driver for a Professor Jefferies who taught occasionally at Gottingen University, West Germany. Frankel doesn't know what he taught. Jefferies carries an American passport, but sounds English. The car, and this is significant, was a large Mercedes limousine with a glass partition between driver and passengers. It is significant because in September last year Frankel was approached by members of a terrorist organization. Whether they were the remnants of the old Baader-Meinhof lot, the Red Brigade or whoever, he doesn't know. They enlisted him and . . .'

Fiona Langley seemed suddenly to remember her coffee. She sipped it, then drank it down and put the empty cup on the table beside her.

'They enlisted him and wired the car so that he could listen to conversations in the back. He was required to report on everything he heard, every place Jefferies went and everyone he met.'

'What was the inducement?'

'The usual thing. His continued existence in return for his co-operation and silence.'

'So he feels safe from them in this country.'

'No, he does not.'

'Yet you persuaded him to break that silence.'

'Mrs Trelawney, he "*died*" this afternoon, right up to the point of unconsciousness, and has no desire to repeat the experience through to its conclusion. Do you want the details?'

'No thank you,' Jane said. 'You've made your point.'

As though she had not been interrupted Fiona Langley went on, 'The three most regular passengers in the car with Jefferies were a Japanese named Shigeru Hatoyama, a Mrs McDowell, Christian name unknown, probably American or Irish – Frankel has difficulty in distinguishing between the accents – and a German referred to only as Gesner. He seems to have been on the closest terms of the three with Jefferies and was in general charge of some major project. Frankel couldn't remember the English expression and used the word "*gleichschaltung*". Doesn't that mean co-ordination?'

'Yes.'

'Well, that was Gesner's responsibility and I think it *is* connected with the unauthorized manufacture of nuclear weapons you mentioned to me.'

'Why, Miss Langley?'

'The conversations with Mrs McDowell were mainly about finance. Those with Gesner partly technical, partly – um – I think logistical is the word I want. With Hatoyama they were all technical. Now, Frankel has neither a technical background nor vocabulary. The same applies to me, but words like "uranium" and "critical mass" kept cropping up. Others too which I don't remember at the moment, but you'll get them off one of the tapes. Would you like some more coffee?'

'Yes please.'

Still talking Fiona Langley poured it for her.

'Critical mass seemed to be used more in the sense of a production target to be achieved than a point at which nuclear fission takes place. I inferred from this that . . . No, that's your job.'

'That a single bomb was under discussion? Is that what you were going to say?'

'In Germany yes, but it's a flimsy inference based on talk of the difficulty of obtaining some kind of ore both in Germany and at what was called the American plant. I pressed Frankel very hard about the American plant's location, but he has no idea where it is.'

'And the German plant?' Jane asked.

'Possibly in an industrial complex north-east of Kassel. That's only a few miles from Gottingen and it's where Frankel most frequently took Jefferies and the others. He always dropped them at the same place where they were met by another car. The driver of the other car stayed in the Mercedes with Frankel until they returned so he was never able to follow, but he thinks the terrorist people did. However, after these visits Jefferies and his guests usually had grey powder on their shoes. There's a cement works in the complex. He forgets the name.'

'Just a minute,' Jane said. 'Has your scrambler been installed yet?'

'By the bed.'

Fiona Langley lay back in her chair, hands behind her head, stretching luxuriously. It had, she thought, been a satisfying day, but she was tired now and, as there was no chance at all of persuading the Trelawney woman to spend the night with her, she wished she'd go away.

She listened to the voice in the bedroom saying, 'Please call Diestel in Cologne, Mr Prideaux. There's a cement processing plant in an industrial estate north-east of Kassel and some miles from Gottingen. There may be several estates and several plants in the area. I don't know, but I want him to check company records as soon as offices open in the morning and let me know at once if there's one with a Professor Frederick Jefferies on the Board, or listed as a shareholder or anything else.' 'Yes.' 'Yes, that's right. Oh, on second thoughts, ask him to check any cement works first and if he draws a blank to check every other company in the district. If they have something similar to the "Directory of Directors" over there he may save himself some trouble. Classification Red.' 'Thank you. Good night.'

'So you knew about him,' Fiona Langley said. 'I didn't know his Christian name was Frederick.'

'Yes, we knew about him, but not in connection with Kassel. Please go on with what you were telling me.'

Twenty minutes later Jane Trelawney got up to leave.

'Thank you very much. You're very efficient.'

'Yes I am, aren't I?' Fiona Langley said.

Near the bottom of the last flight of darkened stairs Jane snatched her skirt above her knees and jumped, her gun coming up to cover the dimly-seen figure crouching by the front door.

'Stirling, Miss.' Stirling always called her 'Miss'.

'You gave me quite a start. I came with Reid. You're different shapes.'

'Sorry. He's waiting in the car. I'll just see if it's still all clear.'

'Look, I don't need *two* of you playing nursemaid!'

'Reid gets a bit panicky alone in the dark, Miss, and in view of your husband being a large awkward customer I thought I better make sure nothing goes wrong while he's away.'

He went out, returned almost at once and said, 'Okay. Reid'll see you safe home. I'm going to stick around for a bit to make sure *she* wasn't followed.'

Jane saw the upward jerk of his head, touched him lightly on the arm and left the building.

The car was passing Marble Arch when she took a piece of paper from her bag and held it close to the dashboard lights.

'I've got four addresses here. I want them pin-pointed precisely in case we have to hit any of them at short notice. We'll need to know approach routes, availability of waiting cover, traffic . . .'

'Yeah, yeah,' Reid said. 'Where are they?'

She read them to him.

'First one's in Islington where we picked up that bunch of comedians. That was the house they came out of. The others sound like they're down towards the dock area. I'll tour around a bit after I've dropped you off. Let you know in the morning. The boys can check out the traffic patterns in daylight when there's some traffic to check.'

'That'll be fine,' Jane told him, 'but please be careful. All these places are owned or rented by the same organization.'

'And we don't want to tip 'em off that we're interested.'

'Right.'

Reid turned south off Oxford Street, circled four blocks and pulled into the side of the road.

'Keys, please.'

'What keys?'

'The ones to your pad. I want to look it over.'

'Now really I . . .'

'Just give me the keys, Mrs Trelawney. It's no trouble. I have to do this for Stirling nearly every night. He'd never go to bed otherwise.'

She surrendered them meekly, touched by the two men's concern for her. At Rafferty's request she had agreed to use a Department chauffeur-driven car, but nobody had instructed these Grade III operatives to act as her bodyguards.

CHAPTER TWENTY-THREE

It was past noon and an hour since the man in the bar had helped him across the sidewalk back to the Buick. Trelawney was very grateful to that man and ashamed of himself for his own gross deceit. The second sentiment he recognized as a warning that he had not yet fully recovered his balance because deceits, gross and petty, were his stock-in-trade.

But the man had been kind. The brandy for which he would accept no payment. The use of a private bathroom. The assistance in stripping him of his clothes and dressing him in fresh ones from the bag fetched from the car. Kind.

Trelawney put down the charred piece of wood he had been using as a poker and shuffled on his bottom through three hundred and sixty degrees. It was easier than trying to stand up. Nobody.

Sedona was still close, its big, strangely shaped outcrops of rock very red in the sunshine. Giant's Thumb, Tea Pot and Merry-Go-Round had been three of the names on the pamphlets he had pocketed at the bar to start his fire with. Another, obviously Bell Rock from its configuration, was not far away.

He looked at the tables and benches of the deserted picnic site wondering what he was going to try to do next, hoping nobody had noticed the smoke from his burning clothes. The brushwood and coarse grass around him were highly inflammable, but it had been essential to burn the clothes. Particularly the trousers stained with blood which was not his own. Return to Sedona, abandon the Buick, buy provisions, go to ground in one of the clefts in these blasted red rocks until they took the checkpoints off the roads? His legs and back told him they didn't want to do that. Then what? An area of great scenic beauty. Stuff you, Purvis!

The police car stole along the dirt track behind him. It was within fifty yards before he heard it and that, he thought, was a fair reflection of his physical state.

'What in hell do you think you're doing, mister?'

He turned his head slowly towards the two officers, one young, the other with grey hair.

'I'm helping to keep Arizona beautiful. It's wicked the amount of junk tourists leave around these places.'

'Very funny,' the older man said. 'I suppose you – Hey! Take a look at his face!'

They flung themselves from the patrol car simultaneously, guns out, the younger sprawling across the bonnet holding his two-handed, doing the talking.

'Get those arms up above your head!'

Trelawney raised his right arm slowly.

'I'm afraid the other one isn't working too well. I can't move it.'

'Get it up!'

'Take it easy, Joe. I'll handle this.' The grey-haired patrolman had spoken quietly, but his voice carried authority and Trelawney was glad of his presence.

'Stand up, mister, and turn around.'

'I can't do that either. Not without something to pull myself up on. My back's hurt too.'

'You been in a fight?'

'Yes.'

'Now that's real interesting. Know anything about three dead men up in the woods above Sedona?'

'No, should I?'

'Well, I guess you shouldn't, but I asked you if you did.'

'No.'

'So where was *your* fight?'

'I got mugged in Flagstaff,' Trelawney said and received a non-committal nod in reply.

'Lie down flat on your back.'

One continued to point a gun at him while the other searched him for weapons and went through his pockets.

'He's clean. British passport in the name of Armitage. Admitted New York yesterday. Sure gets around.'

'Okay. Read him his rights.'

Trelawney almost laughed during the recitation, remembering his thoughts during the past night, but it was the wrong kind of laughter and he held it in.

They handcuffed his wrists in front of him because he lost consciousness for a moment when they tried to force his left arm behind his back, and helped him to the patrol car.

'Let's go,' the older man said.

The laughter burst out of him then, three sharp barks of it, quickly suppressed.

'Sounds like a great joke. You wanna share it?'

'I'm sorry. It's just that you never get more than a few minutes into a police movie on television, British or American, without someone saying that.'

'Saying what?'

'Let's go,' Trelawney said and guffawed again.

The policemen looked at each other and raised their eyebrows.

'All right, Armitage. We'll run through it one more time. You flew into Kennedy yesterday you say.'

There were four of them, all in shirt-sleeves, one sitting across the table from him, three alternately leaning against walls and prowling about. It was like television again, but he no longer had any desire to laugh.

'You said "one more time" five times ago.'

'Answer my question.'

'You didn't ask me one. You made a statement.'

'Did you fly into Kennedy yesterday?'

They had been over his story eight times now and taken two and a half hours to do it, picking points at random. It had been after the third that the man had started saying 'one more time'.

'No.'

'What do you mean "no"?'

'Oh my God,' Trelawney said. 'You don't need a suspect, you need a lexicographer. If you can't understand simple words like "no", a dictionary isn't going to help you. You'll have to have it explained.'

'Are you saying you didn't arrive in New York from London yesterday?'

'That's right. I knew you could figure it out if you tried.

"No" is the opposite of "Yes". The Immigration stamp in my passport and that Air India ticket are both forgeries.'

The plain-clothes officer was watching him with no particular expression on his face. No anger, no amusement. Possibly a trace of curiosity.

'Am I boring you, Armitage?'

'Yes, ever since the second time around.'

'That's too bad. I'm not bored. You bored, Dougal?'

'No way, Lieutenant.'

'You see? I'm not bored. Dougal's not bored. The other two guys ain't got the brains to be bored. How come you're bored?'

Trelawney said, 'I want to see a doctor.'

'Yeah, so you said before. Funny thing, most guys we pull in here start yelling for a lawyer. Don't you want to see a lawyer?'

'Not really, unless you know one with a medical degree.'

'I don't think I do. Why did you say you didn't get into New York yesterday?'

'Because saying I did get in yesterday seems to fascinate you and Dougal so much you make me say it over and over again. I thought if I told you I didn't you'd get bored too and go away.'

'Sure. Tell me some more about these three guys who jumped you in Oak Creek Canyon.'

The pains were beginning to worry Trelawney seriously now and he wondered who the fool had been who had claimed that the human body was incapable of registering more than one at a time. His shoulder pulsed drum beats of intense discomfort at his brain. The molars, or what was left of them, in his right upper jaw sparked viciously into his nervous system like a faulty carbon arc. When he shifted his position on the hard upright chair the shock from his back obliterated the other two sensations. Perhaps, he conceded grudgingly to himself, that was what the fool had been talking about.

'Apart from a lexicographer you also need a recording system,' he said.

'Why so?'

'Because you're the first person I've met who is neither

literate nor numerate, but, if you got yourself a tape-recorder you could keep on playing it back in the hope you'd get everything memorized. It was two men, not three, and now you've got me forgetting how many times I've told you that. As to Oak Creek Canyon, well, if that's the name of the street in Flagstaff where they jumped me it means one of two things. Either your people have arrested one or both of them, or they've found the witnesses. I don't know the name of the damned street.'

A fifth man came into the room while Trelawney was talking and propped himself on a corner of the table.

'What have we got?'

'A hostile smart-ass,' the lieutenant said. 'What's a lexicographer, Captain?'

'A word merchant. Writes dictionaries and such.'

'Is that right? Well, here's what he's been selling me. Arrived Kennedy yesterday from London, England. Took a flight to Phoenix where he picked up that Buick and a case containing photographic equipment loaned to him by a guy called Robert Purvis, First Secretary at the British Embassy, Washington DC. All that's been checked and is correct assuming the Embassy man is telling the truth. Here's a list of the contents of the case he gave Dougal over the phone. Usual camera buff's junk.'

Trelawney sighed softly. At least Thayer Street knew where he was. He wondered if they'd heard about the factory yet.

'What was Armitage going to do with it?'

'When he was all through giving me a load of crap about photographing the missile silos near Tucson he settled for the Grand Canyon. That at least is the direction he was headed.'

'Something the matter with his own camera?'

'He says it's old and cheap and was kind enough to inform me that the Grand Canyon is a subject to be treated with respect.'

'Okay. What then?'

'He ate at a restaurant called the "Jumping Cholla" in Cave Creek. That is correct. We checked with the waitress. Then he says he drove straight through to Flagstaff, stopped to ease his legs and got mugged by a coupla guys with pick-handles. They took off when some other people arrived, taking the camera case with them and leaving him lying on the sidewalk. Seems these other people didn't want to know and Armitage reads me a lecture about "The Good Samaritan". Anyway, he sets off back towards Phoenix and...'

'Wait a minute. Didn't it occur to him to report this to the police?'

'It occurred to him, Captain, or so he says, but he thinks what the hell can they do when he can't give any sort of useful description? He might even have a point there.'

'Why the night driving?'

'Slept a lot on the plane, light traffic, short vacation. It figures.'

It was an interesting experience, Trelawney thought, hearing himself discussed as though he wasn't there. Interesting too that he was being discussed by a police lieutenant and captain. He doubted that Sedona was large enough to rate a captain or, even if it was, that a lieutenant would address him by his rank. So they were probably strangers and that meant that the authorities were moving into the town from outside. He hoped that many more of them would do the same thing and that they'd do it very soon because every passing minute pushed the possibility that he had failed closer to probability. Volchak. The 'Melody' file. All nonsense? Mustn't think that way. Keep the aggression going and pray that they don't come across the one factor which would destroy his story completely and him with it.

'What was he burning when the highway patrol picked him up?'

'Clothes he tells me. Threw up all over himself and dirtied his pants after he was beaten up. There are traces of urine on the car seat, so could be.'

'Well, a big boy like him!'

The lieutenant gave a small shrug and said, 'Okay, you men. Take him along to the doctor.'

They led Trelawney out, supporting him on each side, with the man called Dougal following behind.

When the door closed behind the group the captain eased himself stiffly off the corner of the table, walked to the chair Trelawney had occupied and sat on it.

'What do you think?'

The lieutenant placed his hands palms down on the table in front of him and stared at them for several seconds before saying, 'He reacted the way an innocent man would react. A little scared at the start the way your average Joe is when he's brought in whether he's done anything or not. Seemed to think he'd been booked for creating a fire hazard and was very apologetic about it. When I straightened him out on that he gave a reasonable account of his movements, not perfect like he'd rehearsed it, just reasonable.'

He took a cigar from his breast pocket, rolled it absently between finger and thumb, then put it back.

'Looked real worried at that time, real worried. So I started in on him and after a while he started in on me, beginning to get a little mad at me, giving with that horse shit I told you about. The missile site bit, hunting spooks at Jerome because it's a ghost mining town and he never saw a ghost miner, that kinda thing. The longer I went on the worse it got. Resentment, sarcasm, and he never once asked for a lawyer. Just one angry citizen with nothing bad on his conscience. Well he ain't a citizen, but you know what I mean. Captain, he acted exactly the way I guess you would if you were pulled in on some charge you didn't know a darned thing about just because you got beat up by some punks.'

'You think he's in the clear?'

The lieutenant produced his cigar again and lit it before saying, 'No, I don't. I think he's about as guilty as you can get.'

CHAPTER TWENTY-FOUR

'I'm not really looking sombre, Raff,' Jane said. 'I mean I'm not feeling it. Listening to those tapes was rather a shock and I didn't think I was shockable any longer, that's all. You'll see what I mean when you have time to run them through. It's just that we both know that you can break people down slowly and get the right answers. We also both know that you can break them down very quickly with extreme pain and get nothing but mental confusion, but . . .'

Rafferty watched her silently, saw her shake her head in wonderment, then heard her say softly, 'That woman knew exactly what she was going to do almost before I had finished telling her what I wanted. What sort of a mind has she got, for heaven's sake?'

'It was you who wanted it done – er, I seem to remember that "fast and vicious" was the expression you used. You also saw fit to remind me about Carlson and Ellis.'

'Oh, I'm not complaining. I got it done faster than I believed possible and nobody got hurt much. Not physically anyway.' She shrugged her shoulders dismissively and gave him a lopsided smile before adding, 'Well, never mind about all that. I'm wasting time. Here are Reid's maps of three of the locations she got out of that little man called Boyd. The Islington address isn't there because I can't see them using that again. Reid doesn't know whether they are occupied or not, but I've set up long-range surveillance.'

'Now I wonder,' Rafferty said, ' why somebody like Boyd who runs off at the mouth would be given information like that. He was the one who told me how they traced Langley and . . .'

'He wasn't given it, Raff. He was trying to find out what was going on and followed Beshir Mahmoud from the Islington address on a number of occasions. These were the places Mahmoud visited.'

'Can we believe that?'

175

Jane Trelawney glanced down at her desk, then slowly raised her eyes to meet his again.

'I think we can believe every word they spoke.' She shuddered and added, 'So will you when you've listened to them. Now tell me how you and Fenner got on with your police impersonations.'

'I thought you'd never ask,' Rafferty said. 'We eventually found all four names. Gesner, Heinrich S. Gesner, has been the most frequent visitor which fits in with Langley's description of his job. He's stayed at the Savoy, the Connaught and the Berkeley during this year alone. A certain Dorothy McDowell favours the Hilton and Shigeru Hatoyama the Ritz. We can't find any record of Jefferies for this year, but he was here twice last autumn. His pub's the Dorchester. Here's the list. Names, addresses, dates. Always Gesner and at least one other of them at the same time.' He handed a sheet of paper to her. 'Gesner, McDowell and Hatoyama were here this week.'

She took the paper from him, but didn't look at it.

'Did you have any trouble with the hotel managers?'

Rafferty shook his head. 'Why should we? Senior police credentials will get you most places. Nobody questions their authenticity. I said we were trying to trace some people thought to be travelling on forged passports. They're quite used to the routine. But you know that.'

Vaguely Jane said, 'Yes, I know that,' then asked, 'Did you have to name names?'

'Certainly not. Why?'

'I heard from Diestel in Cologne this morning. Jefferies *is* on the Board of the Kassel cement works. It occurs to me that we might send Stirling and Reid.'

'To sign him off?'

'Yes, if he's there which he probably isn't,' she said. 'I was thinking more of Gesner. He appears to be the organizer.'

Before Rafferty could reply the speaker on Jane's desk buzzed softly and she flicked down the tab below the indicator light.

'Yes?'

'Prideaux, Mrs Trelawney. Is the Director with you?'

'Yes, he is.'

'Oh, good. I've got a "most immediate" here from Purvis in Washington. It's in the Director's code. Shall I bring it along?'

'I'll come and get it,' Rafferty said, glanced sharply at Jane and walked out.

Trelawney lay flat on his back staring at the mountain through the window of the recovery room. Most of the pains had gone from him but that, he thought, could be the effect of the anaesthetic remaining in his system. He hadn't liked it when the doctor had filled the hypodermic syringe because they might have been going to question him under narcotics. The memory made him frown at its irrationality. Local police forces didn't use those techniques and he doubted if he was yet in the hands of people who did.

Experimentally he tried raising his left arm. It lifted from the bed without effort and with no more reaction from his shoulder than a mild burning sensation. He blinked and flexed his knees. They worked too. Slowly he pushed himself into a sitting position, eased his legs over the side of the bed, breathed in deeply and stood upright. No outraged scream from his back, no lightning searing from it down into his thighs. Only when he was flat on the bed again did he release his breath.

So he was more or less whole once more and that was good, but it was not something he would admit to the doctor. They'd want to use a lie-detector on him next and it would be useless to them as long as he claimed a source of stabbing pain, pain which would drive the stylus right off the paper. His back would be best he decided and turned his attention to the view from the window.

There was no column of smoke rising from the mountain now and he watched idly as the plane with US Air Force insignia on its wings swung into his field of vision in a banking turn. It levelled off and flew in a straight line with black dots, blossoming into white like anti-aircraft fire, trailing behind it.

Trelawney blinked again, then gave a long shuddering

sigh. He had won, the Department had won, and whatever happened to him now wasn't really very important.

The door opened and the big, fair-haired young doctor Trelawney, who knew little or nothing about American football, had classified as an All-American something or other, came into the room.

'How're you feeling?'

Dragging his gaze from the window Trelawney looked at him and reached the totally inconsequential conclusion that the English pack could certainly use him in the coming season's Rugby internationals.

He put the farcical notion down to his own intense relief, pushed it out of his mind and said, 'Come over here and look at this, doc.'

The first man of the string of paratroopers was nearing the ground very close to where he thought the factory site lay, the rest angling skilfully in to join him.

'Well I'll be darned!'

'Bloody dangerous place for a practice drop.'

'You're not kidding. Hey, wait a minute. They're dropping right in on where they had those explosions last night. Could be this is no practice.'

'Fire fighters?'

'Uh-uh. But I don't see why. The fires are out.'

'I drove past there last night,' Trelawney said, 'after I'd been duffed up in Flagstaff. Police cars, ambulances, fire appliances, the lot. What happened?'

The doctor turned away from the window and looked at him. 'Duffed up?'

'Worked over. Mugged.'

'Oh. Oh sure. No, I don't know what happened. Aren't you a suspect or . . . Forget it. Let's take a look at you.'

Fingers, almost as big as bananas, as gentle as a girl's, closed on Trelawney's shoulder, probing.

'Hurt?'

'No.'

'Try raising your arm. Good. Slowly now. That's great. Any pain?'

'None at all.'

'Good. Thing is we have a ball and socket arrangement at the shoulder and . . .'

'Ball and socket had parted company.'

'Nearly,' the doctor said. 'Half in, half out. Painful I guess. You're heavily muscled which prevented a clean dislocation. Now let's see if you can sit up.'

Trelawney resisted the steady pressure of the big hand in the small of his back, grunting and hissing through his teeth. Slowly he permitted himself to be levered into a sitting position, said, 'Jesus!' and wiped his forehead with the back of his wrist.

The doctor was standing looking down at him, a puzzled expression on his face, when Dougal came into the room.

'Ah, that's dandy. He's surfaced. The Lieutenant wants him downstairs, doc.'

Almost to himself the doctor said, 'I don't get it. The disc wasn't even extruded. That means squashed out sideways like toothpaste. Just displaced a little. We manipulated it back. Should be okay.'

'Doc, the Lieutenant . . .'

'Shut up, Dougal. I'm trying to think. Better still, go tell the Lieutenant he can have my patient when I say he can and not before. Now get out of here before I knock your roof in.'

Dougal grinned and left. The doctor hadn't so much as glanced in his direction.

A third man had joined the two police officers in the room where Trelawney had been questioned. Someone had found a chair for him and he was straddling it, folded arms resting on its back support.

'Fingerprints?'

'Not on record with your people and I got a negative from Scotland Yard a half hour ago,' the lieutenant said.

'Why burn his clothes instead of throwing them away?'

'Says he was ashamed of himself. He didn't want anybody finding them.'

'Ah nuts. You don't buy that, do you?'

The lieutenant shook his head. 'No, I don't. On the other hand as Armitage points out himself a man on the run who sits around sending up smoke signals has to be some sort of lunatic. He claims he's not a lunatic.'

'I just thought of something,' the man from the FBI said. 'If this guy shits his pants like he says there should be traces of excreta on him, or are you going to tell me that he stopped off at some place and asked if he could take a shower? If he's as crippled as you say I don't see him paddling around in the creek – if there's any water in it. Urine on the seat's no problem but . . .' He broke off at an impatient flick of the lieutenant's hand.

'He tells me he cleaned himself off with the windshield-spray solution. The container's empty.'

'Thorough, isn't he?'

'Yeah, or innocent.'

'But you don't believe that.'

'Right,' the lieutenant said.

The FBI man rested his chin on his forearms, turning his eyes towards the police captain. 'You got anything to say?'

'Nope. I came in on this late. Lieutenant Hart here has the ball. He's running with it. But I think our best chance still lies in tracing where those two guys made that call to your office from. I suppose you wouldn't tell us what they said and why this town is full of the military.'

'I'm not authorized to do that. Anyway, the call was made hours after the explosions and could have come from any place.'

Lieutenant Hart said, 'I'm prepared to bet it came from right here in Sedona. We're searching all over.'

'Why?'

'Because the sabotage bit has been taken out of my hands, but I still have a triple killing to solve. The two things are surely connected and I don't like doing half a job, but that's the way it is.'

'I didn't mean that. I wanted to know why you think the call was made from here.'

Hart stared at the table for a moment before saying, 'Search me. I have this feeling about Armitage. He's as big as Doc Cotterell upstairs and about twice as hard. He just could have killed those men. Every darned bit of circumstantial evidence points to him, but he has an answer for all of it. It's too neat and he does it too well. He makes me think my line of questioning is kid's stuff he learned how to handle way back when.'

He scratched his head irritably, making his hair stand up as though he had been out in the wind, before adding, 'I think he made that call, and I think he made it from the Sedona area because the schedule's too tight for him to have made it from some place else and driven to where he was picked up.'

'We'll find out,' the FBI man told him.

'Could be. I'll check if the doc's through with . . . Hey, that reminds me. Tell me something. Are the British bad at dental work?'

'Not that I've heard. Why?'

'Just wondered. This tooth had been knocked part-way out of Armitage's jaw. The doc removed it. There's a filling that looks like nothing I've ever seen which was put in with a monkey-wrench or something.'

'Let me see that.'

Hart slid the tooth down the length of the table then waited, his expression curious.

'Hart?' The name was spoken quietly.

'Yup?'

'Will you have this taken to Phoenix right now? I want it examined professionally. Then will you check out Armitage's prints with the CIA?'

'Sure. Care to tell me why?'

'Because,' the FBI man said, 'I think our friend's a Russkie. That's why.'

CHAPTER TWENTY-FIVE

'Good and bad,' Rafferty said and looked down at the decoded message in his hand because he did not want to meet Jane's gaze. 'First the bad. Purvis says that . . .'

'That they've got Al.' There was no emotion in her voice at all and that made him wince inwardly.

'Yes.'

'And the good?'

'I'm afraid there's more bad news yet.'

'Yes?'

'Three bodies have been found grouped together in woods close to the centrifuge plant. The killings look like the work of someone trained in unarmed combat, except that one was a knife job.'

He looked up. Large grey eyes, black-fringed, burning into him like searchlights. No moisture forming in them.

'But he wasn't due to go near the place until tomorrow, Raff, and then only for reconnaissance. Before dawn on Monday was . . .'

She stopped talking at the shake of his head. 'I know, but he must have changed the plan for some reason. Perhaps he thought he had been recognized. Perhaps he *had* been recognized.'

'Perhaps.'

Rafferty found her fixed stare unnerving and was wishing that she would at least blink when she added, 'It doesn't really matter how it went wrong. We've failed. There's nothing left to do now but go to the Minister.' She glanced at her watch. 'It'll probably mean getting him out of bed. Poor old Minister.' Her voice was still flat.

'No,' Rafferty said. 'We'll let the poor old Minister, who is about ten years younger than I am, snore on for a bit. You've forgotten about the good news.'

Jane raised an enquiring eyebrow at him.

'Al blew the place to glory, sweetheart.'

'Good old Al.'

'You're making everyone sound like geriatrics tonight.'

Her eyes closed then and opened slowly again.

'Give me a minute, Raff. This is the first time I've lost a husband. Just give me a minute to get used to the idea.'

He sat down, waiting, not watching her.

After a moment she moved and he turned his eyes towards her, saw her take a compact from her bag and examine her face in its little mirror. Her expression seemed to indicate surprise that she hadn't changed.

She snapped the compact shut and said, 'Sorry. All right now. What's Purvis got?'

'The police did what you hoped they'd do if they picked Al up. They called Purvis about the contents of the case. He gave them the photographic equipment bit as arranged. The attack on the plant and the killings are national news.'

'Extent of damage and casualties?'

'No casualties reported. Thirty per cent of the factory destroyed by explosions and fire. Accident has been ruled out because the explosions were widely spread. One eye-witness described it as being like an attack by several heavy mortars with, and here's an odd thing, a ranging shot falling outside the factory site boundary some minutes before the main barrage.'

'Not odd,' Jane said.

'What do you mean?'

'That would have been Al's way of warning them. How long do you propose to sit on our connection with this, Raff?'

'Only a few hours now. If Al succeeded in making his telephone calls there may be some indication that they've found what they're supposed to find. If it's there to find of course and . . .'

Jane's desk-speaker buzzed.

'Yes?'

'Prideaux, Mrs Trelawney. Is the Director still with you?'

'Yes.'

'Purvis from Washington again. On the blower this time. Will he take the call there, or in his room?'

'Here,' Rafferty said.

'Okay, sir. He's on the scrambler.'

Purvis could have been speaking from inside the building. Heads close together Jane and Rafferty listened to the voice coming from the receiver.

'I don't know what's supposed to be going on, sir, but I thought you might want to hear this quickly. According to the latest newscast road-blocks have been set up all around the Sedona-Flagstaff area with National Guard units assisting the police. Paratroops have been dropped on to the factory site and are being joined by ground units. No press or television crews are allowed in and they've put up fighters to chase off inquisitive planes. That's all I've got. Any instructions?'

'Yes,' Rafferty told him. 'You're finished in Washington. Square it with the Ambassador any way you like and catch the earliest possible flight home. With your diplomatic passport you'll have no trouble.'

There was silence for several seconds before Purvis spoke.

'That'll make it look pretty bad for Trelawney, sir.'

'No it won't,' Rafferty said. 'You've just sprung him.'

He didn't glance in Jane's direction when he rang off, picked up a black phone and dialled. She recognized one of the numbers of the United States Embassy in Grosvenor Square.

'Yes, please. My name's Patrick Rafferty. Mr Kravitz is visiting from the States. If he's still at work this late I'd like to speak with him.' 'Yes, I will. Thank you.'

Cradling the instrument on the speaker attachment he folded his arms and waited. Jane sat, eyes on his face, conscious of the heavy beating of her heart, afraid to hope but doing it all the same.

'Patrick, this is Chuck Harris.' The words blared into the room and Jane turned down the volume control. 'Paul Kravitz is in conference and likely to be there quite a while yet. You want I should take a message for later?'

'No, I want you should take a message for now,' Rafferty said. 'I don't much care if he's in conference with the President. Get him out of it.'

'Now, Patrick, there's no way Paul is . . .'

With no added emphasis in his voice, 'Shut up,' Rafferty

told him. 'You haven't heard the message yet. It's "Critical mass".'

A pause, then, 'I see. Stay right there.'

Rafferty nodded his agreement at the desk-speaker.

The next voice was as quiet as the first had been loud and Jane turned up the volume.

'You have something to say to me, Rafferty?'

'Yes I do, Kravitz. I want my man Trelawney in this office in good working order no later than this time tomorrow.'

'Trelawney, eh? Would that be this Armitage guy who's been causing us some grief?'

'As if you didn't know.'

'Well, I'm afraid that what *you* want doesn't coincide with *our* plans for him and I don't think this conversation is the kind we should be having on an open line.'

'I'll be circumspect,' Rafferty said, 'but you're right to worry about open lines. Failing your agreement to my request the next call I make on this one will be to the press. I'll give them everything we know, which is a lot. Considering the trouble you are going to to keep the wraps on I don't think you'd like that much.'

'It could be embarrassing,' the quiet voice agreed. 'I'll check with the brass Stateside and get back to you.'

'Stop stalling, Kravitz. You're across the proverbial barrel and you know it. What's more you carry enough clout yourself to start a private war. I'm not asking for that. I'm asking only for the return of a man who's done you a great big favour. What's Trelawney to you except a potential source of information which I can give you the easy way?'

'When can you give it to me?'

'When he walks into this building.'

Rafferty knew that he had won, had known that he would win from the moment Purvis had finished his brief report, but nerve-ends were still tingling all over his body. The sensation had nothing to do with the silence of the box on the desk, it stemmed directly from his awareness of eyes watching his face. He wished she'd look somewhere else.

Eventually, 'You have a deal, Rafferty.'

Beside him Jane Trelawney made a strangled sound and he

followed her with his eyes as she ran from the room.

'But,' the box went on, 'I'd take it kindly if you'd tell me one thing.'

'You can always try me.'

'Okay. Do you have any hard intelligence on the intended delivery destination? Your man mentioned Israel, but that could have been smoke-screen stuff. That's why the wraps are on. We don't need national – er – concern.'

Amused both by the euphemism and his own theatricality Rafferty let five seconds go by before he said, 'You're at "ground zero" right now, Kravitz. *We* didn't need delay, disbelief or token searches. That's why we forced your hand.'

When she came back into the room Jane found Rafferty still staring at the desk-speaker, but the indicator light was off. She kissed him lightly on the bridge of his nose and sat down.

'How did it end?'

It was a relief to be able to look at her again.

'They're putting Al on the first flight for home. Paul – we finally got back on to Christian names – is coming straight round here after he's arranged that and we'll give him the dope tonight. There was no point in holding out on him once he'd agreed. He can't renege on us.'

'Is he a friend?'

Rafferty moved his shoulders as though he had been going to shrug but had changed his mind.

'That would be asking a lot in the present emotional climate. He's a strong ally who understands our motives. That's enough. We can start to tie this thing up now.'

'There's still Germany to think about, Raff.'

He smiled at her, the first relaxed smile she had seen from him in what seemed a very long time.

'There won't be once the *Bundeswehr* starts rolling, which it will do most efficiently as soon as the German authorities are told what we know.'

'You're *really* going to the Minister at last?'

'Why not? We aren't working on a hunch which grew out of a sordid incident now. Ministers aren't noted for their interest in hunches. We have facts. They go for those and the story starts at any logical point we choose.'

She returned his smile. 'Thank you. Thank you for everything. Well, if you don't mind, I'll leave you to brief Paul Kravitz. I mustn't keep Stirling and Reid waiting.'

'What does that mean?'

'I'm playing the field,' Jane said and kissed him on the nose again.

CHAPTER TWENTY-SIX

The room in Phoenix they pushed Trelawney into was high, windowless and without furniture of any sort. There was a ventilation grille near the top of one wall, a single light countersunk into the ceiling and the closed door fitted closely enough to be almost airtight. He didn't like that kind of room.

As there was nothing else he sat on the floor and began to think about the drive from Sedona in the police car. He hadn't seen the Arizona desert by daylight before with its backdrop of mountains and its mile after mile of saguaro cactus. But he wasn't in the mood for scenic beauty. The mountains were just mountains and the cactus mile after mile of phallic symbols. Stuff you again, Purvis.

That subject disposed of he searched for something else for his mind to work on. Not Jane. Definitely not Jane, his usual mental haven when he was away from her. She would be very distressed by now, but there was no point in thinking about that until he could do something about it. When that would be he had no idea. They had brought him to play with the big boys now. Well, he had played with them around the world and these, by the standards of his trade, were civilized.

The door opened and the man from the Sedona bar came in, a policeman holding his arm.

'That him?'

'That's him.'

'You sure?'

'I'm certain.'

They went out and the door closed.

'That does it,' Trelawney said, but he said it to himself.

It seemed a long time before the door opened again and he found himself looking at two other men, the first white, average height, burly, the second black, tall, slender. They glanced at each other and the black man nodded.

The white man said, 'So this is Alaric Trelawney. What the hell kinda name's Alaric, for Pete's sake?'

The black man considered the question for a moment before saying, 'I guess it must be Trelawney's kinda name.'

'Yeah, that would explain it. Get up, Mr Alaric Trelawney. We want to talk to you.'

Trelawney watched the speaker interestedly, but stayed where he was. Nor did he move when a shoe thudded into his stomach.

'I don't give orders twice, fella.'

'Now, Jim,' the black man said, 'I don't think that was the most sensible thing you ever did.'

'No? Why not?'

'It's liable to annoy him.'

'So what?'

'So if Trelawney gets annoyed he'll likely tear your head off your neck. We wouldn't want that now, would we?'

'Oh for crissake! Quit kidding around.'

'No, I mean it. Look, I think maybe it'd be best if you went away and let me talk to him.'

The white man stared, shrugged and said, 'Okay. You're the boss.'

When he had gone Trelawney got slowly to his feet and took the cigarette offered to him.

'Thanks, Mike.'

'Sure.'

Neither spoke again for a quarter of a minute, then, 'Al?'

'Yes, Mike?'

'What the fuck are you trying to do, old buddy?'

Trelawney recalled his thought about playing with the big boys. He hadn't been wrong. The pleasant black face in front of him belonged to someone well up the scale, someone for whom he felt affection and by whom the feeling was returned. He wished the last was not the case because enmity was easier to deal with.

'I was trying to visit the Grand Canyon and take some photographs,' he said, 'but it's a prohibited area. Some secret government scheme. A couple of security guards in Flagstaff beat me up for asking the way there.'

Mike Driscoll nodded. 'Right. They're filling it in with polystyrene waste as a pilot project for bridging the generation gap.'

'Fiendish, but I suppose it had to come. Now do you mind explaining why the CIA is interested in me?'

'Identification is all. The local cops and the Feds were aggravating their ulcers over this guy Armitage when some bright boy found a tooth Armitage had left lying around. A cavity filling in that tooth made him think Armitage's real name could be Boris Godunov or somesuch, but when they cut the tooth in half the dental work was identified as English. You know, the kind of stuff you Brits and we stick in our people's faces when we don't want them to advertise themselves too much on foreign tours.'

'Then the FBI decided to send you my prints.'

'Right, and I came to look at your face.'

'That must have made your day. All right, Mike, what happens next?'

'I dunno, Al. I've made the identification like I was asked to do. You're not the Agency's responsibility. Not here you're not.'

'Then why are you hanging about?' Trelawney asked him.

'Thought you might listen to some advice from me. You know, for old time's sake.'

'I'm listening.'

'Co-operate with the cops. Give the Feds what they need to know. In other words, talk.'

'What about?'

The black man ignored the question and said, 'You know something? At first I couldn't figure out why your people didn't just send a postcard telling us where to look, but I understand now. Nobody would have found it if you hadn't blown the place to hell and gone. That puts us in your debt. Fill in the blanks for us and it could change the look of your charge sheet some. It makes depressing reading at the moment. Illegal entry, illegal possession of explosives, breaking into private property, sabotage, three murders and endangering twenty-three other human lives. That's only the basics. It'll read longer than that before they're through.'

There was, Trelawney supposed, a lot to be thankful for. From the moment the parachutes had opened behind the Air Force plane he had known that the job had succeeded but now, without being aware of the details, he also knew that it *had* been necessary. 'Nobody would have found it,' Mike Driscoll had said and he had no reason for saying that if it hadn't been true. More. He had used the word 'endangering' and that meant that nobody had died in the explosions.

As if in confirmation Driscoll said, 'That initial blast of yours was a neat trick. The maintenance crew got out of there with nothing more than one broken ankle and a coupla cases of shock.'

'I'm so glad,' Trelawney told him. 'Do I take it that you're talking about the place above Sedona where they've been having all this excitement?'

Driscoll sighed. 'You catch on real fast, pal.'

'How did you come to mislay it?'

'Mislay what?'

'The place you've been telling me about. The one you couldn't have found if we'd sent you a postcard, but got right on to when it was blown up. How do you lose a place? All you need is a map and . . . Oh, I get it. It's some archaeological site, or an abandoned mine.'

'Knock it off, Al. You've been identified as the man who made the call to the FBI about the manufacture of illicit nukes by the guy they brought in a while back. He put the call through for you because you couldn't handle the phone.'

'Oh my God!' Trelawney said. 'That makes two of you who've been out in the sun too long. I never saw him before. He's probably part of a frame-up to drop those three killings everybody's carrying on about in my lap.'

As Trelawney had done earlier Driscoll sat down on the floor and rested his back against the wall. He yawned.

'If you mean to stay for much longer why don't you have them send in a camp-bed?' Trelawney asked him. 'Or do they still need the space for beating me up?'

'I don't reckon we'll be here long enough for them to work you over. I'm waiting for some orders.'

'I thought you were giving me advice.'

'That too. You know, Al, you were lucky with those three men. Questioning has elicited the fact – hey, that's pretty good British English, isn't it? – the fact that the next night, or maybe the night after, you'd have run into forty of them. All unfriendly characters recruited from the more dubious sectors of our society to guard the joint. The three were marking out positions for them. Seems you arrived a coupla days before they expected you. What would you have done if you'd found the place cordoned?'

Trelawney felt suddenly very cold and experienced the sensation of his brain rocking as though it were set in gimbals. He stood rigidly, fighting for mental and physical balance, wanting to believe that he had misheard, knowing that he had not.

It was several seconds before he trusted himself to say, 'I'd have thrown one of the illicit atom bombs you tell me I manufacture at them.'

Dimly aware of Driscoll saying something about people who deliberately misunderstood everything that was said to them being boring he dragged his mind back from five thousand miles away when the door opened. He watched Driscoll take an envelope from the hand of a uniformed policeman, tear it open and read the contents.

'Okay, Armitage. We're leaving.'

As though by reflex the policeman's hand moved towards his gun, then dropped to hang at his side again.

'I'm sorry, sir. I have no orders to release the prisoner.'

'No. *I'm* sorry. Of course you haven't,' Driscoll said. 'Point me the way to the Captain's office and I'll get them for you.'

Trelawney propped his shoulders against the wall, staring at the closed door, not seeing it, repeating silently to himself the words 'Seems you arrived a coupla days before they expected you'.

Suddenly he was back in England again, lying on the gravel outside Professor Morris's house, looking at the device taped to the exhaust pipe of the Lotus. 'Knowing what I do about you, you weren't followed here,' Morris had said and he had agreed to the extent that he knew he had not been tracked visually. He had assumed that it had been done electronically although he had seen no 'bleeper' attached to the underside of the car. That had meant nothing at the time. He could easily have missed it during his cursory examination, or the bomber could have removed the thing when he placed his charge. Now he believed that there had been no 'bleeper'. They had known where he was going that day and they had known why he had come to Arizona.

Oxford faded from his mind to be replaced by a picture of Thayer Street and he thought bleakly of Foster and the other traitors of a couple of years before. All had died in different ways and different places.

All? He was thinking very hard about that when Driscoll returned and he saw that the policeman had gone from outside the door.

In the car on the way to the airport Driscoll said, 'I'd been hoping for a little kudos out of this.'

'Like what?'

'Like getting some information from you. I must have been out of my mind.'

'I'm sorry, Mike. I haven't got any to give.'

'You're a goddam, low-down, stinking, lying, Limey bastard, whitey.' There was no trace of rancour in Driscoll's voice.

Trelawney smiled, then his expression grew serious.

'Mike?'

'Yeah?'

'As this FBI escort who's putting me on the London plane has orders to prevent me communicating with anyone, will you phone a message through to Thayer Street for me?'

Driscoll sighed before saying, 'Don't push it, Al. We're being pretty darned nice to you. Or hadn't you noticed?'

'Just two words, and I promise they hold no threat to the States.'

'What are they?'

'Foster's ghost,' Trelawney told him.

'Kinda combines the crypt and the cryptic. Who's the lucky recipient of this bulletin from the Great Beyond?'

'Jane.'

The black face beside Trelawney broke into a grin.

'You've got it,' Driscoll said. 'That's one lady I'll sit in on a séance with any time.'

CHAPTER TWENTY-SEVEN

Rafferty sat in the outer office staring unblinkingly at the Minister's Private Secretary. He was staring because it obviously made Grenville nervous. What was less obvious to him was why he should wish to do that. They had crossed swords once, with Grenville providing no very adequate opposition and that had been engineered simply to cheer up Sue Mitchell after Havelock-Templeton's death. It was, he supposed, because the man was such an ass, but it was puzzling for all that to find an ass occupying such a responsible chair.

Grenville looked up, caught Rafferty's eye, frowned and bent over his papers.

'How long's his nibs likely to be?'

Grenville looked up again. 'Are you referring to the Minister?'

'That's right,' Rafferty said. 'I requested an immediate interview.'

'Oh, he asked for ten minutes' grace. He had to go across to Downing Street.'

'He asked *who* for ten minutes' grace?'

'I'm sorry. *You*. I should have told you.'

'Yes. You should,' Rafferty said and continued to study the other's face. It was unremarkable except for a cleft in the chin so deep that black stubble inaccessible to a razor showed in a thin vertical line. Trelawney had had trouble with Grenville too, he remembered. Did the man dislike everybody on principle, his job, or just the Department?

The outer door opened.

'Rafferty, I'm so sorry. Got sent for by the P.M just after you telephoned. Come on in.'

The Minister strode towards his own office with Rafferty close behind him.

When both were seated, 'When you people ask for an immediate meeting I feel apprehensive. What is it?'

'It's not very good, Minister. I have reason to believe that it is planned to place a nuclear explosive device somewhere in the Greater London area.'

Apart from a raising of the eyebrows the Minister gave no outward sign of agitation. 'Go on,' he said and Rafferty made his report. It took him half an hour and he was heard out in silence.

When he had finished the silence continued for another minute before the Minister spoke.

'I'd be grateful for clarification on a few points, Director.'

It was the first time outside the Department that Rafferty had been addressed by his unconfirmed title. He wondered if its use implied confidence in him, or was a formality preceding an official rebuke.

'Of course. If I can give it,' he said.

'Very well. Are personal contacts with the KGB, such as the one you have described to me, commonplace?'

'By no means. On the other hand they are not uncommon when a mutual interest is involved.'

Rafferty thought of the many times he had walked, talked and drunk with members of the official opposition in different places around the globe, but he didn't think it would help his present case to develop that theme. Being certain that the Minister had known the answer to his question before he had asked it, he was suddenly aware that he was about to be cross-examined on his story. He had, he believed, covered the gross irregularities in which he had been engaged well enough. To embroider it could easily damage that cover.

'You scratch my back, etcetera?'

'Precisely.'

'Hmm. Why did the Russians come to us instead of approaching the Americans direct?'

'For two reasons. Firstly, they believe us to be the first "target" nation as I have said and they fear misguided reprisals following a military take-over here, as I have also said. Secondly, I imagine they hope to conceal the extent of their knowledge of American production, imports and – um – mislaying of fissionable materials by dealing through a third party – us.'

'That's no sort of concealment. You told the Americans the source of your information.'

'I know, Minister, but it leaves the Russians in a position to deny any connection with the matter. They can say that it's British interference in American internal affairs for which we are blaming them.'

The Minister said, 'Hmm,' again and gestured towards a box of cigarettes on his desk. Rafferty took one. He hoped that this signalled the end of the probing, but the next words spoken destroyed the hope.

'You've taken too much on yourself, Director. I should have been informed immediately of this Russian intelligence, and passing it on to the Americans should have been carried out on a government to government basis.'

Rafferty stood up, walked across the office and leant against a wall before saying quietly, 'That's balls, and you know it.'

He felt no particular surprise when, after a flicker of the eyelids, he received a questioning half-smile. The Minister was neither pompous nor a fool.

'Why, Rafferty?'

'Because if I were to tell you about every piece of misinformation and every deception plan which comes out of Russia you'd never get home to your wife at night. It's my job to analyse, classify, verify or refute. If I get verification, and the classification is high enough, then I come to you. This I have just done. As to government to government approaches, I would respectfully submit that you, as a politician, should know better than I that no government likes being shown to be incapable of enforcing its own laws by another government. On the other hand a friendly hint from a foreign undercover organization that all may not be well is something quite different and much more acceptable. In this case it produced a *quid pro quo*.'

The half-smile was back on the Minister's face when he said, 'I think *you* should have been the politician. You present a strong case and one, on reflection, I find it hard to argue against.'

'Then may I continue to act as I have?'

'In what connection?'

'I'd like to alert the West German authorities to the suspected existence of the Kassel plant and do it through my own channels for the reasons I have given.'

A frown replaced the half-smile.

'Rafferty, you have told me that Kravitz informed you about the place. Are you now telling me that he hasn't shown the West Germans the same consideration? Aren't the rest of our NATO allies part of your "old boy" network? Has the CIA got it in for Bonn?'

Nearly an inch of ash fell from Rafferty's cigarette on to the carpet. Part of his mind registered the fact and instructed his toe to scuff the grey cylinder out of existence. The rest formed a mental picture of a man dying by millimetres as the melting ice on which he stood tightened the wire noose around his neck, a man who had regained consciousness and told everything he knew to the woman who had broken him. Up to his own neck in lies as he was, it was comforting to Rafferty to know that Paul Kravitz, who until that morning had known nothing of Kassel, would substantiate his story. That had been agreed between them.

He said, 'The CIA isn't certain yet, Minister, and they didn't want to raise any hares until they were. We can't afford to be as circumspect with this threat hanging over us. May I take the necessary action? We could be running this thing very close.'

Without further hesitation, 'Yes,' the Minister told him. 'You may.' He stood up and added, 'I'll arrange for MI5 to start digging into your Durham theory at once. I take it that you have nothing more to go on than that this Professor Jefferies teaches there too.'

'Nothing at all. It's just a possibility we can't afford to ignore. I understand that our ability to keep track of our fissionable material is no better than the Americans'.'

'Very well, Rafferty. You will of course hold yourself available to sit on whatever working party the Prime Minister decides to set up. I would expect it to hold its first meeting not later than tomorrow morning.'

'I'll be ready whenever I'm needed, Minister,' Rafferty said.

He was to be needed well before the following day.

Jane Trelawney woke from a heavy sleep at the sound of the door closing, opened one eye and watched Peter Geddes walk the length of the conference room on the first floor of the Thayer Street building. He handed a piece of paper to Rafferty sitting at the far end of the long table, whispered in his ear and turned to leave. She closed her eye.

When he had gone she swung her legs off the sofa, stood up and said, 'Hello. When did you get back?'

Rafferty looked up at her, smiling. 'Nearly three hours ago. Sorry. Did Peter wake you?'

'*You* should have woken me.'

'No, I shouldn't. We're both running short on sleep.'

She yawned, went through the doorway into the washroom and he heard her say, 'Oh my God! How dare you?'

'Are you addressing me or the Almighty?'

'You.'

'How dare I what?'

'See me like this with creases all down one side of my face. And look at my hair! I mean don't look at my hair.'

Her voice sank to a mutter, there was the sound of running water, a minute's silence, then she reappeared looking sleekly beautiful and sat down two chairs away from him.

'How did it go with the Minister?'

The conference room blinds were drawn and a small grey metal box provided by Young connected to a power outlet was standing on the table. Safe from optical surveillance and with the grey box jamming fixed or directional microphones they could talk in safety. Not since Mike Driscoll had passed on Trelawney's cryptic message had they used their own offices.

'He took it all very calmly,' Rafferty said. 'In his shoes I think I'd have shown a little more emotion. You know, like going into catalepsy or being sick on the floor. After I'd had the last rites administered that is.'

She made a small, impatient sound and he glanced at her unsmiling face.

'Sorry, Jane. I'm feeling rather light-headed at being

legitimate again. Paul Kravitz called while you were asleep. The FBI picked up Jefferies earlier today. He was trying to cross the border into Mexico at a place called Nogales. That's south of Tucson.'

He drew a meaningless and only momentarily visible map on the glass-topped table with his forefinger to show her where Nogales was.

'Thank goodness for that. What have they got out of him?'

'Nothing yet. At least nothing the CIA has been told about, but it gave me a break. I fed Kravitz the names of Heinrich Gesner, Dorothy McDowell and Shigeru Hatoyama and asked him to feed them right back at me as having been obtained from Jefferies. That gives us a reason, other than the true one, for knowing they exist. The Minister's been informed and Special Branch and Immigration are watching out for them. The Americans and Germans too, of course.'

Rafferty picked up the piece of paper Geddes had brought to him a few minutes before and said, 'Talking of Germans there's this message from Diestel in Cologne. The *Bundeswehr* has sealed off the industrial estate near Kassel with tanks and infantry. Incidentally, now that we're off the hook I've put Geddes and Fenner in the picture. We can tell some of the lower field grades if the necessity ever arises.'

'You've been busy, Raff. That only leaves the four properties we know they have here. And Durham. They're MI5 territory.'

He nodded. 'The Minister's got "Five" looking into the Durham possibility, but I've said nothing about the London addresses. Nobody's used the places since the Islington snatch, but that doesn't mean they won't and I don't want them frightened off by men in fawn raincoats. They're the only contact points we have.'

One of the telephones buzzed. Rafferty picked up the receiver and said, 'Yes?'

'Patrick?'

'Yes, Paul, but you're on an open line.'

'I know it. Stay put. I'm coming around.'

The click as the connection was cut, followed by the dialling tone, reached Jane's ears before Rafferty could reply.

She watched him get up, walk slowly down the length of the room, then shrug as though ridding himself of the weight of useless speculation about the purpose of Kravitz's impending visit. When he turned to look at her she knew from the blankness of his eyes that she was unseen and she waited patiently for his thought processes to translate themselves into words.

When, after half a minute, he had not spoken she said, 'He'll tell us when he gets here. Whatever it is.'

'What? Oh, Paul. Yes, of course he will. I wasn't thinking of him. We have another lead apart from the London addresses and I rather wish we hadn't.'

Accustomed as she had long been to the almost invariable humorously sardonic set of Rafferty's leathery features Jane Trelawney had been upset by the concern they had betrayed from time to time over recent days. The distress she read in them now troubled her deeply.

She crooked a finger at him. 'I'm not a public meeting. Come back down this end and tell me about it.'

He smiled briefly and rejoined her at the table.

'It's Barry.'

'What's Barry?'

'The numbers file he *found* for me in the safe. The code we can't break. Martha typed it.'

He could sense her eyes on his, but sat staring at his hands wishing, as he had done before, that she would look somewhere else.

'It had to be Martha,' he went on, 'because the boss never even learned how to put paper in a machine.'

'You're not at your most lucid, Raff.'

'Yesterday,' he said, 'I went to my bank and read through the diary of events for this business I've been storing there. I'd recorded the fact that Liz had told me that the numbers were typed on an Olivetti "Lettera 32". For some reason that reminded me that I'd seen one on the desk at their Dorset cottage and don't ask me why I didn't remember it before because I don't bloody well know.'

'And it's the same machine.'

'Yes. It was a long shot, but I sent Prideaux down. Here. Compare the – Oh, don't bother. They're the same.'

'Have you told Charles Barry?' she asked.

'No, and I don't intend to yet. He's denied knowledge of it once and he won't talk now about anything which might incriminate Martha. Same with Martha. I'd never get a word out of her and she's got a George Cross to prove it.'

'Even if you told them what's going on?'

Rafferty shook his head. 'They're both security risks now until proved otherwise. I've held him here for his own safety, but that's no longer the main consideration and I'm taking him back to her before I get involved in working committees and all that stuff tomorrow.' He paused, then added bitterly, 'Taking him back so that I can . . .'

Jane reached out and put her hand on his.

'I know,' she said. 'You don't have to explain to me.'

The telephone buzzed again and she was grateful to it for replacing the unhappiness on his face with sudden interest as he listened to the receiver.

'Of course . . . Fifteen minutes, give or take, depending on the traffic . . . All right. Goodbye.'

As though triggered by his replacing the telephone the desk-speaker demanded his attention.

'Yes?'

'Sergeant Cole here, sir. There's a Mr Kravitz to see you. Shall I have him brought up?'

'No. I'll come down,' Rafferty said, then to Jane, 'The Prime Minister wants me. Mind the store.'

He left the conference room quickly and took the stairs down the single flight to the ground floor. Kravitz, thick-set, sleepy-eyed, was leaning against the armoured glass box talking to Sergeant Cole. Rafferty took him by the arm and turned him towards the entrance.

'Your car outside, Paul?'

'Yeah.'

'Give me a lift, will you? We can talk on the way.'

'Where to, for crissake?'

'Downing Street.'

'So what are we waiting for?' the American said.

Rafferty left Number 10 and walked quickly to Kravitz's car.

The CIA man was sitting, legs stretched across the front seats, staring blankly at a crossword puzzle in his newspaper.

'Five letter word,' he said. 'The clue is H.I.J.K.L.M.N.O. You're the sort of smart-ass who understands these things. What's the answer?'

'Water,' Rafferty told him. 'Get your feet out of the way.'

'Water? Why the hell should it be water?'

'H to O. H *two* O.'

Without rancour Kravitz said, 'Ah, shit,' threw the paper into the back, sat upright and started the engine. 'They've planted their bomb. Right?'

'Right.'

'London, as we expected?'

'Yes.'

Kravitz turned into Whitehall, called his Embassy on the car phone and said, 'Chuck, tell 'em back home "Lariat" repeat "Lariat".' . . . 'Yeah, that's what I said.' Then to Rafferty, 'Want to tell me about it?'

'Yes. I'm authorized to do so. A letter was delivered to the Home Secretary at the House of Commons just over two hours ago. It states that an atomic device with approximately twenty-five per cent more destructive power than the Hiroshima bomb has been placed somewhere in the Greater London area. If all British troops have not been withdrawn from Northern Ireland by three weeks from today it will be triggered. If they have, we'll be told where the thing is and how to dispose of it safely.'

'Is that all?'

Slowly and distinctly Rafferty said, 'You're never going to believe this, but that *is* all. No neutron bomb, no ten megaton hydrogen blast, no cobalt contamination. Just a little old Hiroshima-and-a-quarter World War Two fire-cracker.'

'You finished?' Kravitz asked.

'I've finished.'

'Good. Real good. What I wanted to know was if there was anything else in the letter. People can give themselves away by writing too much.'

'Not these people. There was nothing else. Not even a signature, or the name of some fancy liberation army.'

'What was the general reaction back there?'

'Varied,' Rafferty told him, 'but I think that unless we can find and neutralize it we'll do as we're told.' He sat for a moment staring through Admiralty Arch down the broad expanse of the Mall towards Buckingham Palace, then the Trafalgar Square traffic began to move again and he went on, 'There are about one and a half million British in Ulster, the large majority of whom don't want to become Irish. That's why the Army is there, despite what certain of your countrymen like to imagine. Given that, try balancing a problematically peaceful life for them against certain death for – well, you tell me. There must be ten million in and around this city. I doubt the casualties would be less than a tenth and that's an awful lot of people.'

Kravitz muttered something short and unintelligible while Rafferty continued to speak.

'There was a bit of wishful thinking from one quarter. As there had been no test recorded, maybe the damn thing wouldn't work. The Chief of the Defence Staff shot that one down. He said the principle is so well known now and the mathematics so exact that no testing is necessary for a simple fission device. He's an Admiral, not a scientist, but I expect he knows what he's talking about.'

'He knows what he's talking about,' Kravitz said.

Rafferty smiled without a trace of humour. 'The only bright moment in the whole meeting,' he told the other, 'was when the PM announced that an atom bomb was believed to have been placed in London and, thanks to you, I could say "I know".'

'Don't thank me. Thank the FBI and our friendly neighbourhood anarchist Jefferies. I just wish to God the maniac could give us a lead on the location, but they tell me the operational side isn't his scene. He just likes producing the hardware. What are you going to do, Patrick? I mean you personally.'

'No decision is to be taken by the government for three days,' Rafferty said. 'Amongst other things I'm going to spend them watching. Pray that I'm watching the right places, will you?'

CHAPTER TWENTY-EIGHT

Trelawney passed quickly through Immigration and Customs at Heathrow's Terminal 3, then paused, his eyes scanning the concourse for the gleaming figure he could pick out instantly in any crowd. She wasn't there. He felt enormous disappointment and then a twinge of fear immediately suppressed. There would be more than enough for her to do at Thayer Street without coming out to the airport to meet him.

'Hello, sir. Been walking into doors again?'

He looked at Stirling, smiled and said, 'Yes, one of those plate-glass things with no handle on it. Is my wife all right?'

'Fine. She's waiting in the car with Reid.'

'Why?'

'Reid had this idea we should cover her while you were away. Just routine.'

'I see.'

Stirling took his bag from him and when they left the building he saw Jane waving from the driving seat of a car with Reid sitting beside her. He waved back. Reid left the car and walked towards another, parked closer. Trelawney intercepted him while Stirling went ahead with his bag.

'What's this business about cover, Reid?'

'I dunno, Mr Trelawney. Stirling's orders. He's five days senior to me in the Department.'

'Reid, skip the double act. If something's wrong I want to know about it.'

Trelawney's left shoulder seemed to capture Reid's attention for several seconds before he looked him in the eyes again and said, 'Stirling and me don't know if anything's wrong. We only know that something big's happening and that it smells wrong to both of us. All we did . . . Oh, listen, she's a very nice lady. Why don't you go and say hello to her? She knows a lot more than we do.' He walked away.

'Poor face,' Jane said.

'You should have seen it yesterday. Did Mike Driscoll phone my message through?'

'Yes, darling. Young has been all over the building checking for bugs. There aren't any, but that doesn't rule out directional microphones or whatever other sorts of portable listening equipment might be located inside or outside. Neither Raff nor I have the faintest idea who could be leaking information. That's what you meant, wasn't it?'

'Yes. According to Driscoll I was expected. If I'd stuck to our original plan I'd have found a small army surrounding the place. It's a rotten feeling knowing that we're not secure.'

Jane followed an airport bus down the incline leading to the tunnel with the big 'Welcome to Britain' sign above it. A glance in the mirror showed her Stirling and Reid immediately behind in the second car. They'd have to be told soon she knew.

'There's an even more rotten feeling to worry about now, Al. A very, very horrid feeling.'

He looked sideways at her calmly beautiful profile, mental sirens sounding an urgent alarm for him. There had been nothing in her tone to cause this, there was nothing in her expression, only her choice of words. Early in their life together he had grown accustomed to her way of describing degrees of nastiness as rather horrid, horrid and very horrid. He had never heard her say *very*, *very* horrid before.

'What is it, Jane?'

She didn't answer and half-way through the tunnel under the airport he repeated the question.

'Can't you guess?'

'I see. We were too slow.'

Her hand left the wheel and rested on his thigh.

'I don't think anybody has been slow, darling. Especially you. We started too late, that's all. Now I'd better tell you what's happened since you left for Arizona.'

Jane stopped talking just before the motorway ended and Trelawney sat, lost in thought, until the car slowed in the congested London streets. He sighed then and looked back over his shoulder. Stirling and Reid were so close that the two cars appeared to be locked together.

'They really are unbelievable,' he said.

'Who? My self-appointed guardians?'

'No. The Irish. Most people in this country gave up hating the Germans and Japanese years ago, but the Irish keep right on loathing us. Why can't they let bygones be bygones and start again like everybody else?'

Trelawney recognized the pointlessness of the question and the near-petulance with which he had asked it in the same instant. He scowled in embarrassment and the scowl deepened when a sidelong glance at his wife showed him suppressed amusement flickering about her mouth.

'According to Raff,' she said, 'bygones are all they've got. If they let go of those there would be nothing left. He ought to know if anyone should and I'm sure it's an interesting psychological point, but it's too profound for me. But never mind that. They don't seem to be involved in this.' She paused, shook her head, then went on. 'No, that's silly. Of course they're involved because they are prepared to take advantage of the situation, but they didn't bring it about.'

'So this isn't a Provisional IRA operation?'

'Right. It isn't the Irish National Liberation Army either, or any other Irish para-military group on its own. Light me a cigarette, will you, darling?'

He did as she asked.

'Thank you. It seems to be some sort of international con . . . What do I mean?'

'Consortium? Conglomerate?'

'Yes. One of those. We have Libyans, Germans, Irish, British, Japanese, Americans. You name it. A marriage of know-how, money and urban guerrilla experience. So far we've traced links with the PLO, the Red Brigade and the remnants of the Baader-Meinhof lot.'

Trelawney moved his head back and forth in a slow affirmative movement, letting the picture form in his mind.

'So,' he said, 'as their interest in Northern Ireland must be close to zero this means that we've entered a new phase of political extortion, an extension of kidnapping and hijacking. They've picked a big one to start with to get themselves a reputation. Volchak hinted at other targets.'

His wife reached out and patted him on top of the head. He smiled and went on, 'You know, we owe that man a lot. I wish Raff hadn't pulled that silly misinformation trick on him.'

'It's all right, Al. Raff wasn't functioning very well that day. I gave Volchak the straight stuff before he and Bunin left the country.'

'I'm glad you did that,' Trelawney told her then, suddenly sombre, lapsed into silence, watching the familiar buildings in the familiar streets slide by, wondering if they were seeing them for the last time.

It was several minutes before he threw the mood off with an angry jerk of his shoulders and asked, 'Was Langley any help?'

Jane glanced at him in surprise, then turned her attention to the traffic again.

'Good heavens, yes. How do you think you got here? If it hadn't been for the CIA you'd be languishing in an FBI cell somewhere. Raff fixed it with Kravitz and just how many strings he had to . . .'

'I wasn't thinking of a place called Langley, Virginia,' Trelawney said. 'I was thinking of a woman called Langley, Fiona.'

'Oh! Oh, most definitely she helped. Didn't I say it was she who gave us Kassel, Gesner and company and the three other London addresses?'

'No, you just said we'd got them.'

'Strange. Subconscious revulsion I suppose. Unfair too. You and she have broken this thing wide open between you, but remember that the Minister doesn't know that. He thinks we got it all from the CIA.'

Trelawney grunted, but said nothing. His share of breaking anything open, he now knew, had come about by mere chance. That last bomb inside the factory fencing, tossed almost casually beside the big electrical transformer because 'something would happen when it went up'. Something *had* happened. The transformer had vanished and it had taken them some hours to clear the rubble from the depression where it had stood to find it more or less intact fifteen feet below the surface in the man-made cavern blasted out of the mountainside to store oil.

The cavern had never contained oil and a damaged transformer had not been all they had found in it.

The people working there had gone, gone immediately, it was presumed, after the transformer had fallen through the ceiling of their secret world. They had left through a tunnel leading to a camouflaged cave in the rocky hillside and dispersed in the darkness. Only Jefferies had later been found, because his was the only name available to the FBI directly connected with the place and questioning of the legitimate workers above ground had revealed no knowledge on their part of what was happening beneath their feet.

The FBI would have the names by now Trelawney knew. Jefferies had talked about other things and would have revealed the identities of his co-workers, but locating them could be difficult after the lapse in time. He shrugged mentally. That was an American problem.

He began to think of the excellent equipment in the cavern as described to Rafferty by Kravitz, a nuclear shopping list of items originating in Holland, West Germany, Britain, France and the United States themselves. There had been little of an individually suspect nature but, added together, the components amounted to an installation capable of producing weapon-grade uranium 235. Not just capable of doing so, he reminded himself, it had done it. The quantity of the stuff found had been almost sufficient to achieve critical mass. Had the completed bomb come from Arizona, Kassel or some similar plant hidden in the mountains of the Pennine range near Durham?

They turned into Thayer Street and in an urgent, breathy whisper Jane said, 'Oh my God!'

The car surged forward, angling right to seek a way past the one immediately ahead in the heavy traffic, but was smashed sideways back into line with metal screaming as the off-side front wing was torn away. Trelawney's head cracked against the window glass beside him and it was seconds before his senses cleared enough to recognize the car cutting in ahead of them with the great rent down its side as Stirling's and Reid's.

Reid's head and shoulders were half out of the window and the gun he held in a double-hand grip bucked repeatedly as he fired.

Stupidly, 'How the hell did *they* get there?' Trelawney asked.

'Very quickly,' his wife told him softly. 'But I'm afraid not quickly enough.'

'I'm sorry, Jack,' Rafferty said. 'It's the lousiest job I've ever asked anyone to do. I was going to handle it myself, but I can't leave London now.'

'I know you can't, sir,' Fenner said. 'Better me than you anyway. Sir Charles Barry and Martha are personal friends of yours, aren't they?'

'Yes. Look, try to . . . Oh, shit! Just get the key to that bloody code.'

Rafferty turned away, picked up the phone and dialled two digits.

'Put Sir Charles on please, Sue.' 'Boss, Jack Fenner's ready to run you down to Dorset if you're all set.' 'Good. We'll meet you in the foyer.'

He walked out of the conference room ahead of the other, contemptuous of himself for his failure to employ the most suitable tool for this much more than objectionable task. At one point on the stairs he checked in his descent, then moved on knowing that it was not in him to expose his friends to Fiona Langley's talents.

The glass doors of the Department stood open to the warm summer day and they stepped out on to the pavement together, Barry in the centre, Rafferty and Fenner to either side of him. The white van with an open bonnet parked beyond Fenner's car had 'F & D Collingworth – Heating and Ventilating Engineers' painted on its side.

'Would you rather ride in the back, or up front with me, sir?'

The man in overalls slammed the bonnet shut and opened the driver's door of the van.

'Oh, with you, Fenner. You haven't got a chauffeur's cap.'

Fierce urgency in his voice Rafferty snapped, 'Flat on your

face, Fenner!' and threw himself at Barry, hurling him back against the wall of the building, covering him.

The grenade exploded before it hit the ground.

A man in a city suit with an umbrella over his arm stood staring uncomprehendingly at the red stump on his right hand where his thumb had been. A woman with a child at her side died instantly, a fragment entering the brain through an eye. She remained standing for a second then subsided, almost gracefully, to the pavement. The child said, 'Mummy! Get up!' Fenner lay dead, his jaw blown away.

Against the wall Barry squinted at Rafferty's face two inches from his own. Rafferty leant against him trying to identify the white blur of Barry's beard, then began to slide slowly down his body. Barry caught him under the arms, dragged him through the entrance and shouted, 'Sergeant Cole! Get help!' He had pulled Rafferty another three yards before he heard Cole's 'Fuckin' 'ell!' and then his voice on the telephone.

Trelawney reached him first, stooped and gathered up Rafferty's long, limp frame in his arms.

'You all right, sir?'

'Yes thank you, Trelawney, but tell me...'

'Later, sir. Sergeant Cole, get those people back upstairs. Pass the word nobody is to use the lifts. I want them for casualties. You, Latimer and you, Prideaux, stay. Prideaux, my wife's outside sorting out what's happened to who. I think a man's been killed. Give her a hand. Latimer, I want doctors here within three minutes, any doctors, then I want our own medical staff at the rush. Sir Charles, fend off the police until I get back and send Stirling and Reid to me as soon as they arrive. They're chasing a van.'

He turned and ran for the lifts, cushioning Rafferty on half-extended arms.

'F-Fox and D-Delta Collingworth, Heating and Ventilating Engineers,' Rafferty said. 'White van, red lettering. Didn't get... didn't get number or make. Seen the driver before though. Can't remember who...'

'Thanks, Raff. Quiet now.'

In Hospital Section Trelawney placed Rafferty gently

face downwards on a bed. There was blood oozing from a wound at the back of the head and areas of it soaking his clothes from shoulder to knee.

'I'll say something for you Navy types.' Rafferty's voice was partly muffled by the pillow. 'You can certainly yell orders at people when you want to. Comes of battening down the bollards and luffing the main t'gallants in a high wind I suppose.'

A glass-fronted stainless steel cabinet containing surgical instruments stood against one wall. It was locked.

'That's right,' Trelawney said and smashed the glass with his elbow.

The scalpel sliced effortlessly through the cloth of Rafferty's jacket, then his shirt. Trousers and underpants followed and he lay like a peeled fruit on its own skin. A damaged fruit with its juice running out of it. Nine punctures including the head wound Trelawney thought, but it was difficult to be certain because of the blood. He was thankful to see that none of them was pulsing.

'You look like a pepper-pot, but there's no arterial bleeding.'

'Just instant bed sores.'

'Right.'

'How's the boss, Al? I mean Barry.'

'Not a scratch.'

'And Jack Fenner?'

Trelawney hesitated before saying, 'That was Fenner, was it?' then turned his head towards the door, willing the medical staff to come. He barely heard Rafferty whisper, 'Poor bugger. He really shouldn't have been there at all.'

When he looked back at the bed Rafferty was unconscious.

CHAPTER TWENTY-NINE

'Who's the girl?' Rafferty asked.

'Mrs Partridge. She's a fully qualified theatre sister employed by Special Branch.' The Department's doctor raised his voice and called, 'Sister, come in here a minute and meet the patient, will you?'

She came out of the little operating theatre into the preparation room, smiling.

'Hello, Mr Rafferty.'

'Hello, Sister. Will you do three things for me?'

'If I can.'

'Good. Forget my name, forget you were ever here and go home to Mr Partridge. Nothing personal. Just go.'

The smile faded and she looked questioningly first at the doctor, then at the surgeon.

There was silence until the surgeon said, 'Have you any idea of the gravity . . . ?'

'*Shut up, Kent!*'

The surgeon sighed and turned to the girl.

'I think you had better do as he says, Sister. Please accept my apologies for the unnecessary inconvenience we have caused you.'

'Mine too,' Rafferty told her as she left the room. When the door closed behind her he began to speak slowly.

'Listen to me, Kent. You as well, Fordham. You both seem to have forgotten that the purpose of maintaining this medical set-up is to provide our people with treatment without advertising the fact. To introduce somebody from outside is to advertise and to advertise is a breach of security. Apart from the two of you nobody comes here without my express permission. Is that quite clear?'

'As you happened to be unconscious until a few minutes ago the question of obtaining your permission hardly arose,' Fordham said.

Rafferty ignored him and looked at the surgeon.

'How much does that girl know about my condition?'

'Nothing at all. She was preparing the theatre. How much do *you* know about it?'

'Enough.'

The surgeon snorted impatiently, switched on a projector and the image of a skull seen from the side appeared on a small screen.

'That's you, Mr Rafferty. Do you see this fragment?'

His forefinger indicated a black patch slightly above the junction of head and back-bone.

'Yes.'

The finger moved inwards.

'Do you know what that area is?'

'It's the hypothalamus,' Rafferty said.

'As you say that's the hypothalamus which, as you may or may not be aware, controls many of the body's metabolic functions. If that splinter moves . . .' He shrugged and added, 'It's got to come out and I have no intention of operating without the assistance of a theatre sister.'

'Why can't Dr Fordham help you?'

'Because Dr Fordham will be fully occupied as anaesthetist.'

'Oh,' Rafferty said, 'if you're thinking of something complicated like a craniotomy, forget it. The convalescent period's too long.'

The surgeon raised a quizzical eyebrow.

'Perhaps you do understand your situation. Are you a failed medical student by any chance? These words seem very familiar to you.'

Rafferty yawned. 'No. It comes of having a lot of American friends. They're into medical terms in a big way. If you get a blood blister they tell you you're suffering from haematoma. Now will you kindly get out your pliers and pull at least some of this junk out of my back? I can't waste any more time.'

'You may have no more time to waste, Mr Rafferty.'

'Noted,' Rafferty told him, then said, 'There's one more thing. Apart from the three of us, nobody inside the Department or out is to be given the slightest reason to believe that I'm not in perfectly good shape. That is a direct order.'

Both men nodded and pushed the trolley on which Rafferty lay into the operating theatre.

Stirling's eyes began to water again and he dabbed at them with the handkerchief he had been using to clear the mist from the lenses of the big binoculars on the tripod. He decided to tell Trelawney that he thought three hours over-long for constant, efficient observation.

The name brought back the memory of the abortive car chase. There had been no choice but to side-swipe Mrs Trelawney's Cortina out of the way, firstly because he wanted to be where he could cover her from whatever was going on outside the Department's doors and secondly it had been essential to get Reid into a firing position. In Stirling's opinion Reid could shoot the knee-caps off a reasonably sized fly, but would have resigned from his job rather than admit any such thing to Reid.

It had been just chance that jagged metal from the Cortina's torn wing had ripped the wall of his own back tyre, a tyre which had collapsed a mile further on leaving them watching helplessly while the white van disappeared into the traffic. According to the papers the abandoned vehicle had been found to have seven bullet holes in it, but no blood and no sign of the driver. Perhaps, he thought, Reid was slipping. He grinned and resumed his watch of the house diagonally across the street.

As usual, there was nothing to look at except empty curtainless rooms and a derelict garden fronted by a straggling hedge. Had not Mrs Trelawney explained certain things to him and Reid earlier that afternoon he would have wondered what he was doing there, as previous watchers had. Not now. Definitely not now. Now a lot of things made sense. His own Islington caper the press had labelled as gang warfare, the alleged Hopi Indian riots in Arizona they'd had to use troops to crush, the German army manoeuvres in the province of Hesse which had included a simulated attack on an industrial complex and the setting up of a command post in a cement works. Now he knew the answers to the events causing so much media speculation. Even why a certain Herr

Heinrich Gesner, who had made a brief public statement about co-operating in a military exercise, was subsequently unavailable for comment on the closure of his factory.

Lucky break that, Mrs Trelawney had told him and Reid. Gesner had been the planner and with him removed the opposition might make mistakes. Stirling stepped back from the binoculars and moved round the edges of the room to the window. With the side of his head pressed against the wall he could see across the Greenwich Marshes to the barges moving on the Thames and the shipping in the Royal Albert Dock beyond, but his mind did not register what his eyes saw until the removals van turned into the street from the Woolwich Road, passed beneath the window and stopped outside the house he had been observing.

When one of the six men who got out of it crossed the small unkempt garden and unlocked the front door he picked up the telephone.

'Stirling. Observation point B–Bravo. Record.'

'Recording,' the ear-piece said.

'Right, put me through to Mr Rafferty if he's out of the anaesthetic. If not, give me Mr Trelawney.'

It was Rafferty who answered and Stirling asked, 'Are you *compos mentis*, sir?'

'Batting about average, Stirling. Fire away.'

'Okay. I'm watching house B–Bravo. A furniture van pulled up in front of it two minutes ago and six men got out. One has unlocked the door and gone inside. No sign of him in any of the rooms, so he's either in the hallway, on the stairs, or down in the cellar. The other five are . . .'

'What about the back rooms, Stirling?'

A flicker of worry passed over Stirling's face.

'There are no back rooms, Mr Rafferty. Remember the B–Bravo location off the Woolwich Road? One of a row of mid-Victorian terraced houses, two up, two down, backing straight on to the houses in the next street. Probably dockers' accommodation last century.'

'Yes. I remember now,' Rafferty said. 'What did you say the others are doing?'

Stirling stopped himself saying, 'I didn't.' Not knowing

that Rafferty had received only local injections he decided to give him the benefit of his growing doubts, give him time to sober up from the anaesthetic.

'They're carrying things indoors. So far mattresses, blankets, pillows, cartons of provisions. That is to say there are provisions at the top of the cartons. Could be anything underneath. Could be anything in the mattresses and pillows for that matter. Now what are they up to? Hold on.'

Two men had clambered into the van to join the one already there. Something heavy to be moved Stirling decided, but only a metal tool-box and a coil of electric cable were handed out and he took up his commentary. The heavy object appeared over the tail of the van a few moments later and the sixth man was summoned from the house to help with it. They waited for a small group of pedestrians to go by then, three a side, carried it on their shoulders through the gateway.

'Wooden crate about eight foot by three foot by – say three foot again. They look like bearers at a basketball player's funeral. Alternatively, they look like they're carrying what we're after.'

Rafferty thought about the drawings Paul Kravitz had given him of the containers found at the subterranean plant in Arizona. The metal boxes with their complex wiring systems connecting three separate timing devices to the conventional explosive, explosive which would blast the two stable sections of uranium together to form a devastating unstable mass. They were fitted with a manual trigger too, a fifth actuated by remote radio control and a number of booby-traps. All that was lacking was the fissile material. He thought about all these things and he thought about the dimensions shown on the drawings.

'I think we can rule out the basketball player,' he said. 'We'll hit them as soon as it's dark.'

'Wouldn't it be better to do it now before they get the bloody thing wired up, sir?'

'No, it wouldn't,' Rafferty told him. 'It's got a manual firing device. They may be the types who fancy being dead heroes.'

*

'Think they'll mind if I smoke this in here?'

'Probably have screaming hysterics, boss,' Rafferty said, 'but you can always pull rank, or say you're a visiting gynaecologist. Go ahead and smoke it.'

Barry glanced around the little ward which served both as preparation and recovery room, looked at the door to the operating theatre, then back at Rafferty propped up in bed.

He thought how ill, how much older, he seemed than the man who had driven him up from Dorset not so many days earlier. Slipping the pipe back into his pocket he rolled a cluster of hairs between finger and thumb until they stood out like a stake from the surrounding hedge of his beard.

'Came to say "thank you", Rafferty. Get a medal for you if the Department went in for that sort of thing. Don't know anyone else in the world who would have done that for me.'

'I didn't have a rush of gallantry to the head, boss. There wasn't time to do anything else and I didn't want to have to answer to Martha if you got hurt. Simple as that.'

'Martha? What the devil's Martha got to do with it?'

'She . . . she sort of put me in charge of you when I talked to her at the cottage.'

'She did what?'

'I think you heard me.'

'Then what did she *say*?'

'That,' Rafferty told him, 'can only be revealed after my death or posthumously, whichever is the sooner.'

'Rafferty!'

'Steady, boss, steady. I'm not supposed to get excited. They won't even let me see a nurse under seventy.' Rafferty paused, then in sudden irritation added, 'Oh, for God's sake! You know she's dotty about you. Go back to her. Jane Trelawney will drive you down this evening.'

Barry took his pipe from his pocket, looked at it and put it away again.

'Is that wise? I mean . . .' He made a fluttering motion with one hand. '. . . you and poor Jack Fenner. I'd rather drive myself, or go by train. I can't stand the thought of anything happening to Jane.'

'It won't,' Rafferty said. 'I hate to puncture your ego, but I think that grenade was meant for me, not you. Still, there's no point in taking chances and she's a brilliant car handler which I don't think you ever claimed to be. If there *is* any trouble she'll get you out of it. As for trains – well really, boss. How do you lose a tail on a train?'

When Barry had gone Rafferty wiped away the sweat which had gathered on his forehead and upper lip. He felt mentally sullied and wondered if Judas had experienced the same sensation. Angrily he pushed the thought out of his mind and reached for the telephone. Less than three hours to darkness and so much to think about.

'Jane, there's something I'd like to ask you to do. Would you mind coming down to this antiseptic broom cupboard for a few minutes?'

'I'll come at once.'

He closed his eyes and rehearsed what he was going to say to her, opening them again when he heard the handle of the door turn.

'Oh, Raff darling. You look so tired. The doctor said you were fine!'

She was beside him in four long strides, fingers smoothing hair back from his face, then resting against his cheek.

'I *am* fine. Just sore. Those two back-street abortionists we employ have been pulling chunks of old iron out of me. They removed one from what we of the medical fraternity refer to as the *gluteus maximus*, a process both painful and embarrassing. As you're not similarly afflicted, would you stop standing around looking seductive and sit down and listen to me?'

Pulling the only chair close to the bed she sat and looked at him, waiting for him to speak. When, after half a minute, he had not done so she said, 'It's all right, Raff. I'll take care of the Barry-Martha thing.'

'So you're a telepath too.'

'No. He stopped me in the passage and said it was kind of me to drive him back to Dorset.'

Rafferty nodded. 'This hasn't been my day for getting things in the right order. Or for much else.' He hesitated, then went on, 'I couldn't send Fiona Langley. I just couldn't.'

It was an enormous relief to him to see her smile the very

faintest of smiles and to hear her say, 'It's a strange thing. I seem to have grown harder than you over the years, but I couldn't have sent her on this job either. Now forget about it until I get back.'

Her words made him wonder bleakly if he would ever see her again, then he shrugged off the cold hands of foreboding and self-pity before they could grip, thankful for her presence now as he always had been when they had worked together. Strongly attracted to good-looking women, he had known many, loved some and been affected by each to varying degrees. Not much more than a week earlier he had been staggered by the slashing impact of Fiona Langley's sexuality, but had recovered quickly. It was the woman sitting beside him who had kept him off balance throughout the years by the simple fact of her being.

Content at having so successfully concealed his feelings for his friend's wife, he would have been dismayed to know the memory forming behind the face looking down at him, the memory of a conversation which had taken place a long time before.

'I believe Raff's in love with you,' Trelawney had said and been asked what was surprising about that.

'Well, is he?'

She had nodded her head vigorously. 'For absolutely years. I was rather gone on him myself at one time.'

He had wondered aloud why she hadn't married him and been told there were three reasons for that. 'First, he never proposed. Second, you needed me and he didn't. It's important to be needed.'

'And third?'

'Don't fish,' she had said.

Rafferty eased himself lower on the bed, winced, then, 'I'm very grateful,' he told her. 'We're going to be busy around here tonight. Stirling thinks he's spotted the bomb. So do I.'

'How shall you tackle it?'

He talked for several minutes, explaining what he intended to do and she was aware that he was doing it more for his own benefit than hers. She was his sounding board but, when he had finished, she asked only one question.

'Why you, Raff?'

'Because I'm still the best. I still have the edge on that big ape you're married to. If I hadn't, it would be him.'

He had spoken without conceit, stating a plain fact, but as though afraid of being considered arrogant he added, 'Anyway, the bloody man's always blowing things up. *That* we can do without tonight.'

It was true, she mused, that as a field agent Rafferty had been superb. What had Barry said? The best in Europe and amongst the three best in the world? Totally self-sufficient, he had asked for little and needed nobody other than a competent Mission Controller. But in the exalted and unwanted rank of Director he had floundered and sought her and her husband's help. Now he was going back into the field. No doubt he was content to do so, but this time it was clearly written in his face that he needed something from her, if only her garter to carry into battle. She didn't have a garter.

Jane Trelawney knelt by the bed and, careful not to touch the square of gauze behind one ear, gathered his head in her arms and drew it to her breasts.

The action broke the habit of years.

'Jane, I've always...'

'Hush, darling. I know.'

She felt the tensions draining from him one after the other like a series of strands parting until he lay passive, his breathing slow. Trelawney came almost soundlessly into the room. It never failed to surprise her that so big a man could move so quietly. At the shake of her head he went as quietly out again.

Five minutes later she released Rafferty's head, kissed him on the mouth and stood up.

'I'll take Charles Barry back to Dorset now,' she said.

He smiled up at her, but didn't reply.

One hundred and fifty minutes until he had to be at observation point B-Bravo. It felt better to him to think of it as one hundred and fifty minutes because it sounded longer than two and a half hours, more time to decide if he was right to act as he intended or if he should drop the whole thing in Whitehall's lap.

Three of the minutes slid by when he pulled the sheet up to his chin and his nostrils caught the lingering fragrance of her scent. He lay remembering, calling back the softness of her against his cheek. The time was not wasted because at the end of it he realized that he had been given her tacit agreement. 'Why you, Raff?' she had asked, not 'Why the Department?' and that had been all. It would not have been all had she believed any other organization better fitted to deal with the situation. She had never yet failed to tell him, even threaten him, when she thought he was pursuing the wrong course.

This was no wrong course. He pictured the alternative, the telephone call to the Minister, the emergency Cabinet meeting attended by the head of MI$_5$, the Chief of the Defence Staff, the Commissioner of the Metropolitan Police, all people who would, of necessity, need time to consider, to argue, to plan, when there was no time for any of those things. While the planning proceeded the men in House B–Bravo would be turning it into a fuse so delicate that to approach it too closely would result in detonation. He also would be at that and subsequent meetings, shackled to a conference table, impotent. And the troops, as slowly as the government dared, would withdraw from Ulster, setting the seal on the gravest example of international blackmail in history, setting a precedent for similar actions elsewhere, because there would be other Jefferies, other Gesners,

Another picture formed of himself required to explain why the Department had not revealed the existence of the suspect houses it had watched so carefully. That would come up eventually in any case but not, if he could help it, until the job was done. They could have his resignation then and anything else they demanded of him by way of restrictions on his personal liberty. Given luck the Service by which he set such store would remain unscathed.

'So that's that,' Rafferty said and startled himself by saying it aloud. He was surprised again when a glance at his watch told him how few minutes had passed since Jane had left. Moving with extreme caution he eased himself off the bed and began to walk slowly up and down the little room. The pain, the concentration it took and the rapidity with which he tired made him frown. He went back to bed, picked up the telephone and asked for Dr Fordham.

The doctor's face showed nothing but concern and Rafferty liked him better for that. He had expected resentment after the earlier exchange with him and the surgeon.

'Have you been trying to get out of bed, Mr Rafferty?'

'That's what I want to talk to you about,' Rafferty said and did so while the doctor felt his pulse.

'It's out of the question, Mr Rafferty. That head wound is very dangerous. As I've told you, you should be in a collar. The other one in your side is bad too. The splinter's lodged too close to the spinal column for safety and internal bleeding along the path of entry will . . .'

'Save it for your consulting room, doctor. You know the terms and conditions you are employed under. Just do as you're told.'

'I'm afraid I have to refuse. My terms of reference do not include helping you to commit suicide.'

Rafferty sighed, picked up the telephone, said, 'Send Reid here, please,' and replaced the receiver.

'Who's Reid?'

'A consultant.'

Neither man spoke again until Reid came into the room, then Rafferty said, 'Reid, I've had various bits and pieces of that grenade removed. A couple are still inside me. The general result is that it's difficult, painful and tiring to move around. I have to move around, but Dr Fordham here declines to help me get mobile. We have to make him change his mind.'

'What do you want him to do, sir?'

'I want him to give me a two-millilitre injection of Lignocaine beside each of the punctures you'll see when I turn over, except for the one at the back of the head. That doesn't hurt. Then I want a Dexedrine inhaler and a cocaine nasal spray to take along with me. When we've got that far he's to inject me with a one-millilitre one to one thousand solution of adrenalin. Have you got that?'

Reid repeated it back to him.

'Right. Now if he tries altering any of that, you remonstrate. Okay?'

'Okay, sir.'

Rafferty looked at Fordham and said, 'Let's get on with it, doc,' then addressed Reid again. 'One other thing. I don't want to seem to be a bad loser, Reid, but if he fools both of us by switching bottles or something and I appear to be anaesthetized as a result, kill him for me, will you?'

Reid nodded, took a gun from under his arm, a silencer from a pocket and screwed the two together.

CHAPTER THIRTY

The headlights of Jane Trelawney's replacement Cortina fanned across the country lane and illuminated the gate to the cottage. She slowed and parked beside it.

'I'm going to make a little driveway up to the foot of the terrace next,' Barry said.

'That'll be nice.'

'Dropitsir' appeared from somewhere, lumbered over the gate and cantered round and round the car like a small horse, barking in a frenzy of welcome.

'I should stay where you are for a minute, my dear, or you'll get covered in paw marks and slobber.'

'Very well.'

The terrace light came on, then Martha was running down the steps and along the path, her progress so fast that her limp was barely noticeable.

'Charles! Oh, Charles!'

Jane sat rigidly in the driving seat listening to the endearments, the questions, the assurances. She hoped fervently that she wasn't going to be sick on the road.

'Jane. Beautiful Jane. Thank you with all my heart for letting me have him safely back.'

She got out of the car and looked at Martha, hoping now that she would neither be sick nor cry. As steadily as she could, 'Thank Patrick Rafferty, not me. I'm only the taxi service,' she said.

'Well, come in. Come in. You'll stay the night of course.'

'Thank you, but I can't stay long. I must get back to Town tonight.'

'Dropitsir' attached himself to her as she followed the couple slowly towards the cottage and she patted his big, shaggy head absently. At the entrance Martha pushed the reluctant dog outside and closed the door on it.

'Drink or wash first, Jane?'

Jane's voice sounded like a polite schoolgirl's when she

answered, 'Neither, thank you, Martha. I'd like you to go and sit on the sofa. Charles, would you please sit beside her?'

They stood where they were, looking calmly at the gun in Jane's hand. The hand was steady and the gun pointed at Martha. Barry raised an eyebrow.

'I'm perfectly serious,' Jane said. 'Sit down, both of you.'

They moved to the sofa and sat down side by side.

'What's all this about, Jane? What do you want?'

'Two things, Charles. First, the key to the numbers cipher. "Codes" think it's some form of "one-time pad". They can't break it.'

'I haven't the remotest idea what you're talking about and if you feel you must point that thing at someone kindly point it at me, not at Martha.'

'Very gallant, Charles, but I shall do this my way. The cipher I'm talking about is the one you found in the Director's safe and drew Rafferty's attention to. It was typed on the portable you keep in this cottage, presumably by Martha as you don't type.'

'You're mistaken, Jane. I don't know where you got this misinformation, but I assure you that you *are* mistaken. Now please put that gun away!'

Jane stood, long legs astride, the gun held almost at arm's length in both hands pointing unwaveringly at Martha's right shoulder.

'You have fifteen seconds,' she said.

'To do what?'

'To tell me the key.'

'My dear girl, I . . .'

'Twelve seconds.'

'And what will happen after twelve seconds?'

'I shall shoot Martha,' Jane said, 'and that will be very horrid. I'll try not to hurt her too much, but I shall shoot her again and again until you tell me what I want to know. Five seconds.'

Barry lay back on the sofa looking at the lovely woman he had known and admired for so long, a woman Martha had unsuccessfully conspired to marry him to because she imagined herself to be unacceptable to him in the crippled state to which the Gestapo had reduced her. Jane was incapable of causing her further injury. It followed, therefore, that she was bluffing.

The slam of the gunshot was shocking in the small room. Martha gave a tiny shriek, then was silent, staring wide-eyed at Jane. Blood seeped between the fingers clutching her shoulder. Outside, 'Dropitsir' ran twice up and down the terrace barking, then subsided with a rumbling growl, his duty done.

In a breathy whisper Barry said, 'You wicked, wicked woman.'

'Yes, Charles, but don't let's fuss about it. Martha has experienced much worse. It's only a skin graze.' Jane shifted her aim fractionally before adding, 'But I'm afraid the next one will be a bit more severe.' The weight of the gun was dragging at her arms, but she shut the discomfort out of her mind. 'Only ten seconds this time.'

Dully Barry said, 'It isn't a "one-time pad", it's the marked pages of a book. Havelock-Templeton and I had identical copies.'

'What book?'

'Bulwer Lytton's *The Last Days of Pompeii*. It's on the shelf there.'

Not quite aloud, 'How appallingly appropriate,' Jane said.

'What did you say?'

'Nothing at all.'

She let the gun hang loosely at her side, walked to the bookcase and found the volume. The margins of the pages were filled with neatly printed digits joined individually by ruled lines to a letter in the text. 'A' to 'J' numbered randomly nought to nine, 'K' to 'T' the same and so on, she assumed, for the remainder of the alphabet. Each number had been crossed out as its corresponding letter had been used and the letter was represented by a different digit when it appeared again. Cumbersome but unbreakable without the key.

'May I get Martha a brandy, please?'

Jane gestured with the gun towards the oak chest which served as a bar. 'You'd better have one too and it might be an idea to clean that wound of hers with some of it. You can fix it up properly when I've gone.' She dropped the book into her bag and watched while Barry poured the drinks and soaked his handkerchief with cognac.

'Don't take this too badly, Charles,' she said.

The top of his body jerked furiously towards her.

'How dare you? We invite you into our home, you threaten us, you shoot Martha and you have the gall to . . .' Abruptly he stopped talking and, for a moment, she thought he was going to cry, then he breathed in unsteadily and returned to the sofa. Both sipped at their drinks before he began to wipe the blood from the furrow the bullet had ploughed in Martha's upper arm.

'Jane?'

'Yes?'

'Please don't decode those figures.'

'Why not?'

'The whole thing's a list of names and activities of extremely dangerous people connected with the Trades' Union movement. It was compiled at Julian Havelock-Templeton's request and consists of British and foreigners. He had plans to discredit them or, if necessary, dispose of them when they were abroad. It hadn't occurred to me that he would authorize a killing in this country.'

'So?'

'I'll give you every name on the list. Just *please* don't decode it.'

'Why not?' Jane asked for the second time.

Barry gulped down the rest of his brandy before saying, 'I gave Rafferty to understand that I had obtained the details of the Pole Dyboski from contacts in MI5, the CIA and my then opposite number in Paris. Only Dyboski. There are, in fact, many others. I . . . We . . .' He scowled and fell silent.

Martha put her hand on his and he turned to her and said, 'I'm so very sorry, my dear.'

She smiled at him, then spoke to Jane.

'He's trying to tell you that much of the research work was done by me through my contacts, including old friends from the French Resistance days. It was necessary to quote sources in the list to grade the reliability of the information. These sources implicate me and that, I imagine, is what Charles is so anxious to avoid.'

Loudly Barry said, 'Every successive government has known for years that some of the labour leaders are dedicated to the destruction of the democratic system. They couldn't care less about the welfare of the workers. Other Western countries handle such matters with discreet force, but we're inhibited by something called a "public conscience" which is a succubus sapping the nation's strength. Havelock-Templeton and I were in complete agreement that the time had come to exorcise that demon and act.'

Under different circumstances Jane would have smiled at such an oration coming from Barry, but there was no humour in her now and she heard him out gravely.

'Due to the irregularity of the position,' Barry went on, 'it was impossible for Julian to confide in his own staff and that's where I came in. Very willingly I might add and it's a tragedy that, after so many years of service to the country, Martha and I have been unable to render this final . . . Oh, what's the use? It's all gone sour on us now, but I warn you, Jane, if any connection is made between that list and the killing of Dyboski it will do the Department irreparable harm.'

'He really does believe that that is what this is all about,' Jane told herself. 'I suppose that's something to be thankful for.'

Aloud she said, 'Perhaps you should have thought of that before you involved yourselves in this idiocy. Where's your typewriter?'

'On the floor beside the desk. Why?'

'Because I said there were two things I wanted. We're now going to deal with the second.'

She fitted paper into the Olivetti and placed the machine on an incidental table beside Martha.

'Type as I dictate.'

Martha glanced at her blood-smeared left hand, shrugged and waited.

'To whom it may concern, I, Charles Henry Barry, and I, Martha Louise Cartwright, did, as private citizens . . . in collusion with other parties . . . plan and carry out the murder . . . of Vernon George Whiteoaks previously known as . . . Piotr Gregor Dyboski, a Trades' Union official . . .'

Jane Trelawney spoke for nearly two minutes, her words interspersed with the rattle of the little portable, then, 'Don't date it. Both of you sign it,' she said.

Barry took his pen from his pocket, scrawled his signature, handed the pen to Martha and looked coldly at Jane.

'You'll never use it. You'd destroy the Department if you did.'

She shook her head. 'Don't delude yourself, Charles. We'd destroy you and Martha who no longer belong, and Miss Langley who is a Director's appointment unknown to the Minister. The only other participant is dead. Remember this piece of paper if you ever feel like stepping out of line again.'

Picking up the signed confession she folded it, put it in her handbag and walked to the door.

Before she reached it Martha said, 'Thank you, Jane.'

The words sounded genuine and she turned and looked at the small elderly lady questioningly.

'That was very difficult for you. You knew that the only way to make one of us talk was to hurt the other.'

'It had occurred to me.'

'And you have never liked hurting people. It was good of you not to take the easy path and send Fiona Langley.'

Letting herself quickly out of the cottage Jane walked down the terrace steps and along the path to the gate. 'Dropitsir' went with her, his stump of tail flicking back and forth like a metronome.

She drove towards the village which, a signpost told her, was a mile and a half away. In the darkness of the midnight street it took her a moment to identify the general store which served also as a post office. Parked in front of it she took an envelope from her handbag, addressed it to Barry and stamped it, then set the confession alight along its top edge, watching it burn until only parts of the last three lines and the signatures remained. She extinguished the flame, put the blackened fragments with the remaining scrap of paper into the envelope and sealed it.

Driving through the lanes she thought about the envelope now lying in the red post office box set into the wall of the village shop and hoped that it would reach them by the afternoon post. They had had to be taught a lesson, to be shown that any attempt to *use* the Department for any purpose, mistaken or otherwise, brought retribution, but she had no desire to prolong the punishment. Her message would be clear to them and there would be no question of their interfering again.

When she reached the M3 she drove steadily towards London, holding her speed precisely on the 70 mph limit, wanting no delays while a policeman laboriously wrote her out a ticket, wanting to reach the city at the earliest possible moment to be near her husband and the rest of the people who made up her life. Losing, as she assumed she must have done, two friends in one day, the thought of losing more, all of them really, was unbearable. If they were to die she would rather die with them.

She had no very clear idea of what it looked like when it happened, except for long-range shots of mushroom clouds seen at the cinema or on television. But there had been another, hadn't there? A government information release so unbelievably awful that, until now, she had chosen to forget about it. With no warning at all the entire screen had turned glaringly white, then slowly, very slowly, the sky had begun to reappear at the edges of the brightness, moving inwards to outline the heaving boiling horror of the fireball.

The brilliant undipped headlights of a car joining the motorway from a slip-road flicked across her eyes and she cringed. The cringe was followed by a shudder and Jane Trelawney, who rarely swore out loud, said, 'Fuck the police!' and pressed the accelerator flat.

CHAPTER THIRTY-ONE

The door of the room designated observation point B–Bravo opened to Rafferty's tap and he found himself facing Stirling's gun. He knew it was Stirling because the back glow from the pencil-torch which played for a moment on his own face glinted briefly on blond hair.

'Why are you still here, Stirling? You've been on watch for hours.'

'Dunno, Mr Rafferty. Reid was supposed to relieve me. Probably picked up a bird on his way here. Doesn't matter now. I'd like to see this thing through anyway.'

'Reid,' Rafferty said, 'is our new consultant physician. Very good at it he is too.'

'Oh, is that right? Well, talking of physicians, from the glimpse I had of you just now you look bloody awful, if you don't mind my saying so.'

'I don't mind at all,' Rafferty told him. 'Just don't let it break you up.'

Stirling's remark had surprised him because he was feeling so much better, almost exhilarated. He knew that that and the tingling need for action was the adrenalin injection at work in his system, but it hadn't occurred to him that his apparent well-being was not reflected in his face. Nothing was hurting at the moment although, he thought, a little pain would have been preferable to the fact that his left arm seemed to be dying on him. The hand worked all right, but the arm . . . Damage to nerve or muscle in the shoulder he supposed and moved towards the dimly seen tripods near the centre of the room. There were two of them. The first supported an image intensifier, the other a long tubular object he recognized as one of Young's tight-beam listening devices.

Across the road, lights in a few windows glowed through curtains and a grimy street lamp added its quota of illumination. House B–Bravo was dark, the furniture van gone, taking, as Stirling had reported to him before he had left Thayer Street, three of the men with it. It was this last fact which had convinced him that he was right to go in alone. The odds had shortened and two people could get in each other's way in the darkness.

'Any change, Stirling?'

'They've rigged an alarm system on the downstairs left-hand window, sir. I watched them do that. It's possible they've fixed the door too from the noises I got from this thing of Young's, but I couldn't see them at it. When it got dark they packed it in. Didn't want to show lights I suppose.'

'Where are they now? In the cellar?'

Rafferty could just make out the affirmative movement of the fair head. 'I think so. There was some noise from down there half an hour ago. Nothing since, not that I've heard anyway and the stylograph's been dead steady.' Stirling shone his torch briefly on the recorder and added, 'Still is.'

'They've probably nodded off with the grinding boredom of it all,' Rafferty said. 'Is that van down the road Trelawney's lot?'

'Yeah. They arrived just before you knocked.'

'Okay. Signal them to move in the moment you hear the trouble start.'

On his way down the stairs to the ground floor Rafferty paused at Stirling's quiet call.

'Yes?'

'Suppose they manage to take you silently, Mr Rafferty. What then?'

'That's right. Ruin my heroic bit,' Rafferty replied. 'There's no way they can take me silently. Now get back to your ear-trumpet.'

Rafferty strolled across the road towards his target. There were few people about and none of them close except the uniformed figure of Peter Geddes moving towards him from the direction of the van with the slow stiff-legged gait policemen seem to acquire. That presence would keep the curious away until he was inside the house. He turned into the tangle of vegetation which had once been a garden and pushed his way through it to the right-hand downstairs window.

Three things, he thought, were in his favour. They would have no reason to anticipate an attack, at least yet, because they did not know that, out of the whole vast expanse of London, some or all of their houses were under observation. Then they were badly led. It had been an error in co-ordination to deliver their ultimatum before the bomb had been safely housed. Gesner's arrest had probably resulted in that muddle. And here at this house why had they wired one window and the door, instead of both windows, leaving the door bolted? Stupid.

Finally, and most vital of all, was the human desire to stay alive. However much of a fanatic a man might be Rafferty considered that, from the moment the cellar door blew in, the most dedicated would require a minimum of two seconds to reach and carry out the decision to vaporize himself. In their shocked condition he didn't think it would be very difficult to kill three men in two seconds.

Before he began work on the window with a glass-cutter he took the bottle of cocaine solution from a pocket and squeezed a spray up each nostril.

Stirling saw Reid leave the van and start in his direction, then turned his attention back to Rafferty. The big pane of glass had been cut along three sides now and a rubber suction cup was fixed to it. He was watching the cutter begin its travel across the top edge when Reid tapped for admittance.

'Trelawney's appointed me "runner",' Reid said. 'I wonder when somebody will invent radio.'

'You want to broadcast this?'

'Hmm. Maybe you have a point for once.'

Stirling went back to the sniperscope and said, 'Oh, for Christ's sake don't start over-acting, Geddes.'

'What's he doing?'

'His impersonation of a copper. There's some people coming and he's standing in the gateway going up and down on his toes. I just hope he can resist saying, "Hello, hello, hello. What's going on here, then?"'

Reid yawned audibly and said, 'Trelawney wants to know how Rafferty was just before he went over there.'

'He was okay. He sounded a little dopey on the blower from Hospital Section. Asked the wrong questions. That sort of thing. I was worried, but it was only the anaesthetic. Either that or he's taken a crash course in rejuvenating pills for the over forties. His face looked drawn, but he . . . Oh, my God! I should have guessed! He told me there was no way they could take him without us hearing. The stupid Kamikaze bastard!'

'What are you talking . . . ?'

With quiet authority Stirling said, 'Shut up. Get back to Trelawney. Tell him Rafferty's cut his way through the glass and is going in with a grenade in his left hand with the pin out. If they hit him over the head we'll hear all right. You'd better move up to the garden and . . .'

He stopped talking at the sound of Reid's feet clattering down the stairs.

They'd taken the door at the top of the cellar steps off the hinges. A glance at the house plans had shown that they'd have to do that to get an eight-foot object down, but what pleased Rafferty was that they hadn't bothered to put it back on again. He stood without moving for a full five minutes, listening, waiting for his eyes to adjust to the darkness. There was nothing to be heard from the direction of the cellar, but very gradually the second door began to take shape. After another minute he knew only that it was a door, a closed door, and that he'd learn nothing more about it by staying where he was.

The beam of his pencil-torch danced flickeringly down the steps then was immediately extinguished. Stone. No trip-wires. No reaction from the cellar. They could, he thought, have stretched black cotton threads connected to some alarm from wall to wall at waist height, but he had no intention of using his torch again to find out. He put it away, eased himself to the ground, clasped the American M3 submachine-gun hanging from his neck against his stomach with his right hand and began to slide feet first from step to step.

'It isn't a good combat weapon, sir,' Young had told him 'Looks like a grease gun. In fact that's what they call it – a grease gun.'

'What have its looks to do with anything?'

'Nothing, sir, except it's too short, it's inaccurate and it kicks up so hard you have to force it down all the time you're firing.'

'I like it,' Rafferty had said.

He did like it. He liked its shortness which had made it easy to conceal under a raincoat, easy to handle now and which would enable him to pivot readily. He liked the heavy .45 calibre slugs it fired too. Young had given him lead ones with concave noses and he doubted if he would need to hit anybody more than once.

His back was hurting badly by the time he reached the bottom. There was no pain in those places where he had received injections, but further in from one of them it felt as though a cat was extending and retracting its claws. For a while he lay still, fighting the pain, subduing it, trying to will it out of existence. Partially he succeeded, but the effort left him dizzy and he used the cocaine nasal spray again. When his head cleared he crawled cautiously to the door and took a lump of plastic explosive from his pocket. As he did so a twitch of cramp in the fingers of his left hand told him of the appalling mistake he had made. The realization of it brought on a strange calmness because, he supposed, there was nothing to be done.

The grenade he had instructed his left hand to grip, to hold the lever down, then virtually forgotten about, had never been part of his attack plan. It was to have been a fail-safe warning device for those above had he been struck down before he reached his present position. It could not be used against the three men on the other side of the door.

He had asked Young if a grenade could detonate an atomic bomb and been told that it was highly improbable, but that it might cause a radiation leak. One booby-trapped with a trembler fuse? That had been a different matter. A trembler fuse's basic purpose was to prevent one moving a bomb. A grenade exploding close might move it enough to activate the fuse and there was no way of telling where a grenade might roll.

His mood changed and he thought of the thing in his hand with sudden loathing because its presence deprived him of the right to die, even to lose consciousness when the job was done. If he did either the start of Doomsday could be seven seconds after his fingers lost the power to keep the lever depressed. How much of London would go in the blast it might cause? How many hundreds of thousands of people would go with it? He had no idea and knew only that the metal pineapple he was holding was at the root of potential world disaster.

As quickly as it had gone reason returned to him. Weapons were neutral. They were better than neutral, they were blameless. But for his own stupidity this one could have been rendered harmless by re-inserting the split-pin he had so casually tossed into the weeds outside the house. For a moment he toyed with the idea of disposing of it upstairs, timed to go off when the plastic explosive did. No go. A second's miscalculation and . . . He winced at the mental picture of Trelawney blasted back out of the window he had just vaulted through. Resignedly he worked his tiring hand into his trouser pocket. At least the grenade wouldn't roll anywhere from there.

Rafferty moulded the small lump of plastic explosive at keyhole level into the angle formed by door and brickwork, then pressed the detonator with its four-second length of fuse into it. The little flash of flame from his lighter which ignited the fuse showed him that the door was close-fitting, handleless, held shut by a cylinder lock. The knowledge pleased him because the use of cyanide gas which he had thought about and discarded would have been impracticable with no ready means of introducing it into the cellar. He was half-way up the steps and turning when the plastic charge exploded. Neither the sound nor the blast effect was sufficient to disorientate him and when he tore the strip from a magnesium flare with his teeth and tossed it downwards he saw by its blinding light that the door was now a single splintered board still attached to the hinges.

Only vaguely aware of the partial paralysis in his legs he went through the opening into the brilliance of the cellar with a crab-like shuffle. The M3 was worse than Young had described it, much worse with only one hand to hold it, but the startled expression on the face of one of the men disintegrated into a featureless red mass.

He was cleverer with the second, firing to the left of his feet, letting the gun stitch its pattern diagonally up and across the man's body. The third of them lay dead, a large splinter of wood from the door deeply embedded in his neck. Rafferty killed him again with a savage burst from the M3 and was thinking of doing the same to the others when Trelawney took the gun from his hand.

'Ah, there you are,' Rafferty said, but didn't hear himself say it because the thunder of the M3 was still reverberating inside his skull.

The machined surface of the long metal box lying against one wall reflected the light of the flare with a dizzying intensity like the rays of a rising tropic sun on water. Rafferty looked at it, nodding his head and smiling.

'It didn't go off,' he said, heard the words that time and repeated them as though imparting some crucial piece of information.

'Where's the grenade, sir?'

Rafferty turned to the speaker. 'Hello, Stirling. What grenade?'

'You had a grenade. You pulled the pin and threw it away. I watched you do it.'

'Yes, of course. It's in my hand in this pocket. Could you help me with it? Be careful. I pulled the pin and threw it away. What's that policeman doing here? Oh, it's you, Peter.'

Reid and Stirling eased his hand from his pocket and slowly prised the grenade free of fingers that refused to open.

'Be careful with that thing. I threw the pin away,' Rafferty said and Trelawney caught him as he fell.

He was outside the house before he realized that someone was carrying him. The blurred face above him looked like Trelawney's, but much more clearly he could see the face of the man who had thrown the grenade. Not his grenade. That wouldn't go off because he was holding the lever down. The one that *had* gone off. The one from the white van. Better tell someone.

'Is that you, Al?'

Trelawney's mind jumped back over the years and he remembered another man he had carried, an Arab who had never been able to pronounce his name. 'Is that Mr Trorny?' he had asked and died shortly afterwards. He pulled himself sharply back to the present.

'Yes, Raff.'

Rafferty giggled. 'We can't go on meeting like this.' He giggled again at the old, old joke, then quietened. That hadn't been what he wanted to say. Frantically he searched amongst the clouds drifting in his brain, but it seemed an age before he found what he needed.

'Al?'

'Yes, Raff?'

'The man who threw the grenade was Grenville. Pull him in, squeeze him dry, then bury him. When he's dead tell Jack Fenner's girl.'

'Are you quite sure it was Grenville?'

There was no reply and, when Trelawney felt for it, there was no pulse.

Somebody hadn't closed the gates of the old lift properly on one of the floors and it ignored the stabbing of her finger on the call button.

'Damn and blast the thing!' Jane Trelawney said and took to the stairs, running the whole way up to their studio apartment on the eighth floor. She had her keys in her hand before she reached it, slid one into the lock and flung the door wide. For a moment she stood smiling happily at the sight of her husband and the look of pleasure which leapt into life on his face, then her legs gave under her and she found herself sitting on the floor with tears running down her cheeks.

He strode to her side and lifted her as though she weighed nothing, whispering, 'Jane, Jane, Jane.'

She sniffed loudly once and in a perfectly calm voice said,

'How bloody stupid. I'm so sorry. I've been doing some very horrid imaginings, but as you're here at home it must be going to be all right.'

'Yes, it's all right. The bomb disposal people have disarmed the thing and taken it away, but I'm afraid that . . .'

He frowned, black eyebrows almost meeting over his nose, and looked at the face so close to his own as if seeking help.

'Poor Raff,' she said.

'You knew?'

'Not *knew*, darling. We've been together a long time now and you aren't difficult for me to read. Also I think he was saying goodbye to me in Hospital Section. How was he killed?'

'He killed himself. Dr Fordham tells me that there were two pieces of metal in him he wouldn't let them touch. Exertion could have caused either one to kill him.'

Trelawney began to pace slowly down the room.

'Al?'

'Mmm?'

'Are you going to carry me around until breakfast?'

'Oh,' he said, kissed her where her neck joined her shoulder and set her on her feet. She turned at once and walked to her handbag lying where she had dropped it near the door.

'Raff asked me to bring you this from Dorset. It's the key to the numbers cipher.'

Taking the copy of *The Last Days of Pompeii* from her he moved his hand up and down as if judging the weight of the book.

'Barry gave you this?'

'Yes.'

'Then why the blazes didn't he produce it before?'

'He didn't *want* to give it to me, darling. He . . . It was rather horrid. I had to shoot Martha before he would.'

He smiled at her. 'Martha can't be very badly damaged.'

'Why do you say that?'

'Because it was only *rather* horrid.'

Unsteadily Jane said, 'Don't tease me, Al. Not now. Not tonight. It's been a . . . a tiresome day.'

'It's been all of that,' he agreed. 'Let's have something to eat, then we'll have a go at the numbers. I've got a photocopy of them here.'

An hour and a quarter later Trelawney put down his pencil and looked at the list of twenty-two names and the notes relating to them. He picked the pencil up again and struck out Dyboski and Gesner. Jefferies and Hatoyama did not appear on the list, but Dorothy McDowell did. Of the remaining nineteen he knew of only four, all of them public figures of no great distinction. There was no mention of Grenville. It did not surprise him. Had there been, Havelock-Templeton would have warned the Minister of that at least. He added the name to the end of the list and picked up the telephone while Jane watched him curiously.

'Good morning, Reid. This is Trelawney. Sorry to wake you so early, but I've got a job for you and Stirling.'

When he had given his instructions he told his wife what Rafferty's last words had been.

CHAPTER THIRTY-TWO

A group of five girls went up the steps, faces animated, heads close together, maintaining direction without observation as only girls can. A middle-aged man followed them, looking at their legs. Two, slightly younger, came behind, arms and brief-cases swinging in unison.

'Stop!'

The figures on the conference room screen froze and Trelawney turned to face the slits in the projection box wall.

'I think that's him in the dark pin-stripe, going through the door now with his head turned away. Let's see if you caught him from the other side, Stirling.'

A minute later, 'Yes, that's Grenville,' he said. 'Well done. Have that printed and take it round with pictures of anybody to the outfit that leased the white van. See if they pick him out. We're past the stage of worrying about scaring people off, so play it straight. You're just a couple of cops looking for a man. Have you got your police warrants from "Documentation"?'

'Yes, sir,' one of the slits said, 'Reid's a bloody Inspector again. I'm getting cheesed off.'

'Never mind, Stirling,' Trelawney told him. 'You get a positive identification on Grenville and I'll let you be a Chief Superintendent.'

Less than two hours had gone by when Trelawney answered a call from Reid.

'Stirling says to tell you he's been promoted Chief Superintendent, sir.'

'Thank you very much,' Trelawney said. Then untypically explaining the obvious, 'I had to be absolutely sure.'

The Minister listened to Trelawney's report in silence and when it was done his remarks were guarded. Whatever relief he had felt when first he had been told the outcome of the night's events had not lived in him strongly enough to survive into the afternoon. He was attentive but not congratulatory, polite but not cordial, sorry about Rafferty's death but not saddened by it. When he left the inner office Trelawney knew that the cones giving warning of an impending storm had been hoisted and hoped it would not break before the following day. Given luck he would be ready for it by then.

He stopped by Grenville's desk and said diffidently, 'Could we have a word?'

Grenville looked up at him, saying nothing, and Trelawney went on, 'I'm afraid I rather got off on the wrong foot with you when I came here the other day. I was extremely officious. State of shock probably. Anyway, I'd like to apologize.'

'Very well. I accept your apology.'

Trelawney smiled, made as if to leave, then said, 'Look. I've got a few friends coming in for drinks tonight. Would you care to join us? I mean it would help me to feel that I'd made amends. Six-thirty if you can manage it.'

He stood, the idiotic smile fixed on his face, watching the wheels turn in the other's mind. Trelawney's in trouble. So's the Department. He needs a 'friend at court'. A look into his private life might tell me something, something I could pass on to the Minister.

'Civil of you, Trelawney. I'd like that very much.'

'Not a bit of it. It's civil of you,' Trelawney told him and walked out of the room.

The man stopped just inside the doorway of the studio apartment looking at the group of people standing at the far end of the big room, listening to the voices, to the quiet laughter. Nobody paid any attention to him. Absently he surrendered his hat to Trelawney.

'Where on earth did you find them?'

'Find what?' Trelawney asked.

'Those two stunning women by the window.'

'Oh. Well, the one on the left is my wife. I found her in Libya a long time ago. Go over and introduce yourself while I get you a drink. Gin or whisky?'

'Whisky, please, with water. No ice,' the man said then added, 'That was a pretty tasteless observation of mine. I didn't know. My turn to apologize.'

'I don't see what's tasteless about a compliment,' Trelawney told him. 'Anyway, I agree with you.'

The new arrival nodded and moved in the direction of his hostess.

At his approach Jane Trelawney said, 'Excuse me,' to the other woman, half turned and held out her hand to him.

'You must be Mr Grenville.'

'Yes, I'm Christopher Grenville, Mrs Trelawney.'

'How nice of you to come. Now let me see, I don't think you know Fiona Langley, do you?'

She stayed for a moment, hearing the couple talking to each other, not hearing what they were saying. She was thinking of a day at the zoo when she had watched through the armoured glass while a keeper dropped a live mouse into a compartment containing a snake. The result had disgusted her and, illogically, she had hated the keeper for doing his job. Now she saw herself as that keeper and wondered how long it would take the mouse she had dropped to die. Nausea moved in her stomach, but she felt no compassion. The memory of Rafferty, and the imagined fireball like an after-image on the retina, were too vivid for that. The doorbell rang again and she walked thankfully away from them to answer it.

Grenville and Fiona Langley left together after ninety minutes, but another half an hour passed before the last guests took their leave. Jane closed the door behind them and leant her back against it.

'And Barry was claiming that we were inhibited by a public conscience,' she said. 'Admittedly his assumed circumstances were rather different.'

Trelawney nodded, not speaking.

She watched him for a moment, then pushed herself away from the door and gave him a darting kiss before saying, 'Off you go. I'll tidy up this clutter. You've got a large slice of that conscience to keep now.'

He nodded again. 'But possibly only for a few hours.'

'I know, darling,' she said. 'You'd better use them carefully.'

'It had AU/80 stencilled on it,' Trelawney said and heard Paul Kravitz's voice in the ear-piece saying, 'Uhuh. Reads like good news to me. We have BU through EU stroke 80 at Sedona. Seems maybe Jefferies was telling the truth and yours was the only one that got away. I sure as hell hope so.'

'Don't you *know* if he was telling the truth, Mr Kravitz?'

'Paul. Make it Paul. I can't swear to it. The FBI handled the interrogation, not us.' Kravitz hesitated before adding, 'Oh hell, I guess I know it all right. We and the Feds say some hard things about each other from time to time, but they ain't stupid. With Kassel not yet in full production and nothing found around Durham I guess you're in the clear as of now.'

Trelawney made two more calls before putting the bomb out of his mind and turning his attention to the mass of material on other matters which had accumulated over recent days. He decided to work until 2 a.m. and then go home. His phone rang at 1.27.

'Yes?'

'Darling, your presence is required here. One is given to understand that your failure to arrive in twenty minutes will make you a widower. Coming accompanied or armed will have the same distressing result. Oh, and you're to come through the door, not the skylight, for the same reason.'

The connection was cut before he could say anything, not, he thought, that there had been anything worth saying. Her voice had been controlled, but pitched higher than was normal. That told him that she was very frightened, but she had also told him something very important. Never in his life had he heard her use such an expression as 'One is given to understand'. It meant that there was only one person with her and the knowledge produced a faint flicker of hope. Taking a knife from a drawer in his desk he left the building, his mind as blank as he could make it because he was afraid of what thought might do to him.

He remembered little of the journey to their flat, driving

like an automaton, moving like one when he left the car outside the apartment block. Once he had spoken her name aloud, spoken it without expression as though it were a password he was called upon to give, not repeating it.

The knife had slit the material of the inside pocket of his jacket and dropped until the hilt had halted its fall. Trelawney took it out, put it inside his sock behind his right leg and forced the point down into the heel of his shoe. Then he pressed the call button for the lift.

Jane, wrists and ankles tied, was sitting on an upright chair in a pool of light cast by an angle-poise lamp. She was naked.

'Shut the door, Trelawney, and go and stand by your wife.'

The voice coming from an armchair was instantly recognizable. He did as he was told, moving cautiously, his whole attention on the barrels of the sawn-off shotgun pointing steadily at Jane.

'Take your coat off and throw it behind you . . . Now your shirt and tie . . . Turn round . . . Face me.'

Each command was obeyed slowly, reluctantly, but it was obeyed.

'Raise your trouser legs.' At that one he held his breath, but it was all right.

'Run your hands down the insides of your thighs . . . Good. Very good indeed. We can get on with the job and it's this. You are going to kill your wife in a fit of passion. I think we'll have the rest of your clothes off for that. More realistic. How you do it is entirely up to you. Strangle her if you wish, or use one of those clever hand chops you're so good at. I don't mind and I'm sure she'd prefer you doing it rather than being shot in the stomach by me. It would take her a long time to die that way.'

The voice stopped and Trelawney stood watching light glinting dimly on the gun until it came again.

'When I am satisfied that she is quite dead you will blow your head off in an anguish of remorse. I shall assist you in that. Now strip!'

He spoke for the first time. 'Do you mind explaining why you are doing this?'

'Not at all. I'd like you to know. You and your friends took away from me the only thing that made life worth living. An opportunity to exact retribution for that came my way. You two will be part of that retribution and also the means of gaining me a little credit with my employers. I need that because, thanks to you, the assignment I was given hasn't worked out as well as it should have done. Strip! I shan't tell you again.'

Trelawney stood on one foot fumbling with his right shoe. He was trembling visibly and not all of it was acting. When, with a viciousness he didn't know he possessed, he had thrown the knife he launched himself after it, covering Jane from the blast of the gun.

There was no blast. The only thing to hit him was the gun itself tossed away as if rejected by the figure that lurched forward from the chair before sagging to the floor.

He stood looking down at the dead girl. One arm lay by her side, the other at a hundred and eighty degrees to it as though she were doing the back stroke. The knife had entered just below the sternum and from the downward angle of the handle he knew that the point of the blade had pierced her heart. There was almost no bleeding when he pulled it out. No more than enough to form a small circular stain on the material of her dress. It occurred to him that her Olympic Bronze medal would be about that size and would have hung just there.

'What a very horrid experience for you, my love.'

Jane's voice came from behind him. 'No, just *rather* horrid. On occasions there's something frighteningly implacable about you, darling. The moment you came into the room I knew who was going to die.'

Lightly Trelawney said, 'Well, you might have mentioned it at the time.' He paused before adding, 'It never occurred to me that Sue Mitchell could be Foster's ghost. But it should have done. She went through a very unstable period after her chap – what was the name of that trainee she lived with?'

'Matthews.'

'That's him. Jerry Matthews. After he was killed in that practise mobile surveillance pile-up in Surrey. She should have been suspended indefinitely. I could kick myself!'

'I'm sure you could, darling, but would you untie me first? I'm getting awfully cold.'

Trelawney turned slowly away from the body on the floor and smiled at his wife's spot-lit form.

'Did I,' he asked, 'ever tell you that you have elegant breasts?'

EPILOGUE

'Consequently, with a split vote the decision rests with me and it is with considerable regret that I have to tell you it is thumbs down. My recommendation will be that you be asked to resign.'

'I think such a recommendation would be ill-advised, Minister,' Trelawney said.

'No doubt you do, but the matter is not open to argument. Nobody is denying the fact that a remarkable job was done by Rafferty, you and others in the Department, or that we are deeply in your debt. Having said that, however, it is equally true that a government agency which acts on its own initiative over a situation from which the most appalling consequences might well have ensued with no reference to those in authority over it is in need of new leadership.'

'We followed the course we believed to be right, Rafferty died for that belief and there were no appalling consequences. Why cavil at success, sir?'

The Minister moved irritably in his chair and said, 'Oh, come on, Trelawney. You and Rafferty knew the location of the bomb for some hours before you condescended to tell me. You must have known of their "safe" houses for days and I have no idea *yet* what other vital information you withheld. We don't do things that way in this country and you haven't got a leg to stand on.'

He snapped his fingers sharply before adding, 'In any event, as I have told you, the matter is not open to argument. Nevertheless, I can tell you that you will be offered full retired pay as appropriate to the Director of the Department. This is partly a mark of gratitude, partly compensation for loss of office. Although you never filled the post you were very likely to have done so had circumstances been different. Are we agreed?'

Without hesitation, 'No,' Trelawney told him. 'I'm not prepared to consider retirement. The situation isn't completely defused yet. There are things to do and people to be dealt with. Too many know about this as it is. If you want to keep it from the public, as I assume you do, don't bring anybody else in. Just let the Department and its contacts tie up the loose ends.'

His voice had been rising as he spoke, countering the Minister's angry attempts at interruption and he ended by saying, 'Please don't tell me again that the matter is not open to argument. Let me tell you that if I go down you will have more to answer for than your political career could stand.'

For a moment there was silence then, as if the question was of little consequence, the man behind the big desk asked, 'Are you threatening a Minister of the Crown?'

Ignoring the question Trelawney asked one of his own.

'What excuse did your secretary, Mr Grenville, give you for not coming to work this morning, Minister?'

'*Grenville?*'

'Grenville.'

'He said he was ill. Sounded it too. Very jittery. But what's he got to do with anything?'

'Look in your bottom left-hand drawer.'

The Minister leant down and pulled it open.

'What is this stuff?'

'That,' Trelawney said, 'is some of the highly sophisticated bugging and recording equipment we removed from this and your secretary's office at seven-thirty a.m. today. The rest is still in place, but inoperative. I don't think your security is very good, sir. In fact, leaks which could only have come from here led to near disaster and to you coming under strong suspicion. There was no question whatsoever of providing you with sensitive information.'

He watched while the other reached down again, took some electronic oddments from the drawer and placed them on the desk in front of him.

'Yes,' the Minister said. 'I can believe that.'

Trelawney felt relief at the words, but no surprise. Having rehearsed the lie so thoroughly he almost believed it himself.

A tiny microphone seemed to fascinate the Minister. He pushed it about with a forefinger and, without looking up, asked, 'How did your people gain access to this building without written authority?'

'They didn't. The officer who took Grenville in charge persuaded him to write a letter.'

'You do play rough, don't you?'

Trelawney made no reply and the Minister dropped the pieces of equipment one by one back into the drawer, then turned and examined the face of the big man he had first met only a few days before.

'Very well, Director,' he said. 'I won't keep you. As you say, there's still a lot to be done.'

In the outer office Grenville's desk looked forlornly bare as though its occupant had died. He wouldn't be dead yet, Trelawney knew, but he would die, as would those at 'The Abattoir' and the people named in the numbers file, as soon as they were no longer of use. How many others, he wondered, would experience that euphemism 'termination with extreme prejudice' because of this affair? There was no way of telling yet.

He walked out of the building into a particularly lovely summer's day.